CHINA MIKE

BOOK TWO OF
ABNER FORTIS, ISMC

P.A. Piatt

Theogony Books
Coinjock, NC

Chris Kennedy/Theogony Books
1097 Waterlily Rd.
Coinjock, NC 27923
https://chriskennedypublishing.com/

Publisher's Note: This is a work of fiction. Names, characters, places, and incidents are a product of the author's imagination. Locales and public names are sometimes used for atmospheric purposes. Any resemblance to actual people, living or dead, or to businesses, companies, events, institutions, or locales is completely coincidental.

Cover Art and Design by Elartwyne Estole.

Ordering Information:
Quantity sales. Special discounts are available on quantity purchases by corporations, associations, and others. For details, contact the "Special Sales Department" at the address above.

China Mike/P.A. Piatt -- 1st ed.
ISBN: 978-1648552069

"Just say no."

—*First Lady Nancy Reagan*

"Liberty call, liberty call!"

—*Word passed over the internal communications system on U.S. Navy ships, greeted with cheers.*

DINLI

DINLI has many meanings to a Space Marine. It is the unofficial motto of the International Space Marine Corps, and it stands for "Do It, Not Like It."

Every Space Marine recruit has DINLI drilled into their head from the moment they arrive at basic training. Whatever they're ordered to do, they don't have to like it, they just have to do it. Crawl through stinking tidal mud? DINLI. Run countless miles with heavy packs? DINLI. Endure brutal punishment for minor mistakes? DINLI.

DINLI also refers to the illicit hootch the Space Marines brew wherever they deploy. From jungle planets like Pada-Pada, to the water-covered planets of the Felder Reach, and even on the barren, boulder-strewn deserts of Balfan-48. It might be a violation of Fleet Regulations to brew it, but every Marine drinks DINLI, from the lowest private to the most senior general.

DINLI is also the name of the ISMC mascot, a scowling bulldog with a cigar clamped between its massive jaws.

Finally, DINLI is a general-purpose expression about the grunt life. From announcing the birth of a new child to expressing disgust at receiving a freeze-dried ham and lima bean ration pack again, a Space Marine can expect one response from his comrades.

DINLI.

* * * * *

Chapter One

International Space Marine Corps Second Lieutenant Abner Fortis keyed his throat mike. "Go, go, go!"

Breaching charges blew open the front and back doors of the building simultaneously, and Space Marines dressed in all-black tactical armor flowed inside. There were several bright flashes and sharp cracks as stun grenades preceded the assault troops into interior rooms and up the stairs. Short bursts of gunfire announced the discovery of "enemy" troops concealed inside.

"Clear!" called Assault Team Alpha Leader, responsible for the first floor.

"Clear!" echoed Assault Team Bravo Leader from upstairs.

"Clear!" came the call from the Overwatch Sniper Team Leader.

"All clear, all clear," announced Fortis. He consulted his watch. "Good job, Marines. Twenty-six seconds. All teams, muster at the rally point." Cool air washed over his head as he pulled off his assault helmet and swiped at the sweat on his face. The new-style assault helmets were full face, with a bulletproof visor and a hermetic seal. Great protection, but heavy and stifling.

The assault teams and sniper overwatch gathered together and shared a laugh at Private Modell, who had a bright orange blotch on the chest of his battle armor. The Space Marine trainees used training rounds loaded with bright green paint, while the training cadre opposing force, or OPFOR, used orange.

After the assault teams formed up, the training cadre commander approached Fortis. He was a business-like warrant officer named Tarkenton, with a critical eye and direct manner, and he wasn't shy about pointing out trainee mistakes. He nodded to Fortis.

"You mind if I address your troops, Lieutenant?"

Fortis motioned to the formation. "Be my guest, Warrant."

Warrant Tarkenton faced the Space Marines. "You ladies think it's funny that one of yours got hit?"

Everyone froze, and Fortis got a hot feeling around his neck as the blood rushed to his face. Tarkenton began to pace in front of the formation and every eye followed him.

"This Marine is dead," he pointed at Modell, "And you're all standing around, grab-assing." He put his hands on his hips. "Third Platoon failed this exercise." He turned to Fortis. "*You* failed this exercise, Lieutenant. Your casualty planning was inadequate and your failure to take appropriate measures with a casualty cost the Space Marines a man."

Fortis opened his mouth to protest, but he stayed silent. He didn't learn about the casualty until after the exercise, but if he argued with Tarkenton it would just shift the blame to the men. The simple truth was that Fortis, as the officer in charge, was responsible for the failure, no matter the reason.

"You didn't brief casualty procedures, did you?"

It was more accusation than question, and Fortis shook his head and cleared his throat.

"We did not, Warrant."

"Let this be a lesson for all of you," said Tarkenton raising his voice. "Even on a training mission, you have to be ready for anything." He slapped Fortis on the shoulder. "Don't be too hard on yourself, sir. Once you get more experience it will get easier." He turned back to the formation. "When you return tomorrow, we'll run this scenario again, and this time you better be prepared for anything." With that, Tarkenton turned and joined the training cadre on the other side of the dynamic training compartment.

"With some more experience, Lieutenant, you'll be a jackass like me." Private Queen, Third Platoon jokester and expert mimic, mocked the warrant for the amusement of his comrades.

Fortis fought the urge to smile. "Knock it off, Queen. You all heard the man: We fucked up. I fucked up. We need to be better than that. Third Platoon, atten-hut!"

As one, the platoon snapped to attention.

Fortis eyed the formation. *A lot of new faces.*

After Fortis was relieved of platoon commander duties during his recent court martial, Third Platoon had received replacements to fill gaps left by the meat grinder on Pada-Pada. The new guys were a mixed lot: veterans and cherries, chronic fuckups and genuine head cases. Whatever else they were, they were now his responsibility to train and mold into an efficient fighting unit, and assault exercises like the one they had just completed would help accomplish that mission.

"Corporal Ystremski, take charge and dismiss the platoon."

Ystremski saluted, and Fortis returned the military courtesy.

"Aye, aye, sir." The corporal faced the formation. "Third Platoon, stow your gear and muster in the hangar in ten minutes for PT. Fall out!"

* * *

I n the pre-dawn darkness on the industrial planet of Eros-28, a black-clad figure crouched behind a low stone wall and checked her watch.

Three minutes.

Dust devils swirled and danced in the beams of the searchlights mounted above the underground garage entryway and cast crazy shadows across the featureless landscape. The dust-laden breeze gave the white beams a dull orange glow, and the surrounding darkness swallowed the light after a few meters.

The woman didn't notice the squad of troops that had surrounded her until it was too late. They slammed her to the ground, restrained her arms and legs, and waited.

A hovercopter approached from the east and settled onto a lighted pad next to the garage entrance. The 'copter raised more dirt and dust as the troops dumped her in the aircraft and piled in behind. The machine rose smoothly into the dark sky and sped off over the desert.

Forty seconds later, a series of explosions rocked the underground garage and collapsed the structure. Tons of dirt buried a hundred pieces of newly refurbished mining equipment and wiped out two weeks of work. No lives were lost, but the sabotage was a severe blow to facility productivity and a major escalation in the ongoing struggle between the Galactic Resource Conglomerate, GRC, and the resistance on Eros-28.

Unbeknownst to facility management, the true target of the attack was several hundred kilos of China Mike, a highly addictive drug, hidden in the machinery.

* * *

The morning after the failed training scenario, Fortis sighed and leaned back in his chair in the Foxtrot Company XO's office. He had ground away all night at the mountain of paperwork on his desk, but it didn't look any smaller. The amount of administrivia necessary to operate a company of Space Marines was overwhelming, and it sat squarely on Fortis' shoulders as the acting executive officer. He stood up and stretched, and all of his muscles protested.

There were three sharp raps on the hatch, and Corporal Ystremski stuck his head inside.

"Hey, LT, what's going on?"

Fortis gestured at his desk. "Death by a million paper cuts. What's up with you?"

"Every day's a holiday."

"DINLI, dickhead."

Sticklers for ISMC protocol would have frowned at the casual banter between the officer and the enlisted man, but Fortis and Ystremski had recently spent two weeks in a fight for their lives on the jungle planet Pada-Pada. They had been battle tested together and their shared experience in combat had scoured away the patina of pro forma bullshit and left behind a solid professional military relationship.

Corporal Ystremski sank into the chair opposite Fortis and pointed. "It looks like that pile of paper has grown since the last time I stopped by, sir."

Fortis scowled. "Yeah. Reese has the paperwork pump in recirculation mode, I think."

Captain Reese, the Second Battalion Administrative Officer, hated Fortis and took immense pleasure in tormenting him.

Reese had been Foxtrot Company commander when Fortis and a detachment of two platoons dropped to Pada-Pada on a training mission in support of the Global Resource Conglomerate, or GRC. The mission went sideways, and the Space Marines became embroiled in a battle with vicious bugs and deadly cloned soldiers.

After several appeals for guidance from his company commander went unanswered, Fortis transmitted a status report of events on Pada-Pada directly to the Battalion commander. The report resulted in Captain Reese's reassignment to administrative duties, for which he blamed Fortis.

Because of a Fleet-wide shortage of junior officers, Foxtrot Company only had two commissioned officers: Captain Brickell, the new commanding officer, and Second Lieutenant Fortis. Which meant Fortis was forced to assume duties as the company executive officer, a job which included mountains of paperwork.

As a result of Reese's grudge, Foxtrot Company paperwork had ground to a halt. Personnel action requests were returned for minor errors, routine reports were rejected, and supply requisitions were delayed or just disappeared.

The current Foxtrot Company CO, Captain Brickell, had made it clear to Fortis that he was on his own in the ongoing battle with Reese. Brickell wanted no part of any fight with Battalion HQ, even when he was obliged to make Fortis the acting company XO. "Nothing late, nothing lost," had been his direction, and Fortis worked tirelessly to meet that standard, even though it was like bailing the ocean with a bucket.

"Why doesn't the CO say something? Reese is fucking over the whole company with his bullshit."

"The CO has enough to do without worrying about a bunch of paper," Fortis replied. He sat back down and sighed as his leg muscles relaxed. "Commanding a company with only one officer and two warrant officers can't be easy."

"How are the workouts coming along, LT? Feeling good?"

"Not bad. I definitely feel the enhancement, and I'm lifting more weight than I ever have."

Fortis had received his Level Six Strength Enhancement the previous week and was under strict orders from the Battalion medical officer to exercise to muscle exhaustion twice daily. This was critical for two reasons. First, it was the only way to determine whether his body would accept or reject the enhancement. If his body rejected the enhancement, it was better to find out while the Fleet hospital ship was in range. Second, it was crucial that his musculoskeletal system develop to tolerate the stress the higher enhancement levels could put on his body. Superhuman strength was dangerous in a weak body.

There was a third, unofficial, reason why the exercise was important to Fortis: it gave him a bulletproof reason to walk away from his desk and leave the avalanche of admin behind, if only for a few hours. He *had* to work out, and neither Captain Brickell nor Captain Reese would dare go against the orders of the Battalion medical officer.

The office door banged open, and Captain Reese barged in with a sheaf of papers clutched in his hand.

Fortis and Ystremski stood.

"Mister Fortis, these requisitions are incomplete. You have to submit in triplicate—"

Reese stopped in mid-sentence when he saw Corporal Ystremski.

Years earlier, Ystremski had punched Reese during a drunken confrontation and the resulting charges got Ystremski busted from gunnery sergeant to private. Even without the gunny chevrons, Ystremski had the uncanny ability to project an aura of disdain and contempt at anyone he chose, and Reese was a frequent target of the corporal's attention.

"I... uh... anyway, fix these."

The flustered captain dropped the papers on the desk and backed out of the space before Fortis could even render the customary salute. Ystremski pushed the door shut, and the two exchanged amused smiles.

"That guy is a fucking weasel. I should have hit him twice."

Fortis chuckled. "He's not worth the effort. How many times do you want to make corporal?" He dug through a small pile of completed paperwork. "Before I forget, I have something for you." He found what he was looking for and handed it to Ystremski. "Sorry."

Ystremski opened the folder and saw it was a personnel action request with his name at the top and the word "DENIED" stamped in big red letters across the bottom. Fortis had given Ystremski a battlefield promotion to the rank of gunnery sergeant during the battle on Pada-Pada, but his request to make the promotion permanent had been rejected.

Ystremski gave a bitter chuckle. "At least they let me keep corporal."

"DINLI."

"DINLI," Ystremski affirmed. He tapped his wrist. "It's about time, sir."

Fortis shook his head. Captain Brickell was the only company commander in the entire Battalion that held morning formation in the cavernous hangar bay. He claimed it helped maintain the military bearing of the company in garrison on the flagship. Fortis secretly suspected Brickell did it because the division commander, General Gupta, ran laps in the hangar every morning at the same time the formation was held.

Whatever the reason, the corporal was right. It was time to go.

* * *

Foxtrot Company formed up and submitted muster reports to Lieutenant Fortis. When they were verified, Fortis signaled to Captain Brickell on his communicator. Two minutes later, Brickell entered the hangar.

"Attention on deck!"

Foxtrot Company came to attention, and Fortis saluted the CO.

"Foxtrot Company, all present or accounted for, sir."

Brickell returned the salute. "Very well. Put the company at ease, XO."

"Aye, aye, sir." Fortis about-faced. "Foxtrot Company, stand at ease."

For the next ten minutes, Brickell paced in front of the company and expounded on his theories about leadership, followership, and what it meant to be a Space Marine. Fortis glared at the assembled troops as eyelids drooped and attention visibly wandered.

"Today, Lieutenant Fortis will lead two assault teams on a dynamic-entry training scenario. The rest of Third Platoon will report to the company clerk's office for general duty assignments."

Great.

Normally, Fortis would leap at the chance for more tactical training, but the weight of all the paperwork on his desk threatened to crush him. He began to plot how to slough off the training onto one of the two warrant officers when Brickell said something that got the attention of every Space Marine in the formation.

"The general has approved a ten-day planetary liberty visit for the entire division."

The company held their collective breath.

"In the Eros Cluster."

Military bearing in the formation crumbled, and the Space Marines laughed and whooped. Fortis fought to control his own reaction as the CO held up his hand for silence.

"Company, atten-HUT!" Fortis ordered.

The company popped to attention, and their smiles vanished.

Captain Brickell nodded to Fortis. "Thank you, XO." He turned back to the company. "In three days, the Fleet will arrive in the vicinity of the Eros Cluster. When I receive spaceport assignments from the staff I will pass them on to you." Brickell passed in front of the formation and whirled to a stop facing the Space Marines. "Know this, ladies. Nobody is going anywhere unless Foxtrot Company gear is in tip-top shape, our spaces are pristine, and company business is squared away. Understood?"

The company stood, silent.

Brickell turned on his heel and strode toward the hatch that led to his quarters. "XO, take charge and dismiss the company."

Fortis waited until the CO closed the hatch behind him.

"Platoon commanders take charge. Company, dismissed!"

* * * * *

Chapter Two

After four hours of dynamic-entry training scenarios, Fortis and the two assault teams took a breather while they waited for the colonel in charge of Battalion training to arrive and observe their final training evolution.

The training day had started out rough. The Space Marines were distracted by the news of impending liberty, and they made many basic errors during the first scenarios. Fortis was forced to call a timeout. He delivered a stern warning that they would repeat the scenarios all day if necessary, and the assault teams settled down.

The scenarios had fallen into the familiar pattern of training conducted by the Battalion cadre. The cadre were all over the Space Marines to start. The tiniest mistakes were belabored, and the trainers attributed many of them to a failure of leadership, a polite way of indirectly blaming Fortis.

By the midpoint, the cadre noted fewer mistakes, whether the Space Marines committed them or not. For the final scenario for the colonel, Warrant Tarkenton and his team declared that the assault teams were operating like a well-oiled machine because of the training the cadre had provided.

Fortis wished Corporal Ystremski was there to deflect some of Warrant Tarkenton's bullshit; Ystremski might only be a corporal, but he knew how the game was played.

Maybe that's why Brickell wanted him for admin duty today.

"Lieutenant Fortis!"

Fortis looked up and saw the Foxtrot Company Clerk, Staff Sergeant Cruz, standing by the hatch.

"Captain Brickell wants all platoon commanders and sergeants up in the company room ASAP. The liberty assignments are out!"

Cruz disappeared through the hatch before Fortis could respond. First and Second Squads whooped with excitement, and Fortis cut them off with a wave of his hand.

"Third Platoon, lock it up." He turned to Tarkenton. "What do you want us to do, Warrant?"

"Go ahead and dismiss them, sir. I just got the call, the colonel's not coming. We've been recalled to the training center ourselves."

* * *

Ystremski caught up with Fortis at the company room hatch. "What's the word, LT?"

"Beats me. Cruz said the CO wanted us up here because the liberty assignments were out. What have you heard?"

Ystremski shook his head. "Not a peep. I've been busy with Third Squad all morning."

The two men entered the company room and joined the warrant officers and their platoon NCOs as they waited for Captain Brickell. Finally, the CO arrived.

"I just received the liberty assignments from Battalion admin for Foxtrot Company." He held up a sheet of paper. "Foxtrot Company has been assigned Spaceport Zulu Five on Eros-69."

Everyone laughed and applauded. Ystremski nudged Fortis and smiled.

"Eros-69 is paradise," he muttered to the young officer out of the corner of his mouth.

"I meant what I said at formation this morning, ladies. Spaces clean, equipment maintained, and company business completed."

After Brickell dismissed the group, Fortis held Ystremski back until they were alone in the company room.

"What's on Eros-69?"

"You name it, LT. Booze, real women, everything. The last time I was there, they were building a biodome to hold a beach. Can you believe that?"

"Actually, I can. I was supposed to go work for my father building biodomes after college, but I decided a career in the ISMC sounded like more fun."

Ystremski laughed. "Having fun yet?"

"DINLI."

"You know what's weird about this, LT? Normally we don't stop there so early in a deployment. Usually, it's on our way home."

"Why is that?"

"Imagine what would happen on Terra Earth if five thousand sex-starved Space Marines returned straight home after a two-year deep-space deployment? It would be anarchy. Instead, we go to Eros-69 and blow off some steam. We have to quarantine anyway, so why not do it in a place that has excellent hotels and beautiful beaches, real women and cheap booze, and all of it under a biodome that feels just like home."

Fortis led Ystremski into the passageway to the Foxtrot Company XO's office.

"Huh. Sounds nice. Too bad I can't drink."

"Oh shit, I forgot about your strength enhancement."

One of the restrictions while undergoing physical enhancements was that the recipient could not consume any drugs or alcohol until the doctors were certain the enhancement had "taken." It wouldn't have been a problem on a normal deployment, but the liberty call complicated things for Fortis.

"It doesn't matter anyway. Remember what the CO said about 'company business squared away' at formation? I think I'll be spending my liberty right here."

"I've been meaning to talk to you about that, sir."

Fortis opened the hatch and gaped at his empty desk.

"What happened here? Where did all that paper go?"

"Well, sir, you were busy in the trainer being a Space Marine this morning. And the lads of Third Squad know that you won't get liberty if your desk isn't clear." He winked. "I know some people that know some people, the kind of people who make things work around here. I made a couple calls and got things moving."

"You didn't break any regs, did you?"

Ystremski feigned shock. "Me? Oh, no, sir, I would never break any regs. I'm a by-the-book Space Marine. I divided everything up by subject and got the piles into the right hands."

Fortis chuckled. "I wonder what Reese will say when he finds out?"

"By the time he discovers it, we'll be knee-deep in bacchanal."

* * *

Freed from his administrative bondage, Fortis went to the troop weight room for his first workout of the day. As a commissioned officer, he was entitled to use the embarked staff gym, which was clean and bright, with shiny machines and electro-beats pulsating from overhead speakers. There was even a staff of orderlies who handed out towels and offered personal training services. Users had to remain rank-conscious at all times or risk interfering with a senior officer's exercise time. It rivaled any boutique on Terra Earth, and Fortis hated it.

The troop weight room, by contrast, was a dank, dark space deep in the bowels of the flagship. It reeked of sweat and testosterone. There were no machines or ellipticals; it was all steel bars and free weights. The only music was the clank of weights and grunts of exertion as muscle and iron collided.

Rank didn't matter in the troop gym, only effort. It was a pocket of egalitarianism aboard the highly stratified flagship. Fortis wasn't a lieutenant in the gym; he was a Space Marine building his body to accept the strength enhancements. His fellow weightlifters were eager to help him with a spot, and he endured their good-natured ribbing when they discovered he was an officer. They pushed him hard because someday they might have to follow him into battle. Fortis drove himself hard because he knew the Space Marines wouldn't follow a weak leader.

When Fortis was exhausted and could barely lift his arms, he slumped onto an empty bench. Someone threw a towel at him, and he waved his thanks with a trembling hand. Their laughter followed him as he forced his wobbly legs to carry him into the passageway to make the long climb up several decks to his stateroom.

* * *

Captain Reese was tapping on his keyboard when Captain Brickell entered the Battalion administrative space with an armload of paper and stopped at his desk. When Reese didn't look up, Brickell dumped the pile on Reese's deck without ceremony.

"Hey, Tim, what's all this crap?"

Reese looked up, gave Brickell a look like he had just stepped in something unpleasant before turning his attention to the folders and documents.

"Looks like periodic enlisted performance reports, some supply paperwork, and a few personnel action requests."

Brickell glared. "I know what it is. I signed some of this stuff a week ago. Why is it back on my desk for signature again?"

Reese exaggerated scratching his chin. "Perhaps it was returned because it's not satisfactory. Let me see…" He opened the top folder and scanned the first few pages. "Yep, that's it. These performance reports aren't properly formatted. Each paragraph is supposed to be indented with two spaces not five. I returned them to your XO to correct and resubmit."

"Are you kidding me? What difference does the formatting make? These reports don't go into their personnel files. Hell, most of the guys post them on the walls in the shitter for a laugh."

"What the men choose to do with their paperwork is their business. My only concern is that it meets the standards set forth in the ISMC Correspondence Manual."

Brickell clenched and unclenched his fists and took a deep breath before he addressed Reese in a loud voice.

"What's your problem, Reese? Ever since I relieved you as Foxtrot Company CO you've had a hard-on for Fortis. Don't get me wrong, I'm in favor of training and testing our cherries to make sure they're up to the task, but this—" he gestured at the mound of paper, "—this is bullshit. Your vendetta against my XO is beginning to impact my company, and I won't allow that to happen. From now on, if I sign it, it's good enough. Understand?"

Everyone in the space watched in shocked silence as the blood drained from Reese's face, and his mouth opened and closed without a sound. After a long moment, Brickell turned on his heel and strode out.

* * *

Fortis showered, donned fresh fatigues, and went in search of Major Anders, the Battalion Intelligence Officer. The major was in his office with his feet up while an episode of a holographic Terran reality show floated above his desk. Anders swung his feet down and smiled when Fortis opened the hatch.

"Ah, Lieutenant Fortis. What can I do for you today?"

Major Anders had taken a liking to Abner when he had briefed the lieutenant prior to his deployment to Pada-Pada. Most of the ISMC infantry officers paid little attention to Anders and the intelligence he provided them, but Fortis was genuinely interested. When he returned from Pada-Pada, Fortis had provided the major with a wealth of information about the GRC precision crafted soldiers, or "test tubes," he'd fought there.

"Hello, Major. I guess you heard about our liberty on Eros-69?"

Anders chuckled, and his smile widened. "Indeed, I have. What of it?"

Fortis shrugged. "I've never been there, and the only stories I get from the men involve debauchery on a grand scale. I'm curious to know if there's anything of interest about the place besides the obvious."

"To understand the Eros Cluster you have to know the history. Do you have time?"

Fortis nodded, and Anders gestured at the seat across from him. He keyed his computer terminal, and a group of planets replaced the show on his holograph.

"When humans first began manned deep-space exploration and resource exploitation there wasn't a lot of thought given to the nasty things that might follow us back to Terra Earth. The assumption was that nothing harmful could survive the decontamination procedures we followed before getting back inside our space craft. Nor did we think anything could survive on the exterior of a spacecraft in the vacuum of space. If it did, the thinking was that heat of atmospheric re-entry would finish it. Then came the *Long March* incident."

"The *Long March* incident?"

"Yes. *Long March* was a Chinese deep-space survey mission. This was back before the UNT formed and individual countries still sponsored their own missions. Anyway, *Long March* returned after a four-year deployment and went into quarantine orbit around Terra Earth.

"Just before the crew boarded a shuttle to return to the surface, there was some kind of viral outbreak on *Long March* that killed everyone. They had brought something back with them and, fortunately, it woke up before they brought it to the surface. Some of the crew managed to escape on the shuttle and tried to enter Terra Earth's atmosphere. The Chinese government destroyed it before they could land."

"Damn!"

"The Chinese were determined not to release any more pandemics or plagues on the planet, so their reaction was understandable. Had that shuttle landed and unleashed whatever it was that had killed everyone on *Long March*, our species may not have survived.

"Anyway, three hundred and nine people died as a result. At that point, the governments of every space-faring nation decided that a more rigorous quarantine protocol was necessary."

Fortis scratched his chin. "That's an interesting story, sir, but what's it got to do with Eros-69?"

Anders held up a hand. "Patience, Abner. We'll get to Eros-69, but first I have to tell you about *Cuba Libre*.

"After *Long March*, they reactivated the International Space Station and used it to quarantine crews until they could be certified as safe to return to Terra Earth.

"The first mission placed in quarantine on the ISS was the crew of *Cuba Libre*, a long-range mineral survey vessel. The ship returned from a six-year survey mission and docked with the ISS without incident. After two weeks in quarantine circling Terra Earth, mass psychosis swept through the *Cuba Libre* crew. They attempted to de-orbit the ISS, and it broke apart and burned up on re-entry."

"What drove them crazy, a bug?"

"Nobody knows. It might have been a bug or it might have been the psychological torment of seeing Terra Earth every time they looked out the viewports after six years away. Whatever the reason was, it died with them when the ISS burned up. That's when the Galactic Resource Conglomerate got involved."

"The GRC? As in the guys we fought on Pada-Pada?"

Major Anders nodded. "One and the same. GRC had a resource extraction claim on a small cluster of plutoids at the far edge of the Milky Way known as the Eros Cluster. The claim was a bust, but as they say in the real estate business: location, location, location. The cluster is perfectly situated to serve missions departing and returning to the galaxy.

"At first, they built a quarantine dome on Eros-69 for their own crews. It worked out so well for them that the UNT contracted with the GRC to expand the operation to include a series of pleasure domes for all deep-space missions. Now, crews returning from extended missions stop there to release pent-up energy and pass quarantine before they return to Terra Earth."

"Smart idea. Makes sense."

"And makes big money."

"So that's where we're headed, huh? Eros-69. Ystremski said they have beaches there."

Major Anders leaned back and laid his hands across his stomach. "They have every kind of diversion imaginable, Fortis. It's paradise."

* * *

For the next two days, Foxtrot Company cleaned and trained.

Atlas, flagship of ISMC's Ninth Division, was designed to be self-cleaning, but with Eros-69 liberty on the line, the Space Marines left nothing to chance.

The company paperwork logjam finally broke, and Fortis mastered the art of only handling a piece of paper once. Captain Brickell made no comment about the sudden administrative efficiency of the company. Warrant Officers Takahashi and Taylor, the other Foxtrot Company platoon commanders, did their part to help the paperwork monster lurch along. Fortis began to relax. He intensified his physical training regimen, and it became obvious to him that the strength enhancement had been successful. He wouldn't be able to fully participate in the drunken wildness Third Platoon had planned for liberty, but at least he wouldn't be stuck on the flagship.

He received a hologram from his mother the night before the Space Marines were scheduled to load up for Eros-69. He considered leaving it until he came back from liberty, but if he didn't respond in a day or two, she would follow it up with another, and another, and then another, each more anxious than the last.

It depressed Fortis that his life had been a complete cliché. He'd been a dutiful son who performed well in school and steered clear of trouble. Abner's father had dreamed of him working his way up through the family biodome construction business and eventually taking over. His mother had no opinions of her own, content to parrot whatever his father said.

When Abner announced that he had applied for a commission in the ISMC, his parents reacted exactly as he had expected. His father angrily demanded that he withdraw his application, and his mother disappeared into her bedroom in tears. Two days later, as he prepared to catch the train for the induction center, his mother fought back a new torrent of tears and smoothed his hair.

"Be careful, Abner." She kissed him on the cheek. "Steer clear of danger."

His father waited for him at the door, and for the first time in Abner's life, the two shook hands.

"Stay out of trouble, son. If you need anything, call."

Their private disappointment became public pride when word that he had received the *L'Ordre de la Galanterie* made it back to Terra Earth. His father was on a contract in the Felder Reach, but his mother's holos were filled with stories of her new-found popularity as the mother of a hero, her efforts at matchmaking for Abner, and admonishments to be careful and write soon.

Fortis keyed her latest and sat back to watch. A blue-tinged electronic version of his mother hovered over his desk.

Hello Abner,

I hope this finds you well. Everything is fine here. We all love and miss you.

Do you remember Mrs. Armstrong? Her husband is aide to the territorial governor. Anyway, I saw her at the community center with her daughter Elspeth yesterday. Elspeth is quite the beauty, Abner. I know that you would agree. I promised her that you would holo her when you got time away from your duties. Be a dear, Abner, and write when you can. She comes from the finest sort of people, and I think you two would make a lovely couple. It never hurts to plan for the future. After all, the future will be here before you know it.

Anyway, I'm sure you're busy, so I'll let you go. Please write back as soon as you can.

I love you.

Holographic Mother waved, and Fortis caught himself before he waved back.

He sighed and hit Reply.

* * * * *

Chapter Three

Mikel Chive, the GRC Director of Security on Eros-28, suppressed a smile as he entered the windowless interrogation room. The gray dirt walls swallowed the light cast by the single-bulb light fixture on the ceiling.

The prisoner was standing in the middle of the room, shackled to a heavy eyebolt anchored in the floor. She'd been defiant at first, but two days in the cold, damp cell with no food or water had crushed her spirit. Her face was drawn from fear and exhaustion, and she swayed unsteadily on her feet.

Chive wrinkled his nose at the sharp stench of dried urine.

"Will you give me your name?"

She shook her head and lowered her eyes.

Chive knew who she was from her fingerprints and DNA, but he wanted her to give him information, and it was a good way to start. She was the first member of the resistance he'd captured, and he wanted to squeeze her for every bit of information she had. But, to do so, it was critical that she talk.

He flashed his friendliest smile.

"What harm could your name do? I can't just call you 'woman,' can I?"

No response.

"If you don't answer my questions, I'm going to hurt you."

She stayed silent.

"It doesn't have to be like this, Raisa."

She flinched but still said nothing.

"Oh, yes. I know who you are." He leaned in until he could smell the sweat and fear in her grimy hair, and his voice dropped to a whisper. "I know who you are. I know about Belson, too."

Raisa lunged at the mention of her son. Chive backpedaled until her shackles jerked tight and she fell to the floor. He motioned to the guards standing in the shadows behind her.

"Get her up."

The guards hauled Raisa to her feet by her arms and held her there. Chive stepped forward, paused, and punched her hard in the stomach. Her breath whooshed out as she doubled over and fell to her knees. He gave her a moment to recover and then snapped his fingers. The guards pulled her up, and Chive saw a string of bile clinging to her shirt. He grabbed a handful of her disheveled hair, jerking her head up.

She spat full in his face.

Chive stumbled back and wiped at his eyes as the guards threw Raisa to the floor and started pummeling her.

"Wait!"

The guards stopped and looked at Chive.

"Pick her up."

They stood her up again, and this time Chive didn't hesitate. He drove a fist directly into her face. There was a satisfying crunch as her nose shattered. Raisa clutched her face and collapsed to the floor. Chive delivered a sharp kick to her ribs.

"They told you we would use a mind probe to interrogate you, didn't they?" he said as he stood over her prostrated body. "Maybe some drugs?"

Raisa moaned.

He kicked a hand away from her face and ground his heel into the palm. Raisa squealed and tried to pull her hand away, but he continued to twist his boot until the bones snapped. She screamed and finally managed to jerk her hand free.

He chuckled at her pain.

"You have the power here, Raisa. You get to decide how I treat you. If you answer my questions fully and truthfully, I will treat you well. If you lie to me, I will hurt you. If you refuse to answer my questions, I will hurt you. Do you understand?"

Raisa didn't respond, so Chive kicked her in the ribs again. She cried out and tried to roll away from further abuse.

"You see? I asked you a question, and you didn't answer, so I hurt you. Do you understand now?"

This time, she gave an almost imperceptible nod.

"Good."

He snapped his fingers and two guards picked her up while a third slid a chair underneath her.

"Let's begin."

For the next hour, Chive peppered Raisa Spears with questions about the resistance and her role in the demolition of the garage. When she hesitated or told him an obvious lie, she paid with pain. Chive was careful not to push her too hard until he was certain he had everything he was going to get from the shattered woman. Her answers soon became nonsensical, and she drifted in and out of consciousness. That's when the mercenary knew she was finished.

Finally, he stood in front of her and pulled her head back by her hair.

"I think we're finished here. Time to go, Raisa."

He laughed aloud at the look of hope that crossed her filthy, battered face.

"This isn't an interrogation anymore." He kicked the chair out from under her, and she slumped to the floor. "Now I'm going to punish you for blowing up my garage."

* * *

The GRC planetary governor of Eros-28, a prematurely bald man named Czrk, sighed with frustration and dropped his pen on the open file in front of him. His staff, gathered around the conference table, were somber, except for his security director, Mikel Chive. Chive was his usual expressionless self, and his lack of visible concern tweaked Czrk's nerves.

"Over a hundred vehicles buried by a terrorist attack and nobody saw a thing."

The governor's eyes went from face to face, but none dared meet his gaze except Chive.

"Two weeks' worth of work, ruined in an instant! What happened to our vaunted security force? Where were they when the attack occurred?"

"I only have so many men, Governor. They can't be everywhere. If the maintenance crews had locked the doors behind them, the attack could have been avoided."

The maintenance chief, Blud Leutgen, slammed his beefy palm on the table. "You can't prove that, Chive! We sealed that door after we loaded all the gear in there. Don't pass your failures off on my people!"

The governor held up his hands. "Gentlemen, gentlemen! We can sit here and point fingers, but it won't solve the problem of a hundred vehicles under three meters of dirt. Where are we on the excavation?"

Bob Drager, the governor's executive assistant, chimed in. "Sir, we didn't learn about the attack until after the dust storm started. We thought it was just going to be some wind, but it turned into a full-blown sifter and halted all outside work. As soon as the storm blows out, we'll get crews over there to excavate the site."

"We'll have to clean each piece of equipment again, but I can add extra shifts to get it done as soon as possible," added Leutgen. "Is there space in one of the other storage garages?"

The governor looked at Jan Stepnow, the facilities supervisor, who nodded.

"We can make space in Garage Five. I'll have my folks get started at once, sir."

Czrk gestured to a pudgy man in a bright orange jumpsuit. "Chief Schultz, do you have anything to report?"

The chief of the colonial police force shook his head. "No, sir, Governor. We haven't been able to get out since the sifter started. We will go out as soon as possible."

Governor Czrk nodded and consulted his meeting agenda. "And finally, the weather. Mr. Yuri, please, make the sifter end."

The governor's science advisor was a slight Asian man seated at the far end of the table. He gave a nervous smile and cleared his throat. "Good news, Governor. Our surface sensors detected a significant drop in wind speed over the last six hours, which indicates the storm center has passed earlier than predicted. We'll have more accurate information as soon as I can get a link to the weather satellite, but at this time, I estimate that the storm will abate within twenty-four hours."

The staff traded nods and smiles. They lived in relative comfort and safety in the underground corporate facility, but many of their workers lived in the city. Every day those workers couldn't get to work was another day of reduced productivity. Corporate headquarters was quick to harangue Governor Czrk when he failed to meet production schedules, and they weren't interested in excuses about the weather.

To complicate the situation, a section of the extensive network of access tunnels under the city, known as "the subway," had recently collapsed and killed over two hundred workers before rescuers could dig them out. Tension between the workforce and management was at an all-time high, and the extra work incurred by the garage attack would only intensify the strain.

Mr. Yuri gave a self-conscious chuckle. "The possibility of an Eolian Blast will persist until atmospheric pressure stabilizes."

An Eolian Blast was a small area of extremely low pressure and high winds spawned by a dirt storm known as a sifter. A sifter carried dust and sand, but an Eolian Blast could pick up sizeable rocks and hurl them at life-threatening speeds.

Governor Czrk sighed. "Then we should all take care not to be outside when it does. Thank you, Mr. Yuri." He looked at his agenda again. "It looks like that's it. Unless there's anything else?"

No one spoke.

"Thank you, everyone."

The group stood as one and filed out of the conference room.

Czrk signaled to Chive. "Mr. Chive, a moment please."

When the two men were alone, Chive pushed the door shut.

"Any word about the attack? Have you found the perpetrators yet?"

"Governor, my men are no more capable of operating in a sifter than Fat Schultz and his idiot police force. When the storm lifts and excavation begins, we'll collect what evidence we can. Our prime suspect is Dask Finkle, but until we convince the population to turn him over, he's a ghost."

"Why do they insist on protecting him? Don't they understand that the resistance makes life difficult for everyone, not just the GRC?" Czrk rubbed his pate with both hands, frustrated. "Why won't they cooperate?"

"Governor, just say the word, and my men will *get* their cooperation."

Czrk stopped rubbing and stared at Chive. "We tried that, remember? Your men turned a minor disagreement into a full-blown riot that shut this place down." He shook his head. "No, thank you. Not again. We need to be careful or this thing is going to get out of control."

"Have it your way. I'll keep working my sources; maybe we'll get lucky." Chive turned to leave.

"One more thing, Mr. Chive. Don't call Chief Schultz 'Fat Schultz' anymore. He's a senior member of my administration, and you will show him the appropriate respect."

* * *

Foxtrot Company formed up with the rest of the Battalion in the hangar to embark the personnel transports that would deliver them to Eros-69. The atmosphere in the hangar was carnival-like, and there were smiles everywhere Fortis looked. Even Captain Reese had a smile on his face.

Reese approached, and Fortis came to attention and rendered his best parade-ground salute.

"Good morning, Captain."

"Ready for some liberty, Fortis?"

"Yes, sir."

"What's going on, Captain Reese?" Captain Brickell walked over and stood close to the two men. "Is there a problem here?"

Just then, a group of Space Marines carrying cases of various sizes and shapes entered the hangar and waved to Captain Reese.

"Hey, Captain, where do you want us?" asked the sergeant leading the group.

"Right there is fine," replied Reese. He held up a clipboard and leered at Fortis. "There's been a slight change of plans. The commanding general decided he wants to take the division band with him to Eros-69, so I had to shuffle some liberty assignments." He made a show of examining the clipboard. "Third Platoon has been reassigned to Eros-28."

"What's Eros-28?"

Reese chuckled. "I don't know, but it's not Eros-69."

Captain Brickell looked at Fortis and shrugged. "Tough luck, kid."

* * *

Two men were huddled over a rickety table in the back of a small bar in Boston, the capital city of Eros-28. The bar was hidden behind an anonymous unlit doorway in an alley full of dusty, unlit doorways. It was a place where private conversations could be held and secret deals could be made.

"They got her, Jandahl." The larger of the two, a ham-fisted man by the name of Mandel Spears, punctuated his statement with a thump on the table.

"I'm sorry, Spears, but what do you want me to do?"

"Get her out of there." Spears' hands trembled as he flexed his fists. "We have to get her out of there."

Jandahl laid his hands on the table, palms up. "How do you propose to do that? We don't even know where they have her."

"You've got people on the inside. I know you do! They can find out."

"People on the inside?" Jandahl shook his head with a wry smile. "You give me too much credit, my friend. I'm just a clerk. Even if I could find out where they're holding her—which I can't—why would I?"

"She's my wife!" Spears slammed his hand on the table hard enough to make their mugs jump, and the few other people in the bar looked over. Spears leaned even closer and lowered his voice to an urgent whisper. "She's my wife. We have a son, damn you. That's why."

"She's your wife, and I warned you not to get her involved." Jandahl looked around the room, but everyone had gone back to their own business. "Look, Spears. This thing is bigger than you or me or Raisa. I really am sorry that she got caught up in it, but she knew the risk she was taking. Does she know the identities of the others in your cell?"

Spears shook his massive head.

"Well, that's good news. Perhaps they'll decide she doesn't know anything and turn her loose."

Spears fixed Jandahl in an icy stare. "You don't really believe that, do you."

Jandahl suppressed a shudder brought on by Spears' piercing glare. "No. I don't."

Spears covered his face with his hands and his shoulders heaved as he sobbed. Jandahl waited a few seconds before he patted Spears on the arm.

"Come on, Spears, control yourself. You've got a son to think about."

Spears wiped his eyes. "I moved him to—"

Jandahl cut him off with a raised hand. "Whoa! Uh-uh, don't tell me. The less I know, the better." He stood, pulled some wrinkled company scrip out of his pocket, and threw it on the table. "I have to go. Have another one on me before you leave, okay?"

Spears nodded.

"I'll be in touch."

* * *

Word flashed around the hangar that Third Platoon had been replaced by the band. There were anonymous catcalls and some laughter as Fortis led his men to the adjoining hanger to board a separate transport for Eros-28. The mood of the platoon had turned ugly, but when Fortis looked at Ystremski the corporal shrugged as if saying, "DINLI."

The Fleet had to pass Eros-28 on the way to Eros-69, so the Space Marines of Third Platoon would arrive at their liberty location a day before the rest of the division landed on Eros-69.

The trip to the surface of Eros-28 was short but eventful.

The shuttle pilot struggled to get a fix on the navigation beacon at the spaceport, and when she gave up and engaged the autopilot, the shuttle rolled and nearly dove nose-first toward the surface.

"Are you sure about this?" she hissed through gritted teeth as she struggled with the controls. The shuttle bounced and bucked as it clawed downward through thick clouds of dust. "This dust storm is murder, and there's nobody answering the hailing freqs."

"This is where Battalion ordered us to go. Can you get us down?"

"We're about to find out."

The shuttle slammed belly-first onto the surface, bounced once, and came to a rest.

"Here you go, LT. Get off my ship so I can get the hell out of here."

Third Platoon literally got their first taste of Eros-28 when a whirlwind of dirt flooded into the troop compartment. They cursed and spat as they followed Fortis onto the landing zone, fanning out and crouching as the transport's engines wound up and the craft blasted off.

When the shuttle was gone, the platoon stood and coughed up the dirt that had been driven into their mouths and noses. A strong wind whipped stinging sand across exposed skin, and Fortis squinted as he searched for somewhere to escape the torment.

A person in a white contamination suit and respirator approached the Space Marines and gestured for them to follow. Fortis signaled "follow me" to the rest of the platoon. The white suit led them down some steps and into an airlock. Once the entire platoon was in the airlock, the white suit secured the exterior hatch and crossed to a hatch on the other end.

"Wait here. We need to get you blown down before you can come in." He stepped through the interior hatch, secured it behind him, and stood at the viewport. "Place your bags on the deck. Hold your arms over your heads and close your eyes. Try not to breathe. High-pressure air will blow the dust from your clothing."

Fortis and the Space Marines did as they were told, and air blasted from overhead jets mounted in the ceiling. When gale ceased, powerful vacuum vents removed the dirt and dust that had collected on the floor.

"Exit this way."

The interior hatch swung open, and the platoon entered a large room with rows of chairs. To Fortis, it looked like the passenger lounge in a space port.

Double doors at the far end of the room opened, and a dozen soldiers in black uniforms with pulse rifles at the ready rushed into the room. They lined up shoulder-to-shoulder and leveled their weapons at Fortis and his men.

"What's going on here?" Fortis demanded. The Space Marines behind him growled and grumbled. Ystremski held up a hand to silence them.

A tall blond-haired man strode in and stood before the soldiers. He was also wore a black uniform and a scabbard on his belt with a short sword which Fortis assumed was a badge of rank. He had thick red-purple scars on his cheeks which twisted when he scowled at the Space Marines and put his hands on his hips.

"Who are you and why are you here?"

The reception at the barrels of the guns, coupled with the scarred man's abrupt manner, surprised Abner and he struggled not to react with anger.

"I'm Second Lieutenant Abner Fortis, International Space Marine Corps. These men—" he indicated the Space Marines, "—are Third Platoon, Foxtrot Company, Second Battalion, First of the Ninth. Who are you?"

"Why are you here?"

Fortis fumbled in his pocket for the platoon's travel orders. "We've been ordered here for the next ten days. For liberty."

Scarface snorted. "Liberty? Here? Surely there's some mistake."

"Hmm. This is Eros-28, right?"

Scarface nodded. "Correct. This is Eros-28."

"Then we're in the right place."

A chubby, balding man rushed in and stepped in front of Scarface.

"What's the meaning of this?" he demanded of the blond man.

"They're Space Marines, Governor. Here for liberty, they say."

The governor turned to Fortis. "Liberty?"

Fortis stepped forward and held out their travel orders. "Ninth Division is on liberty in the Eros Cluster. We were ordered here."

The governor studied the document while the two groups of men glared at each other. Finally, he handed it back to Fortis. "It looks like your orders are valid. Still, they must be mistaken. This is not the right place for you and your men, Lieutenant." The governor pulled a handkerchief from his pocket and mopped his brow. "Eros-28 is an industrial planet. We maintain and repair heavy equipment from survey, mining, and construction missions. We even get the occasional asteroid cowboys. The equipment comes here and the personnel go to Eros-69 for quarantine and R&R. When we're finished, we either store the machinery in one of our underground garages or pack it up to go back into orbit. There's no liberty here."

* * * * *

Chapter Four

Fortis and Czrk sat on opposite sides of the governor's desk. Director Chive stood by the closed office door. Ystremski and the rest of the platoon were in a transient crew dormitory with Bob Drager, Czrk's executive assistant and the man in the white suit who had greeted the Marines at the airlock.

"I want to apologize for our reception of you and your men," Czrk started. "When a large military force arrives unannounced, we get nervous. Even though we're a GRC colony, we're not immune to privateers or slavers."

"I'm the one who should apologize, sir. It was a mistake to assign Space Marines to Eros-28. I will do everything I can to get out of your hair." *Like punch Reese in the mouth.* "If you'll show me to your communications center, I'll get word to Second Battalion to send a transport to extract us."

Czrk winced. "It's not that easy, Lieutenant. We're in the middle of a four-day sifter. We can't transmit or receive until it passes."

"A sifter?"

"A sifter is a dust storm. This is an arid planet, and when the wind blows down from the mountain, it creates massive dust storms. We call them sifters because the damned dust sifts into everything." Czrk coughed, a deep, phlegmy cough, and spat mud into a trashcan behind the desk. "Including your lungs, if you're not careful. Frankly, I'm surprised your transport was able to land."

43

"Four days?" Fortis' heart sank. Third Platoon would be unhappy to hear that half their liberty would be spent here.

"Don't worry, Lieutenant. It's been blowing for two days and my weather advisor reported that it won't last much longer." The governor smiled. "Your time here won't be the party you'd find on Eros-69, but we're hospitable here on Eros-28. We don't have a pleasure dome, but the food is reasonable, our gym is top notch, and our VR library is only a few months out of date."

"Governor, we're grateful for your hospitality, and again, I apologize for dropping in on you like this."

"No apology necessary. I have one question for you, though. Are you the same Lieutenant Fortis that led the attack on the GRC facility on Pada-Pada?"

Fortis' cheeks burned as blood rushed to his face. "I was on Pada-Pada, but it was hardly an attack on a GRC facility. I don't know what you've heard, but the test tubes made an unprovoked attack on us. My Marines and I acted in self-defense."

Czrk stared at the lieutenant for a long second before he forced a smile across his face.

"No matter. Pada-Pada is far away, and I assure you that we don't have a clone army here on Eros-28." He stood up to signal the meeting was over, and Fortis followed suit. The two men shook hands and the governor gestured to Chive.

"Director Chive will show you the way to the transient crew dormitory."

Chive gestured at the door. "This way, Lieutenant."

"Welcome to Eros-28," Czrk called as Fortis left the office.

* * *

C hive didn't say a word as the two men walked through wide passageways to the transient crew quarters. The silence was uncomfortable, and Fortis got an unfriendly vibe from the tight-lipped security chief. They arrived at a set of double doors marked "Transient Personnel Quarters A."

"Your men are in there," said Chive as he pointed to the door.

"Thank you," Fortis replied, but Chive was already returning the way they had come.

Fortis shook his head and went through the doors into an open bay barracks. Ystremski spotted him and greeted him.

"Hey, LT, how did it go with Battalion? Are they sending a troop transport?"

Fortis shook his head. "We can't get a message out until this sandstorm ends. The governor said it might be another couple days before we can get a report out."

Ystremski swore under his breath. "The lads won't like that, sir."

Fortis shrugged. "DINLI."

"Yeah. DINLI." Ystremski pointed to an open bunk near the door. "That one's yours, LT. I'm next to you, and the rest are billeted by squad. The mattresses are soft and the shitter stalls have doors. This is the lap of luxury for us grunts. I'm not sure how you'll survive, being a posh officer and all."

Fortis laughed. ISMC enlisted accommodations were notoriously spartan, even aboard Fleet troop transports. The rigid Fleet caste system that provided him with privacy and comfort while his men lived in close quarters embarrassed the young officer. He was grateful that same system didn't seem to exist on Eros-28.

"I put your duffle on your rack. That little guy that works for the governor, Drager, said we've got twenty minutes until the chow hall opens, if you want to unpack. Do you want to address the men?"

In the short time he'd served with Ystremski, Fortis had learned to recognize the difference between a legitimate question and a suggestion disguised with a question mark. Chevrons or not, Ystremski was still the gunnery sergeant he was before he slugged Captain Reese, and Fortis respected his knowledge and experience.

"Yeah, that's a good idea. I didn't get much from the governor, but they need to know what's going on. Form them up."

Ystremski had the platoon fall in.

"Third Platoon all present or accounted for, sir."

"Very well, Corporal. Put them at ease."

All eyes were on Fortis. "You men know we're here because of some kind of foul up." He paused, but there was no response. "The governor expects the sandstorm we landed in to last another two days, and I can't report our status to Captain Brickell and call for an extraction bird until it clears up. Which means we're stuck here for the short term.

"The governor told me their gym is excellent, and the food isn't bad, either." He shrugged. "I will do everything I can to get us out of here as soon as possible, but until then DINLI." Several heads nodded. "I'm going to leave our daily schedule up to Corporal Ystremski. If he says we train, then we train. If he says we lay in our racks all day—"

Ystremski gave an evil chuckle, and the platoon groaned. "Not going to happen, sir. I predict sore muscles in the mornings and tired bodies at night."

Fortis smiled. "There you have it." He tried to make eye contact with every Marine in the platoon. "Does anyone have questions for me?"

Nobody spoke up, so Fortis turned to Ystremski. "Corporal, dismiss the platoon, and let's get ready for chow."

* * *

While the Space Marines ate, Governor Czrk and Director Chive met in the governor's office.

"What do you make of them?" Czrk leaned back in his office chair and made a steeple with his fingers in front of his nose. "Do you believe their story?"

Chive shrugged. "It's the ISMC. They're certainly capable of a screw up like this."

The governor nodded. "You think it's a coincidence they sent Fortis? He looks like a cherry, but he led the ISMC attack on Pada-Pada."

"Anything is possible. He certainly didn't like your question about it."

"Huh." Czrk scratched his chin thoughtfully. "If they came here to cause trouble, you'd think they would have brought more than a platoon. I didn't see any weapons, though."

"It might be a reconnaissance mission. I ordered my men to scan their bags while they're in the cafeteria. We'll soon know what they've got hidden in their duffels."

The governor sighed. "Okay, let me know what you find. I sent Drager to show them around and monitor them. Maybe he can learn something."

Chive's face darkened. "Drager? Drager's not a trained operative. He's a fool."

"He's not there to spy on them; he's supposed to make sure they find what they need and not wander around."

"Drager should be able to handle that. If *he* doesn't get lost."

"I'll get Fortis on the comm link with his chain of command as soon as the sifter blows over. The sooner they leave, the better."

* * *

The affable Drager joined Fortis and the Space Marines for lunch. Governor Czrk had understated the quality of the food on the cafeteria. It wasn't gourmet, but it was far better than the dried ham steaks known as pig squares the Marines subsisted on in the field. It was better than the chow on the flagship, even.

"Your quarters and this dining facility are on a branch off the main corridor of the company facilities," Drager explained to the lieutenant. "Almost everything is underground."

"Why is that?"

"When the GRC first built this facility, they started constructing a standard dome. They were halfway finished when a massive sifter buried everything under five meters of dirt. That's when they decided to build everything underground. Before this latest sifter started, about half of our facilities were underground and half remained uncovered by the dirt. It changes."

After their meal Drager took Fortis on a tour. The corridors were ten meters wide and five meters high, and the floor, walls, and ceiling gleamed with a composite material Fortis had never seen before. A thick double yellow line divided the corridor into two lanes, and black and yellow stripes outlined doorways and hatches.

"There are six attached garages where we store equipment that branch off the main corridor, and twelve workshops where we repair and refit machinery. There are also eight remote garages we use for long-term storage, but we can only access those when the weather is clear."

"How many people work here?"

"Currently, we employ almost five thousand workers. A new group arrived two weeks ago, and we sent two hundred to Eros-69 to quarantine before they head home. Our workforce lives in ten habitat branches on the other side of the main corridor, and a thousand or so live in Boston with their families."

"Boston?"

"The first governor named the capital after his home city on Terra Earth. I guess it was a dirty hellhole, too."

Fortis stared, and Drager laughed.

"I'm joking, of course. We don't have family quarters in the facility, but there's no stopping human biology. Employees who choose to marry and have children live in houses they build in Boston. The first governor also named this facility Fenway, after a sports stadium in the original Boston."

Fortis searched his memory, but he drew a blank. "Never heard of the place."

The pair paused when they reached the door to the transient quarters.

"Hey, Bob, the governor mentioned a gym?"

"Ah, yes. The gym is right down there." Drager pointed at some doors down and across the corridor. "It's open all hours, although it can get crowded when the shift changes at 0800, 1600, and midnight colony time." He gave Fortis a sheepish smile. "It's not much, but it's home. Do you have any other questions, Lieutenant?"

Fortis shook his head. "We appreciate your hospitality, Mr. Drager." He extended his hand, and the two men shook. "It will be a shame to leave all this after the sifter passes."

They shared a laugh, and Fortis entered his quarters.

* * * * *

Chapter Five

Aboard the Fleet flagship *Atlas*, General Gupta tightened his seatbelt and prepared himself for the trip down to Eros-69. Captain Nilsen, his aide-de-camp, was strapped in next to him. The gentle pressure of her leg against his electrified the general, and he allowed his thoughts to wander toward his liberty plans for the young Nordic beauty. One of his Fleet Academy classmates had given Gupta his highest personal recommendation when Nilsen's name appeared on the list of candidates for her current position, but the general had yet to explore the extent of that endorsement. He hoped—

The pilot's voice came over the speakers, interrupting Gupta's fantasy.

"General, sorry to bother you, but there's a staff runner on the way with a message for you."

"Bah! Tell him we're already gone and forward it to the surface."

"Sir, the staff duty officer said it was a Whiskey priority message."

"Whiskey? What the hell?"

Fleet communications were prioritized due to limited bandwidth through the jump gate communications portals. Alpha was the lowest priority and was assigned to routine administrative message traffic. Zulu was the highest priority and was reserved for warning of imminent enemy attack. Gupta had seen a Whiskey priority message only once in all his years in the ISMC, when his Battalion was ordered to track down slavers who had kidnapped all the residents of an agricultural colony.

The hatch popped open, and the runner entered and handed Gupta an envelope. The general looked at Nilsen, who shrugged and shifted her weight so their legs were no longer touching. He tore open the envelope and discovered that the message was a jumble of letters, numbers, and symbols.

"It's double encrypted, sir," the runner said. "Only you have the keycode."

Gupta fought back the urge to vent on the runner. He tore open the buckle on his seat restraint and stood up.

"Don't go anywhere," he shouted at the pilot. "We're leaving in ten minutes."

Eight minutes later, after he'd broken the encryption and verified the message, he dialed the number to the watch center. "This is General Gupta. Immediately recall all 9th Division Space Marines from Eros-69 and set Alert Condition Bravo."

The duty officer acknowledged his orders, then he hung up and punched in the number for the Fleet commander, Fleet Admiral Burle Kinshaw.

"Guppy! Good to hear from you. Why aren't you down on Eros-69 yet?"

"You haven't seen the Whiskey message yet?"

"Whiskey? What the hell?"

"That's what I said. Fleet Intelligence has detected unknown potential hostile activity in the sector where *Nelson* disappeared last month. We've been ordered to investigate and be prepared for action."

* * *

Fortis and Ystremski were the only two people in the cavernous weight room. They could hear the shouts and curses of the other Space Marines through the swinging doors at the far end of the room, who were engaged in a game of Calcio Fiorentino on the highly polished basketball court.

When the ISMC had been formed from the elite military units from all over Terra Earth, many of those units had brought their cultural traditions with them. The kukri, a traditional weapon carried by the fierce Gurkha warriors from Nepal, was so deadly that the ISMC adopted it as their standard edged weapon, with one caveat: A Space Marine had to earn the right to carry a kukri by serving in combat.

Calcio Fiorentino was another cultural tradition that came to the Corps, this time by way of northern Italy. The game dated back many centuries and it is best described as a combination of basketball, bare-knuckle brawling, and rugby. It's a violent sport that is not for the faint of heart. The ISMC required the rules be modified to prevent serious injury among the players.

The Marines had invited Fortis to join their game, but the lieutenant ducked the offer because of his strength enhancement workout requirements. He and Ystremski watched the game long enough to see the ball roll, unnoticed, from under the pile of battling Marines and into the far corner of the room.

"Those guys will kill each other," Fortis observed. "Maybe we should stop them."

The corporal shook his head. "Nah. They'll be okay, sir. It's good for them to roughhouse now and then; helps the cherries earn acceptance. It also sorts out the pecking order among the privates.

They'll fight like hell for an hour and be best friends afterwards. Good way to break in the new guys, too."

"I appreciate you greasing the skids with the platoon," Fortis said as they loaded heavy metal plates onto the weight bar. "It's hard enough to give them bad news, but when it's because of me, it sucks."

"What are you talking about?" Ystremski positioned himself behind the bench as Fortis slipped under the bar.

"You gave them a heads up about our situation here, right?"

"Yeah, I did, but that's not what I meant. The other, about you."

Fortis exhaled heavily and sucked in a deep breath as he lifted the bar and held it above his chest. As he lowered it, he looked up at Ystremski. "We're not here because of an administrative foul up. It was Reese."

"No shit." The corporal guided the bar up as Fortis strained under the weight. "What makes you think it's because of you?"

Fortis hissed as he lowered the bar and pressed it up again. "Reese is pissed off at me, wouldn't you say?"

"Meh, Reese is a petty, vindictive prick, sir. But it's not just you. I slugged him, remember?"

Fortis lowered the bar onto the bar rest and sat up. Raw power surged through his chest and he gasped as he flexed his muscles.

Ystremski smiled. "Feels good, doesn't it?"

"Best feeling in the world," replied Fortis.

"Wait until you get to Level Ten."

Ystremski added more weight plates and Fortis positioned himself back under the bar.

"They have to put up with a lot without me adding to it," Fortis grunted through gritted teeth.

"Don't worry, LT. Nobody is blaming you for this clusterfuck. In a couple days, they'll be drunk as skunks and up to their asses in women on Eros-69, and this place will be a distant memory." He put a hand on the bar and stopped Fortis from placing it back on the rest. "Now, why don't you stop being a pussy and start lifting some real weight?"

* * *

J andahl slipped through the door of the utilities room and it closed behind him with a *click*. Chive was already there, and his presence among the pipes and wiring runs unnerved Jandahl. He was a veteran of numerous undercover missions for the GRC, and he'd made his share of clandestine meetings with unsavory characters, but Chive was a different breed. The scarred mercenary exuded danger.

What scared Jandahl the most was the ease with which Chive had ferreted him out. Jandahl's intelligence collection mission to Eros-28 had been planned and conducted in the strictest secrecy. He had arrived on a routine shuttle with the group of replacement workers and his cover as a logistics and transportation clerk was rock solid. Still, he was only on Eros-28 three days before the security director paid him a visit in the logistics section where he worked and made Jandahl an offer he couldn't refuse: work with Chive to uncover the resistance or Chive would expose him and drive him from the colony in disgrace.

"What's the news?" Chive demanded without any greeting. He was all business, the scars on his cheeks making him look angry, even when he smiled, which wasn't often.

"Spears has gone to pieces since his wife went missing. He moved their son somewhere, but I stopped him before he could tell me."

"Why? That would be good information to exploit."

Jandahl shook his head. "Sometimes you forget yourself, Chive. These people are not the enemy. They're GRC employees. Some of them conduct acts of vandalism, allegedly as part of a half-assed resistance movement, but we're not at war with them. My directive from GRC headquarters was to investigate the overall situation here, not target the children of the workers. You can't always break kneecaps and pull fingernails."

"Where's Raisa Spears?" Jandahl had hoped to provoke a reaction from Chive with his point-blank question, but the security chief didn't flinch.

"I don't know. I thought the colonial police had her."

The spy stared into Chive's eyes and searched for a flicker of prevarication, but he saw none.

"If the colonial police had her, I'd know about it."

Chive shrugged. "Maybe your source cut you out of the loop."

"I doubt it; he doesn't know he's a source. What have you found out about the Space Marines?"

"Their story appears to check out. They don't have any weapons or explosives, and they seem as anxious to leave as we are to get rid of them."

"What about the cartel? Any progress there?"

"Why are you asking me?" Chive scoffed. "You're the intelligence operative. I just break kneecaps and pull fingernails, remember?"

Jandahl took a deep breath to calm himself and then headed for the door. He stopped and looked back. "You know, Chive, when this is all over, I'm going to remember moments like these when I write my final report."

He opened the door a crack, looked up and down the passageway, and left.

The door clicked shut behind him.

* * *

Two hours after the Calcio Fiorentino game ended, Lieutenant Fortis stretched out on the weight room floor and groaned. Every muscle in his body was screaming, protesting at the punishment Corporal Ystremski had meted out during their workout. All Fortis could do was smile at the exquisite, full-body agony. Despite the pain, he felt great.

Ystremski had jumped into the exercise rotation when Fortis reached the upper limit of his own strength. The older man had lifted, pushed, and pulled more weight than Fortis could have imagined. Ystremski was not a large man with masses of bulging muscles, but the power he generated amazed Fortis.

He propped himself up on one elbow and watched as Ystremski curled a loaded bar with ease.

"What do you make of that security guy, Chive?"

The corporal set the bar down with a *clank*. "He doesn't say much. Seems intense for a backwater place like this. It surprised me to see the corporate types had hired a mercenary to run their security."

"Mercenary? How do you know he's a mercenary? Do you know him?"

Ystremski shook his head and sat down on a bench next to Fortis. "No, I don't know *him*, but I recognize the type." He gestured to his face. "The scars gave him away."

"Yeah, the scars. What about them?"

"They're dueling scars. You saw his sword, right? He's a Kuiper Knight."

"What's a Kuiper Knight?"

"Not what, who. The Kuiper Knights are a freelance group of general-purpose mercenary assholes who operate on the fringes of deep space. Dirty deeds done for the highest bidder. They'll do anything for a handful of credits. I've heard they hire out as security forces for survey missions and miners and then jump the profitable claims. A lot of ex-Space Marines and Fleet dropouts are Kuiper Knights. They follow their own weird pseudo-religion which basically means they're a cult. A heavily armed cult."

"Huh. I've never heard of them."

"When I first joined the ISMC, we chased down a bunch who kidnapped an entire farming colony and sold them off as slaves." Ystremski rubbed his hand together as if relishing the memory. "Killed every one of them."

"What about the scars? They get them from dueling?"

Ystremski nodded. "The Knights are a meritocracy, so they have to fight their way up the ranks. They'd run out of guys if they fought to the death, so they duel with dull swords and don't wear headgear. That dude Chive has been in a duel or two."

"You think they're making a move on Eros-28?"

Ystremski scoffed. "That would take some balls. Looting ore cars on some backwater planet is one thing, picking a fight with the GRC is a whole other matter. This place doesn't look like much, but I don't think the GRC would let it go without a fight."

* * * * *

Chapter Six

Governor Czrk looked up in annoyance when Chive barged into his office without knocking.

"You want something, Governor?"

"Close the door."

Chive pushed the door shut and the two men were alone.

"What are the results of your scan of the Space Marines. Anything of interest?"

The security chief shook his head. "No. My men didn't detect anything significant. They have a mini satcom set and a medic bag. The only weapons they have are their kukris. No rifles or pistols, and no explosives."

"Kukris? What are kukris?"

Chive struggled not to laugh at the concern on Czrk's face.

"A kukri is a bladed weapon about this long." He held up his hands about forty centimeters apart. "They're standard Space Marine issue. Nothing fancy."

"Are they dangerous?"

This time Chive did laugh.

"In the right hands, a kukri is lethal, and these guys are experts."

Czrk's eyes widened.

"Relax, Governor. They don't have anything I wouldn't expect them to have on a liberty run; I don't think they're a threat. As hard as it is to believe, I think they really are lost."

* * *

Mandel Spears and his resistance cell, two men and two women, crouched in the dim light of a fluttering candle in the abandoned dome. After a sifter had buried the dome when it was half-finished, some of the colonists had quietly excavated a wide area under the intact roof. The wind whistled outside and dust swirled inside on unseen currents of air, but they were safe, and, to their experienced ears, the storm had begun to weaken.

"What news of Raisa?" asked Pai Choon, a grim-faced woman who wore her blonde hair tied back in a severe ponytail.

Spears pulled aside his dirty filter mask and spat a thick blob of muddy phlegm before he shook his head. "Nothing. It's like she never existed."

Glenn Deale, a hulking mechanic with a square head and flat nose, stood up and scoffed. "To the GRC, she didn't." The other members of the group shot him angry looks. "What? It's true. She didn't work for them, so, in their eyes, she was a freeloader. Not even human."

"Doesn't." Spears rose to his feet and faced Deale. "She *doesn't* work for them."

Deale arched his eyebrows but said nothing.

The third man, Ben West, stood and insinuated himself between Shears and Deale.

"Guys, until we get some solid information on Raisa, I think we need to concentrate on what's next. Is there a what's next?"

Everyone looked at Spears.

"When the sifter lifts they'll add shifts to excavate the garage Raisa blew up. That will give us an opportunity to track the China

Mike back to the source. We *have* to find the lab if we want to put a stop to this."

Deale shook his head. "Man, how many times have we tried this? Four? Five? Every time, it's the same result. We spot the dealers, but they disappear before we can figure out who their suppliers are."

"What would you have us do, Deale? Let's hear your master plan."

"It's easy. We grab a GRC suit and make 'em talk."

Spears scoffed. "Genius 'Make 'em talk.' How do you propose we do that?"

Deale shrugged. "Beat it out of them. Electric shock. Whatever it takes. It's not like we don't have people who have learned the hard way at the hands of those bastards. Let's use their own methods against them."

"That's a brilliant plan." Spears' voice dripped with sarcasm. "Let's grab a corporate executive and torture them. Who did you have in mind, the governor?"

Deale scowled at Spears. "What's wrong with you? Don't you want to stop those sons of bitches from poisoning us with their drug?"

"Of course I do, but we can't do it if we torture a GRC exec, and they call the colonial police down on our heads. I heard they brought Space Marines in, too."

"Space Marines? Why did they bring in Space Marines?"

"Probably because Space Marines kill people," said Ben West. "We just blew up their garage and buried their drugs. They're going to want revenge." He wrung his hands. "This is getting out of hand."

"What about the drugs hidden in the vehicles?" Choon asked.

"Leave it there and let them ship it off-world," scoffed Deale. "We don't want to hurt their feelings."

Spears glared at him. "*Dask* has requested that we don't interfere with it."

Dask Finkle was the unofficial leader of the resistance—a loose network of colonists who were dissatisfied with GRC management of Eros-28. Resistance cells formed and dissolved at will, and they chose their own level of involvement in the ongoing unrest. Spears' cell had formed early in the movement, but they'd been mostly talk until the highly addictive drug China Mike had spread through colony. The destruction of the garage was a big step up for them.

"What the hell? We're supposed to let them have it back?"

"Deale, that's what Dask said. I don't know why, maybe he has something else planned. Either way, this group isn't going to interfere. Got it?"

The other woman in the cell, Shelly Baird, stood up and stretched. "This is going nowhere. The sifter will end soon, and I need to get some sleep before the shift begins." Baird was an electronics specialist, and her shop would be loaded with extra work once crews excavated the buried garage. "I'll keep my eyes open and let you know what I find."

Spears nodded, and she disappeared into the shadows.

The rest of the cell gave Spears similar assurances and vanished in different directions. The tunnel networks the colonists had dug by hand after the subway collapsed ran in all directions. It was only local knowledge that kept them from becoming hopelessly lost.

When Spears was alone, he slumped onto the dirt floor and stared at the flickering candle. Grief squeezed his chest until he couldn't breathe and he groaned at the pain.

Deale is right. Raisa is gone.

He rolled onto his side and hugged his knees as deep sobs wracked his body. A sudden gust of wind blew the candle out as his anguished cries echoed in the lonely darkness.

* * * * *

Chapter Seven

"Lieutenant Fortis? Hey, LT."

A hand was shaking Fortis' shoulder, and he sat straight up out of a deep sleep.

"Wha-what?"

"Sir, it's me, Private Boudreaux. The fire watch. That Drager guy is at the door. He wants to see you."

Fortis swung his feet off his bunk and hissed when they hit the cold floor.

"What does he want?"

"He didn't say, sir. He just said it was urgent."

"Okay, I'm up." The lieutenant stood on unsteady legs and stretched. The transient quarters were dark, the only light the green glow of emergency exit signs at the doors. "What time is it?"

"0320. You want me to tell him to come back?"

"No, no." Fortis reached for his uniform hanging on the end of his bunk. "Tell him I'll be there in a second."

"Aye, aye, sir."

"What's going on?"

Fortis jumped at the voice close to his ear. He turned and saw Corporal Ystremski standing next to him, fully dressed.

"Geez, Corporal, don't you ever sleep?" Ystremski snorted. Fortis fastened his belt and buttoned his shirt. "Drager, the corporate guy, wants to talk to me; said it was urgent."

"Huh. Might be good news."

"Yeah, maybe." Fortis tied his boots and stood, stretching his arms overhead as far as he could. A slight groan escaped his lips.

A normal person would have been paralyzed by muscular soreness after a workout like the one Ystremski put Fortis through the previous day, but the strength enhancements inhibited muscle soreness by breaking down lactic acid and promoting muscle growth and repair, which allowed the Space Marines to string together days of intense workouts with no ill effects. All Fortis felt was mild stiffness that a good stretch would relieve.

Ystremski chuckled softly. "Go see what he wants, sir. I'll be here."

Fortis walked out and blinked in the glare of the lights in the passageway. "Good morning, Bob. What can I do for you?"

Drager gave him a big smile. "Sorry to wake you, Lieutenant, but I have good news. The sifter has passed. Come with me; we've got a carrier signal with the satellite, and you can message your boss."

"Awesome!" Fortis was wide awake now. "Give me a sec to tell Ystremski."

By the time he got back to Ystremski's bunk, a knot of Space Marines had gathered.

"Good news, sir?" a voice from the group asked.

"At ease, numbnuts," Ystremski growled. He put his hand on Fortis' arm. "Let's go over here so we can talk in private, sir."

When they were out of earshot, Fortis leaned close to Ystremski.

"Drager said the sifter has passed, and they've got a satellite signal. I'm on my way to contact Battalion HQ."

"Hmm. Okay, sir. I'll ride herd on the platoon while you're gone. Just make sure you include the entire chain of command on your message. We don't want Reese to ignore it and leave us hanging again."

"Good idea."

Lieutenant Fortis accompanied Drager to the Fenway communications center, a windowless office located in the same hall as the governor's office.

Drager gestured at the racks of blinking screens and scopes. "It's not state-of-the-art, but our communications suite gets the job done." He explained to Fortis how to format and transmit a message to the flagship, then left to give the officer some privacy.

"I'll come back and check on you in a few minutes."

Fortis wrote and rewrote his message several times. He hated spending so much time on a simple task, but he had to choose his words carefully.

Although he strongly suspected Reese had sent Third Platoon to Eros-28 out of spite, he couldn't say that. There might be a legitimate reason why he and his men were routed to the industrial colony that he wasn't aware of. He also didn't want to sound like he was complaining.

The Space Marines had a roof over their heads, the food was good, and nobody was shooting at them—an easy day in the Corps. Fortis addressed the message to Captain Brickell, but that didn't mean he was the only person who would see it.

He finally settled on a short and simple request for extraction which left little to misinterpretation:

From: Platoon Leader, 3rd Platoon, Foxtrot Company
To: Company Commander, Foxtrot Company

Request extraction of 3rd Platoon from Eros-28 to flagship Atlas *at the earliest opportunity. Eros-28 is an industrial colony with limited capability to host deployed troops.*

3rd Platoon is standing by for orders.

*F*ortis

* * *

Thirty minutes later, Fortis returned to the transient personnel quarters and found the lights on and the entire platoon awake and dressed. Their racks were made, and many of them had their duffel bags packed and waiting.

"What the hell is this?" he asked Corporal Ystremski.

"Sir, I tried to tell them, but I'm just a lowly corporal."

He sighed. "Form them up, I'll explain."

Once the men were in ranks and standing at ease, he stepped forward to address them.

"Men, it seems you've all heard the news that the sifter has passed. That is true, and it is also true that I was able to get a message off to the company explaining our situation and requested extraction."

Smiles and nods greeted this announcement.

Fortis continued: "It's going to take time for my message to reach Captain Brickell. Remember, the entire division is on liberty on Eros-69, so it won't be easy for him to round up the right people to make arrangements for our extraction. Who knows, they might decide to leave us here."

There were crestfallen looks and scowls in the ranks, and he shrugged. "DINLI." He motioned to Corporal Ystremski. "In the meantime, we're all awake, and Corporal Ystremski is in charge of the daily schedule. Corporal?"

Ystremski didn't miss a beat. He strode forward with an evil grin on his face. He placed his hands on his hips.

"YOU HAVE TEN SECONDS TO GET YOUR ASSES OVER TO THE GYMNASIUM. MOVE! MOVE! MOVE!"

* * *

Colonial Police Chief Schultz steered his electric cart into a narrow Boston side street and turned off the flashing lights. Dask Finkle, his friend and former shift leader in the pipe fitting shop, slid into the seat next to him. The two men shook hands.

"Good to see you, Schultzy," Finkle said with a smile.

"I see nothing," Chief Schultz declared, and the two men laughed. The pair had been friends for many years and the old joke was comfortable territory.

"What's new?" asked Finkle. "Any problems from the sifter?"

"I have received no reports of trouble except for the explosion in Garage Number Seven. You wouldn't know anything about that, would you?"

"No. I didn't have anything to do with that one."

Chief Schultz knew Finkle was the nominal leader of the resistance. It was Finkle who had organized the first labor slowdowns, and he had led the opposition to the crackdown by Security Director Chive and his mercenaries. Schultz relied on Finkle to keep him apprised of news around the colony. In return he provided the resistance leader with information about the goings-on in upper management. Together, they kept tensions on Eros-28 at a low simmer. Until China Mike had flooded the colony.

"A platoon of Space Marines arrived on a lander in the middle of the sifter," said Chief Schultz.

"Space Marines? So the UNT has sided with the GRC?"

"I don't think so. They claim they're here by accident."

"Accident? Nobody comes to Eros-28 by accident."

"The rest of their division is on Eros-69. These poor bastards got sent here."

"Huh. What are they doing?"

Schultz shrugged. "Nothing right now. They called for a transport back to their flagship, but it's going to take time."

"Interesting."

"You know what's really interesting? The platoon leader is a lieutenant named Fortis. Does that name ring a bell?"

Finkle shook his head. "Hmm, no. Should it?"

"A little while back there was a GRC project to clone soldiers for the UNT. A group of Space Marines destroyed the clones and killed a bunch of humans, too. Fortis was one of those Space Marines."

"Huh. That *is* interesting."

After a few seconds, Finkle continued. "A woman is missing. One of ours, named Raisa Spears. Do you have her?"

"No. We don't have anyone in custody. When did she go missing?"

"The night the garage collapsed."

"Maybe she got caught in the sifter."

"Maybe. I guess we'll find out soon enough."

Chief Schultz extended his hand and Finkle shook it.

"Time to go, my friend. Protect and serve. Lots of dirt to move."

Finkle slid out of the cart.

"Stay safe, Schultzy."

* * * * *

Chapter Eight

Instead of a costly city-wide communications system that required continual maintenance in the dusty conditions of Eros-28, the GRC built a number of towers with speakers mounted. These served as an early warning system for approaching sifters and Eolian blasts. They were also used to communicate news about the repair facility. One long blast on the horn indicated the next shift started work in one hour. One, two, or three short blasts followed to indicate which crew was due to start. It was rudimentary but effective, and, most importantly, it was inexpensive.

Electric plow trucks patrolled the city streets and cleared the main thoroughfares of any dirt left behind by the sifter. When they finished, the plow drivers would use whatever battery capacity remained to clear side streets and back alleys.

The colony police spread out across the city in search of citizens who might need assistance. Blowing dirt could block doors and windows, and more than one dead colonist had been discovered entombed in their home after a severe storm.

A long horn blast sounded, followed by one short blast, and the first shift streamed through the city toward the tunnel entrance to the maintenance facility. Word of the garage collapse had spread from house to house as soon as the sifter passed, and everyone knew there were long, hard hours of labor ahead.

Glenn Deale lurked in an alley doorway just off the main street and watched the crowd closely. A few individuals passed through the mass of workers and appeared to shake hands with many of them. To Deale's experienced eye, they weren't shaking hands. Instead, small plastic envelopes were being exchanged for folded corporate scrip. The exchanges happened so fast that they were almost invisible and the colonial police who monitored the crowds seemed oblivious to the drug trade happening in plain view.

The surge of people tapered off until only a few tardy workers were left running toward the maintenance facility and the street dealers took that as their signal to melt back into the cityscape. Deale saw his chance when one of them chose his alley.

Deale surged out of his hiding place, wrapped one beefy arm around the dealer's neck, and delivered a kidney punch with the other. The dealer gurgled and stiffened in agony from the blow to his kidneys. Deale dragged his prey to his hiding place and elbowed the door shut behind them.

The man went limp and Deale shifted his grip so he could hold the unconscious man under both arms. He kicked open a door, revealing steps that led down into the hand-dug tunnel network.

Twenty minutes later, Deale let the drug dealer fall to the floor of the half-built dome. He struck a match and a candle flickered to life. The semi-conscious man grunted and tried to get up, but Deale planted a boot between his shoulders and drove him back down.

"Don't try that again, or next time I'll make it hurt."

The other man grunted again, but stayed down.

Deale pulled out a length of cordage and knelt on the other man's neck. He yanked his arms back and bound his wrists together with a tight knot. When Deale was finished with the hands, he shifted and straddled his captive's legs. He lashed the ankles together and then rolled the man over until he was sitting.

"What's your name?"

The drug dealer was wide-eyed with fear but said nothing.

Deale poked him in the chest with a thick finger.

"What's your name?" After a second, Deale shook his head. "Man, listen. My name's Glenn. I just want to ask you a few questions, like a conversation, okay? C'mon, what's your name?"

The other man pursed his lips, and for a moment Deale thought he wasn't going to respond.

"Moore. My name's Moore," he croaked through parched and dirt-crusted lips. "I need some water."

"Yeah, yeah, I'll get you some water. After we talk, okay, Moore?"

Moore was silent.

Deale dug through Moore's pockets and came up with a thick wad of scrip and a handful of plastic envelopes. Inside the envelopes were yellow-white crystals.

"China Mike, right?" Deale knew what the crystals were from personal experience, but Moore didn't know that.

The dealer nodded.

"Who do you get it from?"

Moore stiffened and shook his head.

"Come on, you can tell me," Deale said.

"He's just a guy I know. I don't know his name."

"You can do better than that, Moore." Deale leaned in until their noses were almost touching. "Who's your supplier?"

The drug dealer squeezed his eyes shut and shook his head.

"If you don't answer my questions, I'm going to hurt you. Now, who is your supplier?"

Moore twisted away and rolled over onto his side. "I don't know. I don't know!"

Deale pulled him back up. "Okay then, tell me this: where do you meet this guy you don't know?"

Moore clenched his jaw and stared straight ahead.

After a long second Deale slapped him across the face. The drug dealer looked at him with a mix of fear and surprise. Deale nodded.

"Yeah, it's like that. I want answers, and if you won't give them to me I'll take them." He grabbed handfuls of Moore's tunic and yanked him close and snarled, "Let's try this again. Where do you meet your mystery man?"

The sharp stink of urine stung Deale's nose as Moore lost control of his bladder.

"Ah, shit!"

He shoved his captive away, and Moore tumbled across the floor and buried his face in shame. Deale regarded the defeated man for a moment before he hauled him up.

"Where do you meet him, Moore?"

He seized Moore by the throat and squeezed. Moore's eyes bulged, and he made a wet sobbing noise. He struggled, but he was no match for the larger man. Deale relaxed his grip before Moore passed out and let him slump to the floor.

"We can do this all day if you want," said Deale. "I don't know how many times a guy can be choked out before his brain is damaged, but I guess we'll find out."

Moore gagged and gasped.

"Ready for round two?" Deale's fingers closed around Moore's throat.

He squeezed before Moore managed to croak, "Please."

Deale stopped. "Please what?"

"No more." Moore's voice was barely audible. "No more."

"There's plenty more, unless you tell me what I want to know."

Moore nodded, and a tear escaped from the corner of his eye, leaving a clean streak on his dirty cheek.

"Good boy." Deale dug a hydration pack from his jacket, popped the cap, and stuck the nipple in Moore's mouth. His captive made greedy slurping sounds as he sucked it dry. Deale threw the empty pack aside and put his hands on Moore's shoulders.

"You were about to tell me where you meet your supplier."

"The Cock and Tail. It's a pub on Dirt Road."

"I know the place. How do I recognize him?"

"He works the door. Big guy, scar across his cheek." He traced a path across his face with trembling fingers. "Can't miss him."

"Does he have a name?"

Moore shrugged. "I dunno. I hand him the money, and he gives me the stuff. It's not like we're friends."

Deale lifted Moore's face up with a finger under his chin. "See? That wasn't so hard, was it?"

"You'll let me go?" Hope filled Moore's tear-streaked face.

"I never said that." Deale slammed a massive fist into Moore's jaw, sending him sprawling in the dirt. He dug the plastic envelopes of China Mike out of his pocket. "Do you know what the penalty is for dealing drugs? It's death by overdose, and it looks to me like you're about to overdose on your own shit."

* * *

After an intense calisthenic workout at the hands of Corporal Ystremski, followed by a hearty breakfast, Fortis felt a wave of euphoria as he left the cafeteria. The entire platoon was in good spirits, and they laughed and joked through their meal. Ystremski had been right; despite a few fat lips and black eyes, the Calcio Fiorentino had exorcised tension within the platoon. The vigorous pre-reveille exercises had stretched out residual muscular soreness, and morale was high.

"Lieutenant Fortis?"

Fortis turned and saw Bob Drager bustling down the corridor.

"Good morning, Bob. More good news?"

"More like an opportunity," Drager panted. "Now that the sifter is over, you and your men can go out on the surface. There's not much to look at, but it beats being buried underground all the time."

Fortis looked at Ystremski, who shrugged.

"That sounds great, thanks. How do we get out there?"

Drager pointed up with both index fingers and smiled. "How about if we go up onto the observation tower and get oriented, first? Boston is a small town, but it all looks the same when you're down on the streets."

The whole platoon followed Drager up a vertical tube with ladder rungs welded onto the side.

"We built these to make sure we can get out in case of a big sifter," Drager explained as he climbed. "We call them periscopes; you'll see why when we get to the top."

At the top of the periscope Drager opened a large hatch and climbed out. The hatch led to a platform about twenty meters high, large enough to accommodate the entire platoon with room to spare.

From the platform, they could see the entire city of Boston and the surrounding desert.

The surface of Eros-28 was brown and featureless. In the distance, a single mountain towered over the landscape. The top of the mountain was shrouded in brown clouds and the weak light from the planet's primary star cast an orange-hued halo around the solitary peak.

Below, there was a squat collection of buildings close to the maintenance facility. Fortis saw yellow plows at work in the widest roads and orange-clad figures were shoveling doorways clear in side streets and alleys.

"Not much to look at, is it?" Drager smiled. "Not much liberty."

Fortis nodded in agreement. "What are we looking at, Drager?"

Drager pointed at the tall mountain in the distance. "That's Dirt Mountain. It's the highest point on the planet; actually, it's the only mountain on Eros-28. It's also the source of the dirt the sifters blow around. All the dirt you see around you originated up there."

The lieutenant looked around at the mounds of dirt piled up in every direction.

"All this dirt came from the mountain?"

Drager nodded. "Dirt Mountain is what they call a cold volcano. It's a thermal vent that extends to the center of the planet. As the core pressure vents, molten material rises up through the center of the mountain. By the time it reaches the top, it's cooled to the point where it doesn't flow, it sticks to the inside of the vent and adds another layer of rock. The new inner layers create outward pressure and the old layers crumble away. When a windstorm blows, it picks up the loose material and becomes a sifter, which dumps dirt wherever it wants."

"Wow. That's incredible."

"Yeah. Lucky us." Drager chuckled and coughed at the same time before he spat over the side of the periscope. "Don't mind me, Lieutenant. My sense of humor jumps between the gallows and the graveyard."

He pointed at the buildings below. "That's Boston, where some of our workers live. There's not much to see or do. It's just a bunch of mud huts, really. Along the outside wall of this facility is a place we call Dirt Alley. There are several bars there, basically our version of a red-light district." He pointed at the surrounding desert. "The rest of it is a whole lot of nothing.

"And that concludes your tour of Eros-28."

Although he had perked up when Drager said "bars," Corporal Ystremski had a half-scowl on his face. "This is better than being buried underground?"

"Give it a week, Corporal. Then you'll beg to come up here."

Fortis and Drager laughed, and Ystremski snorted. "If we're stuck here for a week, all of these monkeys will be begging to come up here just to get away from me." Several of the Marines standing within earshot nodded their agreement.

"Anyway," Drager continued. "If you want to walk around the city, I'll show you how to get outside the facility. But please remember that at least one third of the city is asleep at any time between shifts. There's no crime and there are always colonial police on patrol. Those are the guys in the orange jumpsuits. If you get lost, look for this platform. There are four main roads that crisscross the city; all you have to do is find one and follow it until you see the tower."

* * * * *

Chapter Nine

The comms terminal at Governor Czrk's elbow warbled, and he pressed the flashing button to answer.

"Governor, it's Chief Schultz."

"Hello, Chief. What's on your mind?"

"Pardon the interruption, sir, but there's been another overdose."

"Oh? When?"

"It's hard to say until the autopsy is completed, but it's recent. After the sifter, for sure. My men found the body buried under a dirt pile in an alley, but the skin wasn't scoured away like he'd been out in the storm."

"He? Do you have an identity?"

"No, sir. We ran his prints and DNA against the database and got no hits. He's a freeloader."

"Well, at least we don't have to report this one to corporate. Are you sure it's an overdose?"

"He's got needle marks on both arms, and there was a rubber hose tied around one of his arms."

"A junkie freeloader."

There was a long silence on the line before Schultz replied.

"Governor, I saw the body when they brought it in. There's more to it than an overdose, I think. He's got some bruises on his face like he was beat up, and it looks like he was strangled, too. His wrists are chafed."

"Chafed?"

"Yes, sir, chafed. The doctor said it looked like he was tied up shortly before he died."

"Hmm. That's odd."

"Yes, sir, it is."

"Anything else?"

"Not right now. Doc has started the autopsy, so maybe we'll know more when he's finished. I thought you'd want to know."

"Yes, thank you, Chief. Let me know the results of the autopsy."

* * *

Captain Brickell smoothed his utilities one final time and cleared his throat before he rapped on the door three times.

"Come."

Brickell opened the door and found Colonel Kivak Sobieski standing over a desk covered with musters, readiness reports, and supply requisitions. The colonel's perpetual scowl looked deeper than usual and dark circles under his eyes gave him a skull-like appearance.

"Sir, Captain Brickell."

"I know who you are, Captain. What do you want?"

"We have a situation, sir. With the recall, I mean."

Four hours earlier, General Gupta had set Alert Condition Bravo and ordered a complete recall of all Ninth Division Space Marines from Eros-69.

"A situation? What situation?"

"Ah…well, sir, one of my platoons, Third Platoon, isn't on Eros-69."

"Where are they?"

"They were sent to Eros-28. They're there now awaiting extraction." He placed a copy of Fortis' message on the desk in front of the colonel.

"Eros-28? Eros-28 isn't a liberty planet. Who sent them to Eros-28?"

"The orders were signed by the Battalion admin officer, sir. Captain Reese."

"Reese?"

"Yes, sir. We were mustered in the hangar getting ready to board the transports when Reese showed up and told Third Platoon they had been replaced by the division band. He sent them to another hangar to board a transport to Eros-28."

Sobieski threw down his pen and leaned across his desk.

"You allowed the division band to replace one of your platoons?"

"Sir, I—well…it was the division band. The general's band. The Battalion admin officer signed the orders."

Sobieski blinked. "Wait a second. You said Third Platoon?"

Brickell nodded.

"Who's the platoon leader?"

Brickell cleared his throat. "Third Platoon is commanded by Lieutenant Fortis, sir."

"Fortis. *That* Fortis." It was an indictment, not a question.

"Yes, sir, Second Lieutenant Fortis."

Sobieski dropped his chin to his chest and slowly shook his head. When he looked up, his eyes flashed with anger.

"WILLIS!"

Staff Sergeant Willis, the colonel's administrative aide, entered the office.

"Yes, sir."

"Get that idiot Reese up here. Now!"

"Aye, aye, sir."

The colonel straightened up and pointed at Brickell with a stiff-fingered motion known in the ISMC as "knife hand."

"Go down to the Aviation Department and arrange for a transport to retrieve Third Platoon. I don't care how much ass you have to kiss or kick, just get it done. Do you understand me, Captain?"

"Sir...uh, I just came from Aviation. There aren't any transports available; everything they've got is tied up with the recall. The air boss told me that a request to divert a shuttle would have to be approved by the general himself before he could release anything."

Sobieski's neck turned purple, and the veins in his forehead popped out. When he spoke, his voice was level and threatening.

"On top of everything else going on, I have to go to the general to request a transport to unfuck your mistake?"

"Sir...I—Captain Reese—"

As if on cue, there were three sharp raps on the door and Captain Reese entered the office.

"Colonel, you want to see me?"

Sobieski fired an angry glare at Brickell. "Brickell, get out of my sight." He pointed to a spot in front of his desk. "Reese, get over here."

As Brickell left the office, he heard Colonel Sobieski shout:

"REESE, YOU FUCKING IDIOT! YOU'RE FIRED! PACK YOUR—"

The shouting became a muffled roar as Brickell pulled the door shut. When he looked at Staff Sergeant Willis, the NCO shrugged.

"DINLI."

* * *

Twelve hours later, Fortis slipped into the darkened transient personnel quarters and paused to give his eyes time to adjust. A VR holograph film hovered above the deck amidst a circle of chairs and the Space Marines hooted and clapped as a squad of movie Marines fought back a swarm of alien bugs. Fortis smiled in spite of himself.

A year ago, as a civilian, he would have watched the film and been enthralled by the heroism and fighting prowess displayed by the VR Marines. Now, after his recent experience fighting bugs on Pada-Pada, Fortis was amused by the portrayal of combat by people who'd never experienced it.

Ystremski was seated on the far edge of the circle, and Fortis walked around until he was behind the corporal. Ystremski saw him approach. Fortis motioned for the corporal to follow him and went into the hallway.

"Great movie you're showing, Corporal." Fortis smiled. "I hope they learn a lot from it."

"It wasn't my idea to give them the night off to watch a film, LT. It was either this nonsense or pornography; I'd rather be in the gym. So, what's up? Something wrong?"

"I was up in the comms center when the response to my message to Battalion showed up." He handed a folded sheet of paper to Ystremski.

From: Commander, Second Battalion, 1st of the 9th
To: Platoon Leader, 3rd Platoon, Foxtrot Company

Your request for extraction is denied. There are no Fleet assets available to effect pick up at this time. Third Platoon will remain on Eros-28 until further notice.

Commanding General Ninth Division has ordered Alert Condition Bravo. All units are directed to maintain four-hour readiness posture until further notice. Third Platoon be prepared for no-notice extraction.

Sobieski sends

"Sonofabitch. The lads aren't going to like this. What do you think this means?"

Fortis shook his head. "Your guess is as good as mine. Whatever it is, they're not kidding around. Alert Condition Bravo means all liberty is cancelled. Those poor bastards are orbiting Eros-69 at four-hour readiness."

"Lucky us, eh?" Ystremski chuckled as he handed the paper back to Fortis. "At least we know it's not Reese fucking with us. Colonel Sobieski signed that one. Give me a minute to stop the movie and form up the platoon and then you can break the bad news, sir."

Fortis stopped him before he could reenter their quarters.

"Nah. Let them finish the film. Nothing's going to change between now and then."

* * *

"Remain on Eros-28 until further notice." Governor Czrk dropped the message on his desk and leaned back with his hands folded across his stomach. "I wonder what that means."

"That they're not leaving anytime soon," replied Chive, without a hint of humor.

Czrk gave him an irritated glance. "I know that, thank you. But what does it *mean*? An entire division of Space Marines placed on high alert in the Eros Cluster. Is there a threat out there?"

"Maybe it's a drill?" asked Drager. "Those guys are always training for something."

Chive snorted. "This isn't a drill. Not even the Space Marines are dumb enough to run a readiness exercise when they've got five thousand men on liberty on Eros-69. They'd have a mutiny on their hands."

"Well, whatever it is, we need to be ready. Bob, make sure the comms center is listening to the standard comms frequencies and the tower personnel are available on short notice."

"Yes, sir." Drager stood up to leave, but the governor stopped him with a raised hand.

"One more thing, for both of you." His eyes flicked between Drager and Chive. "They don't know that we can read their messages. Right now, it's our little secret. Let's keep it that way."

After Drager was gone, Chive stood up and folded his thick forearms across his chest.

"You have something in mind, Governor? Some plan you want to share?"

Czrk shook his head. "Not at all. The Space Marines are our guests and we should extend them every courtesy. Still, I'm curious about why they're here and what has them on high alert. Maybe we can glean some information from their comms; it's leverage. If Fortis discovers we've been reading their mail, he might switch to an encrypted mode we can't break."

*　*　*

Third Platoon took the news of the alert about as well as Fortis and Ystremski expected. There were some disappointed looks and a grumble or two, but mostly they accepted it without complaint. There were even a few smiles when Ystremski reminded them that three hots and a cot on Eros-28 beat the shit out of being trapped on the flagship with all the lifers.

Private Trapp raised his hand when Fortis asked if there were any questions.

"What's the alert about, sir?"

"I don't know," replied Fortis. "I checked the latest news downloads while I was in the comms shack, but I didn't see anything that warranted Alert Condition Bravo. After we finish here, I'm going to talk with Governor Czrk and let him know what's up. He might have some additional information."

PFC Philips raised his hand. "Are we stuck underground then, sir?"

Fortis traded glances with Ystremski.

"For now, yes. We're supposed to be prepared for no-notice extraction, which means our stuff should be packed and ready to go."

Fortis dismissed the squad, and Ystremski followed him into the passageway.

"It would be good for the men to get out of here for a while, LT. Even if it's only out into that dusty excuse for a city to stretch their legs for a bit."

"I appreciate what you're saying, but I can't just cut the guys loose without some way to get them back here on short notice. 'No-notice extraction' doesn't leave a lot of wiggle room." The lieutenant shrugged. "I'll see what the governor has to say about all this, and then we can reevaluate."

* * *

Spears, Choon, and West huddled next to the candlelight in the abandoned dome.

"Where's Deale?" Spears asked. "Baird's on shift, but Deale should be here."

Choon answered. "Hard to say. Things are crazy at the plant right now. Maybe he's working an extra shift."

"Hmm. Maybe." Spears thought for a second. "There was another overdose not far from here. A drug dealing freeloader by the name of Moore."

"Serves him right," said West.

"Yeah, except I heard the colonial police aren't sure he died of an overdose. There were marks on his body that make the police think he died somewhere else and his body was dumped."

West shrugged. "So what? The colony is better off without him."

Spears frowned. "You've been hanging around Deale too much. I don't like the dealers any more than you do, but murder? That's not good. Now the colonial police will be all over the place asking questions and poking their noses in where they don't belong. Who knows, the governor might involve the mercenaries again."

Choon made an angry noise in her throat, and West shifted uncomfortably. The mercenaries who masqueraded as industrial plant security contractors were a violent, heavy-handed force who didn't hesitate to use brutality against the employees. Their appearance in the colony had been a sudden, unpleasant surprise. It had taken a plant-wide labor slowdown to force the governor to restrict their activities.

"If they can prove it wasn't a simple overdose, the governor will blame us," Spears continued. "This movement is hard enough to sustain without more accusations." He stood and Choon and West followed. "I appreciate you two coming on such short notice. If you see Deale or Baird, try to get them aside and find out if they've heard anything. Otherwise, I'll be in touch."

* * * * *

Chapter Ten

Governor Czrk and Director Chive listened as Lieutenant Fortis briefed them on the response to his message.

"I imagine that's not welcome news to you and your men, Lieutenant."

Fortis gave a half-smile. "We're grateful for everything you've done for us, Governor. The facilities are excellent, and the food is better than you admitted when we first met. It's just…"

"It's not Eros-69," the governor interjected. The two men shared a chuckle.

"No, sir, it isn't. But nobody is enjoying Eros-69 right now. As far as I know, Ninth Division has been recalled to the Fleet because of the alert."

"What prompted this alert? Is the Eros Cluster in any danger?"

Fortis shook his head. "I don't have any information about the reason for the alert, sir. The divisional recall makes me think we'll be going somewhere else, though. If there was a threat approaching, the last place I'd put five thousand Space Marines is on nice fat transports waiting to get blasted."

Chive surprised Fortis when he grunted in agreement.

The lieutenant smiled again. "Of course, that's my parochial view as a lowly ISMC second lieutenant."

Czrk spread his hands wide open on his desk. "Lieutenant, it's our honor and pleasure to host you and your men, and I apologize again for the lack of creature comforts that are normally associated with liberty. If there's anything I can do to make your stay here more tolerable, please don't hesitate to ask."

"Actually, there is something. We've been ordered to prepare for a no-notice evacuation, but it's difficult for me to believe they would send a transport all this way and not give us a heads up it was coming."

Governor Czrk nodded.

"I realize there isn't a lot to attract the attention of my men in town, but they've expressed interest in the bars that Bob Drager described as your red-light district. I'd like to let them go out there, at least for a few hours, but there's no way to recall them on short notice. Do you have any ideas?"

The governor thought for a moment. "Perhaps we could use the towers? If we came up with a specific horn signal they'd be able to hear it anywhere in the city. Would that suit your needs?"

Fortis smiled. "It definitely would, Governor. Thank you."

Chive cleared his throat. "Governor, I recommend we put certain conditions on the Space Marines."

Fortis felt the blood rise into his face, but he said nothing.

"Conditions? Like what, Mr. Chive?"

"In the interest of safety and public order, I don't think it would be a good idea for the Space Marines to mix with large groups of our employees, especially those who have just completed their shifts." Chive looked at Fortis. "No offense intended to you or your men, but some of our citizens can get rowdy as they wind down after a long day of work. There are also some anti-conglomerate sentiments among certain factions, a self-styled resistance movement. They might misinterpret the appearance of your Space Marines as a GRC power play."

The governor glared at Chive, and his cheeks flushed. "Now hold on a second, Chive." He turned to Fortis and attempted a smile. "It's true, there are a few malcontents among the population, but they're hardly a 'resistance.'" He made air quotes around resistance. "We work under difficult conditions here, Lieutenant, and, in a population as big as ours, there are bound to be some people who are unhappy." He looked at Chive before he continued.

"Mr. Chive does have a valid point about preventing trouble between the groups, though. I know your Marines are tough young lads, but it would be better if we didn't mix them with a bunch of rough-and-tumble colonists and add alcohol."

Czrk sounded exasperated as he finished, "I'll get together with Colonial Police Chief Schultz and Bob Drager and we'll come up with a plan to accommodate you and your men. How does that sound?"

"Governor, if it will cause problems, then please say so. We don't *have* to go out. Corporal Ystremski has a lot of experience keeping the men busy."

"It's really no problem. I'll have Bob come find you after we get this sorted out, okay?"

* * *

After Lieutenant Fortis left to rejoin his men, Governor Czrk told Chive to close the door.

"What do you think you're doing, Chive?" he demanded. "Why are you talking about the resistance to someone from off-world, especially a Space Marine?"

Chive gave an uncharacteristic shrug. "I was explaining why it's a bad idea to mix his men and the locals."

"That's not what I'm talking about, and you know it. The resistance, such as it is, is a colonial law enforcement matter. For all practical purposes, there is no resistance."

"You called the attack on the garage a terrorist attack, but the resistance is a colonial law enforcement matter? How did you explain it to GRC headquarters?"

Czrk stared at Chive a moment too long before he opened his mouth to answer, and Chive cut him off.

"You didn't report it, did you?"

The governor closed his mouth and shook his head.

Chive scoffed. "You're playing a dangerous game, Governor. If the Conglomerate finds out…"

"I run this colony as I see fit, and I don't need a lecture from the likes of you, Chive. You'd do well to remember your place. One call from me, and your contract is cancelled."

"Why the threats, Governor? I'm on your side, remember?"

Czrk glared at him. "Sometimes I wonder."

"If it's any consolation, I think the stuff about the resistance went over Fortis' head. He's not interested in local problems. He just wants to get drunk and laid before the Fleet arrives to pick them up."

"Regardless, I don't want you to discuss the resistance with anyone. Those kinds of things have a way of taking on a life of their own, and we have enough to deal with as it is."

* * *

Fortis caught up with Ystremski in the gym.

"I just talked with the governor and his security guy, Chive. They weren't thrilled about us staying, but what choice do they have? It's not like we asked to be here."

"True. What about liberty?"

"We talked about it. The way I see it, the biggest hurdle is having a way to get everyone back here if the transport shows up. It makes sense that Fleet would give us advance warning, but anything is possible. The governor said he'd try and work something out with the chief of police and Bob Drager so we can get the platoon out of here, even for a little while."

Ystremski grunted as he heaved a loaded bar over his head and pressed it up and down. "When?" he managed between gritted teeth.

"I don't know. Soon, I guess. In the meantime, let's keep the boys busy."

"Will do, sir."

"You want to hear something strange? Chive said he was worried about us mixing with the locals because there's some kind of resistance movement here on Eros-28. Have you heard anything about that?"

Ystremski set the weight bar down with a clang. "Resistance? What's he talking about?"

Fortis shook his head. "I don't know. Chive brought it up, and Czrk got pretty pissed off. He dismissed it as some malcontents."

"That's probably what it is. So what? You think it's a problem for us?"

"For us? No. I don't think so. It's just odd to me that he reacted that way."

The corporal indicated the weight bar and smiled. "You want to get in on this, or do you want to talk all night, sir?"

* * *

Jandahl was sitting at one end of the bar in the Cock and Tail where he could watch the hallway leading to the bathrooms, the emergency periscope, and the alcove where patrons played billiards and sought privacy for other activities. In the mirrors behind the bar, he could see the door and the stairs leading to the private rooms where customers could satisfy their carnal urges.

Although it was mid-morning, the bar was crowded with GRC employees who had just finished their twelve-hour shift. The crowd was boisterous and the drinks flowed freely. An anonymous techno-beat throbbed from speakers around the room and people had to put lips to ears to communicate.

He sipped his beer and studied the crowd. Jandahl recognized the lingering effects of China Mike on many of the bar patrons. The drug produced an energized euphoria that allowed users to work long hours in difficult conditions, but it was short-lived. Users required frequent boosts of the drug to maintain that feeling.

When users stopped boosting and started coming down, their bodies released residual China Mike, which caused a rush of frenetic energy known as "the edge." Addicts enjoyed "riding the edge," characterized by loud speech, sudden mood swings, and the urge to dance to the point of exhaustion. When the edge ended, they would stagger home and fall into bed until it was time to get up and do it all over again.

Jandahl spotted a familiar figure by the main entrance, and he blinked in surprise. Mikel Chive, dressed in a hooded jacket pulled up over his head as if to disguise his dueling scars, was engaged in a discussion with the doorman.

Chive left the bar, and the doorman resumed his usual perch.

What was that all about?

For the next two hours, Jandahl watched a stream of people enter the bar, shake hands with the doorman, and leave, without buying a drink. He realized he was witnessing hand-to-hand exchanges, but of what? When the doorman turned to speak to someone behind him, Jandahl saw that he, too, had a dueling scar on one cheek.

Why is a Kuiper Knight working the door at the Cock and Tail?

As the action in the bar wound down, and the crowd leaked out the door to go home and sleep it off, Jandahl mixed in with them. He chanced a look at the doorman's face as he passed. It was definitely a dueling scar.

What the hell is going on?

* * *

Chive stared out at the darkness as his driver, Dolph, piloted the crawler along the track to their compound. The crawler was a converted ore hauler abandoned on Eros-28 by a defunct mining company. There was a boxy engine car capable of pulling two ore cars that rode on knobby balloon tires. Chive's men had removed the ore chutes and welded benches on either side of the ore cars. Each car could accommodate ten seated people and four standing in the center aisle. It was their primary means of transportation between Fenway and the compound they had constructed seven kilometers outside of Boston.

"You know, the governor hasn't reported the sabotage of Garage Number Seven yet," Chive said. Dolph remained silent, so he continued. "That works in our favor."

"How so?" replied the taciturn driver.

"It's all about leverage, Dolph. At any moment, GRC might discover what happened and that would be bad for the governor. The governor might give up a lot to prevent that information from getting back to headquarters."

"So, you're going to blackmail him. Very clever."

Chive tried to make out Dolph's face by the console lights, unsure if the other man was smiling or not.

"Blackmail is such an inelegant word. I'm not going to demand he do anything to guarantee my silence, because I'd be lying." He tapped his temple with a finger. "What I will do is file that information away for future reference, perhaps to influence the governor to see things my way. What I won't do is demand he do something *or else.*"

"Isn't he the client? I mean, we work for the GRC, right? Who cares how he runs the place, as long as we get paid?"

"Dolph, you've got to think bigger than the current contract. Strictly speaking, we are well-paid to fulfill our contract. However, when opportunities present themselves, we need to seize them. It's part of our responsibility to the Knighthood. Besides, it's fun to dabble in politics."

"I'm just here to drive this thing and fly the hovercopter," replied Dolph. "I'll leave the politicking to you."

"It's probably better that way."

The two men lapsed into silence as the glow from their compound lights grew brighter. Dolph sounded the horn when they arrived at the gate, but there was no response. After a couple minutes, he sounded it again, with the same result.

"Fuckers are drunk again," he muttered as he climbed out of the crawler. He wasn't surprised to find the gate unsecured, and he shoved it open.

"You know, Mr. Chive, you might want to talk to the guys about securing this place," Dolph said as he steered the crawler inside the compound.

"*Tsk*. You worry too much, Dolph. We're in no danger out here."

* * * * *

Chapter Eleven

Shortly after his shift ended at midnight, Glenn Deale shouldered his way through the people crowded inside the Cock and Tail and leaned on the bar. The bartender acknowledged his presence with the tip of her chin, and moments later a tall glass of beer and a double shot of whiskey appeared before him.

Deale surveyed the crowd as he sipped his drink, careful not to let his eyes linger on the doorman too long. He'd only gotten a quick glimpse of the man's face when he entered the bar, but he was certain he was the scarred man Moore had described.

The volume of the music was turned up enough to rattle the liquor bottles on the shelves behind the bar, and the crowd became more boisterous. Deale's mood soured as his head throbbed in time to the music. People laughed and shouted as they surged and danced, and it was all Deale could do not to lash out at those closest to him.

Fucking junkies.

Deale had tried China Mike along with everyone else when the drug first appeared in the colony. He didn't like it, but, for many others, the drug quickly went from a leisure-time distraction on a bleak planet to a full-time addiction. Deale had remained ambivalent about China Mike until a coworker, fresh off a double boost, caused a refurbished engine block to break free from a hoist and crush Deale's hand. Deale lost two fingers and nearly his job because of it.

Only a timely transfer off Eros-28 had saved the other man from Deale's anger.

Since then, Deale had developed a deep contempt for people who used the drug and a burning hatred for those who dealt it. When Spears approached him to join the resistance, Deale accepted without hesitation. He didn't care about politics, he just wanted to get revenge against those who cost him his fingers.

While he drank, Deale watched a steady stream of bar patrons approach the scarred bouncer and then disappear down the hall toward the restrooms. When they returned, the flush on their faces and gleam in their eyes was all the confirmation Deale needed that they were using China Mike.

The bouncer was much bigger than Moore, so Deale was uncertain how to approach the larger man. He decided to wait outside and follow his prey in hopes of finding an opportunity when the bouncer headed home.

Ninety minutes later, the burly doorman stepped outside, looked up and down the street, and began walking toward the GRC facility. Deale left his hiding place and fell in behind him. He adjusted his pace to overtake his quarry at the last alleyway before the facility entrance. Deale knew of a vacant house a few doors up the alley. A very convenient spot to interrogate his captive.

Deale was two steps behind when he reached out to put a chokehold on the bouncer. The man whirled around, ducked under his grasp, and hit Deale in the throat with a stiff-fingered strike. Deale clawed at his injured neck, desperate to open his collapsed airway. He fell to his knees. He looked up in time to see a knee in front of his face, and then nothing.

* * *

The next morning, Drager beamed at Fortis as he sat down across from him at the breakfast table.

"Good news, Lieutenant. We've come up with a recall signal for you and your men, and the spaceport tower is now manned around the clock. When the Fleet sends your ride, we'll be ready."

"That's great news; thanks, Drager. I'll get the men together after we finish eating and let them know."

"Do you think it would be okay if I tagged along and gave them a short brief about the town?"

"About what?"

"Hmm, well, there are a few eccentricities about Boston, especially the bars. Local customs that your men might benefit from knowing. That sort of thing."

Fortis looked at Ystremski, who shrugged.

"Sure. That sounds fine. We need to respect the local culture, after all."

Lieutenant Fortis briefed the Space Marines on the liberty plan then turned to Bob Drager.

"In case you've forgotten, Mr. Drager is the executive assistant to Governor Czrk, and he's been instrumental in coordinating everything for us during our time here. He's got some important information about Eros-28 and the local customs that we need to observe while we're in town. Mr. Drager?"

Drager smiled and nodded at the Space Marines. "Good morning, everyone. I'm sure you're all excited to get out and see Boston, and we're anxious to see that you enjoy yourselves.

"Most of you will likely end up on Dirt Alley. I hope you have fun there. The bars on Dirt Alley are like bars anywhere, and you can certainly have a good time. They only accept GRC scrip and I've arranged for a money exchange so you can trade UNT credits for company scrip at a one-for-two exchange rate.

"But, before you go, I have two important topics to discuss with you. First, there is a synthetic drug present in certain areas of the city. I can't pronounce the chemical name, but the street name is 'China Mike.' It's strictly illegal and the colonial police aggressively enforce the laws about it. I don't know what the ISMC drug use policy and testing protocols are, but, please, don't get involved with China Mike. Some of the local dealers might offer it to you, perhaps even free samples, but resist the temptation and report the incident to the nearest colonial police.

"The other topic deals with the prostitutes who work some of the bars on Dirt Alley. Prostitution is legal here, and there is mandatory testing to ensure the sex workers are healthy. Customers are required to undergo a finger prick blood test for safety purposes as well. It's all proper and aboveboard. However, what you need to know is that the male-to-female population here on Ero-28 is about twenty-five to one, and most of those females either work here in our facility or are married to people who do. Very few have employment elsewhere."

Drager cleared his throat nervously.

"What this means for all of you is simple, if you meet a woman in a bar, and she has an apple, she probably has a banana."

The Space Marines exchanged puzzled looks, and Drager pursed his lips.

"If she has an apple," he repeated and touched his throat. "She probably has a banana." He pointed to his crotch.

Realization swept over the formation, and the Marines laughed uproariously. Drager held his hands up for silence.

"This is an inclusive colony and we make no judgments about lifestyle choices among consenting adults, but it's important for you to understand what you're getting into ahead of time to avoid any surprises later. Unfortunately, we've had issues with transient personnel before and I would like all of you to avoid any trouble." Drager turned back to Fortis. "That's all I have, Lieutenant. Enjoy your liberty."

After Drager left, Ystremski called the platoon to attention, and Fortis looked them over.

"Okay, Marines, you heard Drager. You know the ISMC doesn't tolerate drug use; stay away from China Mike. And make sure you know what you're dealing with if you get the urge to pay for a date." Fortis looked back to Ystremski. "Corporal, dismiss the platoon and put down liberty call at your discretion."

* * *

Mikel Chive looked up and down the dirt street before he ducked into a building around the corner from Dirt Alley. Shag Wychan, a fellow Kuiper Knight and trusted lieutenant who moonlighted as a bouncer at the Cock and Tail, was waiting for him inside.

"What's the news, boss?"

"The Space Marines are going on liberty in Boston."

"Dirt Alley?"

"Where else?"

"Space Marine credits spend as easily as GRC scrip. Is there a problem?"

"No problem. An opportunity, actually."

Wychan grunted but said nothing.

"Do you still sell to the prostitutes?"

Another grunt from Wychan, accompanied by a nod.

"At some point, I expect some of the Space Marines will go looking for love. When they do, I want China Mike in the room. Fat Schultz and his clown posse will get a tip about drug activity and swoop in to make the arrest."

Wychan chuckled at Chive's nickname for the police chief. "Why do you want the police to arrest the Space Marines?"

"Leverage."

"Speaking of leverage…" Wychan walked over and kicked a tarpaulin-covered lump piled up against the far wall and Chive heard a grunt.

"Who's that?"

"Mechanic named Deale." He handed Deale's identity badge to Chive. "He tried to grab me on the street last night, but it didn't go too well for him."

"Disgruntled customer?"

"No. I've seen him hanging around the bar, but he's never bought from me."

"Hmm. Why would he go after you?"

"Maybe he's resistance, or maybe he just doesn't like Kuiper Knights. Maybe both."

"Okay. Can you stay here with him for a while longer? I'll send a clean-up crew to pick him up and take him out to the site."

"Sure. I'm due at work in an hour."

"They'll be here in ten minutes."

* * * * *

Chapter Twelve

Three hours later, Lieutenant Fortis was smiling to himself as he walked onto the dusty street outside the GRC facility. He could still feel the rush of his strength enhancement from the workout he'd just completed, and it was exhilarating. Fortis wasn't claustrophobic, but three days underground had left him cramped and restless.

He patted the wad of scrip in his pocket, and his smile broadened. Fortis had received the *L'Ordre de la Galanterie* for his actions on Pada-Pada. Along with the medal, the award came with a generous, life-long monthly pension, which nearly doubled his second lieutenant salary. He had been self-conscious to the point of embarrassment when he'd received the medal because any number of the other Space Marines who had been on Pada-Pada deserved it more, so he had decided to use the pension to improve the lives of his Marines whenever he could. Today, that meant putting down a pile of company scrip on a bar tab and inviting the men to drink their fill.

Fortis didn't know which of the half-dozen Dirt Alley bars the Space Marines would be in, so he let his ears guide him. He stopped in front of a nondescript place that looked like every other building except for a large red metal rooster mounted over the door. A faint, dirt-stained sign next to it read "Cock and Tail." Judging from the riotous sounds leaking into the alley from behind the door, the Marines were inside.

A wall of noise greeted Fortis as he stepped inside. He paused to let his eyes adjust to the dim interior. A muscle-bound man met him at the door and looked him up and down before tilting his head to the Space Marines crowded on one side of the bar. The bouncer had a facial scar similar to Chive's and Fortis wondered if he was a Kuiper Knight, too.

Fortis saw Corporal Heisen standing atop a table, waving a mug, and leading the Space Marines in a song.

The One-Legged Lady of Pada-Pada
Splash a taste and toast.
DINLI! DINLI!
Drink to Kilfoy's ghost.

Fortis recognized "The One-Legged Lady of Pada-Pada," the song the survivors of Pada-Pada had composed in memory of one of their fallen comrades, Sergeant Maya Kilfoy. Kilfoy had been popular with her fellow Marines, and her agonizing death from the necrotic sting of one of Pada-Pada's many venomous bugs had deeply affected the Space Marines. It was a silly song that barely rhymed and had no identifiable tune, but it had bonded the survivors of that desperate battle as they came to grips with the deaths of so many comrades for no discernable reason.

"Hey, Lieutenant Fortis!"

Corporal Ystremski and several of the other Space Marines had spotted Fortis and waved him over. He couldn't help but smile as the drunken mob greeted him with shouts and rude remarks. Somebody pushed a beer mug into his hands, and he clinked glasses with everyone in reach.

"How's it going?" Fortis shouted to Ystremski. "Looks like a good time."

"The good times are just getting started," the corporal replied. "We might do some fire walking later, maybe sacrifice a virgin or two. You busy?"

Fortis laughed, loud and long. The corporal drained his glass and set it on a nearby table before he reached for the mug Fortis had been given.

"Here, LT, let me help you with that."

Fortis gave him a reluctant smile as he let go of the mug. He'd almost forgotten about the prohibition against alcohol while undergoing strength enhancement.

"I need to get out of here before I get in trouble," he told Ystremski.

"It's all right, sir. In two or three years, when we stop at Eros-69 on our way home and all your enhancements are complete, you'll be able to drink with the adults."

Ystremski maintained a straight face for a long second, and Fortis almost believed he was serious. Then the corporal's face split into a wide grin, and he slapped the lieutenant on the shoulder.

"It sucks, sir. DINLI."

"Damn right. DINLI." He looked over at the bar. "I need to go talk to the bartender and then I'm headed back to Fenway. Keep these animals from killing each other, okay?"

Ystremski nodded and shouted something unintelligible as the noise level exploded. Fortis looked around and saw Heisen and Lemm standing on adjacent tables with their trousers around their ankles. Long strips of paper hung from between their buttocks, and as Fortis watched, another Marine lit each piece of paper. The flames raced up the makeshift fuses, and Lemm shouted and slapped his out a split second before Heisen did. The Marines cheered Heisen and booed Lemm, and a fresh contestant clambered up on the tables.

Ystremski hooted and slapped Fortis on the shoulder, and the lieutenant shook his head.

When he got to the bar, he leaned across to the smiling bartender.

"These Marines giving you any trouble, ma'am?"

A toothy white smile split her face, and she laughed. "Not a chance. Those guys are gentlemen compared to our usual crowd. The Dance of the Flaming Asshole is a new one, though. What can I get you?"

"Nothing for me." Fortis pulled out his roll of scrip and laid it in front of her. "You can get these guys as many drinks as this will buy."

Her eyes widened. "Are you sure? These guys will be drunk for a week!"

Fortis nodded. "I'm positive. Give them whatever they want, and at the end of the night, what they don't drink is yours. Just don't tell them until I'm gone, okay?"

The bartender gave him a confused look. "Why not?"

Fortis gave her an embarrassed smile. "Doctor's orders. I want to get out of here alive."

* * *

Glenn Deale sputtered and gagged, regaining consciousness when a bucket of frigid water doused his face. The water had a sour odor and left an oily residue in his mouth, and he struggled to breathe without swallowing any.

His throat burned when he choked and spat, and it was then that he remembered his failed assault on the scarred bouncer. By the light of the bare single bulb in the ceiling, he saw shackles on his wrists. When he tried to get to his feet he discovered his ankles were chained, too.

"Where am I?" he croaked, looking around the dim cell, but there was no answer. He swiveled his head back and forth and caught sight of a silhouette standing behind him. "Hey! Hey, you. Where am I?"

A heavy metal bucket passed through the light and hit Deale in the face. He shouted as the bucket spun off into the corner. He tasted blood on his lips.

"What the hell did you do that for?" he demanded.

"Stand him up," the shadow commanded and rough hands jerked Deale to his feet. They attached his wrist shackles to a chain that ran through a pulley on the ceiling and hauled him onto his tiptoes.

The shadow leaned into the light. Deale saw thick scars on his captor's cheeks. "You're a mercenary," he croaked.

"My men and I hire out for certain tasks from time to time," the scarred man said. "My name is Chive." He pulled a GRC employee identity card from his pocket and threw it at Deale's chest. "Your name is Glenn Deale. You're a shift mechanic, and you're a member of the resistance."

Deale hung silently.

Without warning, Chive drove a fist into Deale's exposed ribs. Pain lanced through his chest, and he gasped. Chive punched him again in the ribs. Deale wheezed as he struggled to breathe.

"I might have broken a rib with that first one. Sorry." Chive shrugged and gave an embarrassed grin. "Sometimes I get carried away." His fist smashed into Deale's face, and he felt his nose break. Hot blood gushed down his chin, and his face swelled immediately.

"Wha-what the fuck?" Deale spat through the blood running into his mouth.

"That's right. I know your name, and all the others in your cell. Will you talk now?"

Deale shook his head.

"Good. Very good." Chive nodded. "It makes a dreary job much more fun."

The mercenary delivered punches to Deale's stomach. Searing pain paralyzed the mechanic. His mouth opened and closed as he fought to draw a breath. His chin hung down to his chest as he drifted toward unconsciousness.

"You know who else didn't have much to say at first? Raisa Spears." Chive delivered another series of body blows before stepping back. "Let him go."

The chain rattled through the pulley letting Deale collapse to the cold cell floor. He curled up and clutched his abdomen as he fought to breathe. He heard a screeching whine, and it took him a moment to realize it was the sound of air wheezing through his throat. After several long minutes, the pain in his ribs subsided, and he got his wind back.

"Back up."

The chain rattled and yanked Deale up. Deale screamed as the pain in his ribs became a white-hot spear again.

Chive leaned in and peered into his face.

"I like that you're strong, Glenn, but you need to know something. I can do this a lot longer than you can take it."

Deale responded with a nod, and a stream of blood and snot from his ruined nose ran down to his chin.

"Now that we understand each other, let's get back to it. I will ask you some questions. If you don't answer, I will hurt you. If you lie to me, I will hurt you. Do you understand?"

Deale didn't answer, so Chive flicked his broken nose with a forefinger. He gasped in pain.

"You see? You didn't answer my question, and I hurt you. Get it?"

After a long second, Deale nodded.

"Good. Okay, first question: Are you in a resistance cell with Raisa Spears?"

Another nod.

"How many terrorists are in the cell?"

Deale coughed, and blood dribbled down his chin.

Chive sighed. "I'm a patient man, Deale, and I try to be fair, but you're making this very hard. Again. How many terrorists were in the cell?"

A sob wracked Deale's body. He moaned from the agony in his ribs as tears created tracks down his blood-streaked cheeks.

"Six," he croaked.

"Very good," replied Chive. "Why did you attack my man Wychan last night?"

Deale stood in silence as blood dripped down his face.

"You attacked one of my men last night, Deale. Why?"

When Deale didn't answer, Chive delivered a sharp kick to the inside of his right knee. Deale felt the ligaments give way. His legs gave out and the chains around his wrists pulled tight, which immediately reignited the fire in his abdomen. He forced himself to take his full weight on his toes to alleviate the agony of his body, groaning with the effort.

"Does that feel better, Glenn?"

Chive grabbed the front of the mechanic's tunic and drove a knee deep into his groin. Nausea boiled up from Deale's stomach and foul-tasting bile fountained from his mouth. The mercenary danced back to avoid the reeking vomit. One of the mercenaries holding Deale's chains made a noise in his throat.

Chive glared at him. "What? Do you have a problem with that?"

The mercenary shook his head and looked away. Chive turned his attention back to Deale.

"Why did you attack my man?"

"D-d-dealer. Ch-ch-china Mike dealer." Deale fought to get air into his lungs as spasms of pain from his damaged testicles wracked his body. "Fuckin'…mercenary…"

"Let him drop."

The chains rattled again, and Deale collapsed face-first to the cold, hard floor. The pain in his face barely registered as he fought to breathe through all the pain.

"What do you know about China Mike?" the mercenary demanded.

Deale's head felt stuffy and thick and he welcomed the unconsciousness starting to sweep over him.

"Not so fast, Glenn. Water."

Another bucket of foul water was poured over his face, and the darkness in his mind receded. Chive pinched his cheeks with one hand and looked into his eyes.

"Give him the dope."

Deale felt a prick in his arm. Seconds later, a surge of energy rushed through his body.

China Mike.

"You bastard."

"Ah, you're feeling better. Good. Let's talk about China Mike."

The interrogation went on forever. Chive seemed to know when Deale was going to risk a lie. The mercenary was skilled in inflicting excruciating punishment with minimal effort. Once Deale had surrendered everything he knew about China Mike and his resistance cell, Chive stopped his questions.

"Deale, I appreciate your honesty. You want to hear a joke?"

Deale grunted. His swollen face throbbed where Chive had poked and prodded at his broken nose, and sharp edges of broken ribs tore at him whenever he coughed up gritty, foul-tasting blood.

"Your friend Raisa Spears," the mercenary whispered, and he leaned in until their cheeks almost touched, "she died right here, in the same spot where you're about to die."

Deale summoned the last of his energy and aimed a headbutt at Chive's face. Chive dodged the attempt and laughed as the pain of Deale's last-ditch effort coursed through his body.

"Not today, Deale. Not ever."

The next blow landed on his broken ribs, and more pain detonated across Deale's midriff. Chive's punches landed on his vulnerable body, hard and fast. Deale wallowed in a sea of agony as red crowded the edges of his vision. At long last, the pain faded.

* * * * *

Chapter Thirteen

"Lieutenant Fortis!"

Rough hands yanked him from the depths of a wildly erotic dream starring the bartender from the Cock and Tail, and he thrashed wildly to escape his sheets.

"Fortis!"

Fortis tumbled out of his rack. His feet hitting the cold floor shocked him awake. He shook the vestiges of the dream from his head as he rubbed his eyes.

"What? Who? What is it?"

"Sir, it's Corporal Heisen. Ystremski sent me. We've got big trouble."

"Trouble? What trouble?"

Heisen briefed him as Fortis pulled on his uniform.

"We were partying at the Cock and Tail, trying to drink up that pile of scrip you left on the bar. The place started to fill up, and a couple of the guys went upstairs to do their thing. Next thing I know, a bunch of cops in those orange jumpsuits showed up, blowing whistles and dragging Space Marines outside. They lined us up, and then they dragged Landis and Marx out in restraints. That's when Ystremski told me to come find you, sir."

"Ah, shit." Fortis yawned and started for the door. "Where are they now?"

"I don't know, sir. The last time I saw them they were lined up in the street."

By the time Fortis and Heisen arrived back at the Cock and Tail, the alley was vacant. When they tried to enter the bar, the same burly doorman he'd seen before met him on the steps and held up a meaty hand.

"No Space Marines allowed," he rumbled.

"I'm looking for my men," replied Lieutenant Fortis.

"They're not here. They left with the cops."

"Where did they go?"

The doorman shrugged his massive shoulders. "Wherever cops take drug dealers."

Frustration rose in Fortis' chest and he had a sudden urge to slug the bouncer. Just then, the bartender stepped outside.

"What's going on out here?" she demanded.

"No more Marines," the doorman mumbled. "Too much trouble."

"I just want to find my men," Fortis told her. "This clown is getting in the way."

The bouncer took a step forward, but the bartender stopped him with a hand to his chest.

"Cut the bullshit, both of you." She looked at Fortis. "Your guys are probably at the colonial police headquarters inside Fenway. That's where I would start looking."

"Hmm, yeah. I should have gone there first." Fortis gave the bouncer the same up-and-down look he'd been given when he'd arrived at the bar earlier, and then he winked at the bartender. "Thanks for the tip."

As Fortis and Heisen left the bartender called after them.

"Thank *you* for the tip. You made my year!"

* * *

Jandahl watched the exchange from a shadowed doorway a few doors from the Cock and Tail. After the bartender and the bouncer went back inside, he emerged and headed for the door. The raid on the bar and arrest of the Space Marines interested him, if only because he'd never heard of the colonial police taking such action before.

When he tried to enter the bar, the bouncer stood in his way.

"We're closed."

Behind the massive human doorstop, Jandahl saw the bartender righting overturned chairs and straightening tables.

"What happened here?"

"I said, we're closed."

"Let him in, Shag. He's a regular."

Shag glared at Jandahl but moved aside, and the intelligence operative nodded as he stepped past the bouncer. He straightened up some chairs and tables as he picked his way through the wreckage to his customary spot at the bar. The bartender had retreated behind the bar and greeted him with a tall glass of beer, which he accepted with a grateful smile.

"Some party in here, eh?"

The bartender laughed. "Space Marines being Space Marines, until the colonial police showed up and hauled them away."

"Really? Why?"

The bartender started drying a row of glasses lined up on the sink board. "Some of them were dealing China Mike, if you can believe that."

"Space Marines dealing China Mike? That's hard to believe."

"Yep." The bartender finished drying the glasses and wiped down the bar. "I've been doing this long enough to know the signs of a China Mike user, and none of those guys were using. I don't even think the prostitute they were with is using."

"Huh." Jandahl drained his glass and slid it across the bar.

"Another?"

"Hmm… not right now." He stood up and smoothed back his hair with both hands. "All this talk about prostitutes has got me thinking." He pointed up the stairs. "Which room has time on it?"

"Rooms Three and Four. I don't know if they're still taking customers, but you can try."

A low voice—*Male? Female?*—answered Jandahl's knock on Room Four. He turned the knob and entered.

Inside was a plainly furnished room with a queen-sized bed flanked by nightstands, a small table, and two cushioned chairs. An attractive woman was curled up in one chair holding a long-stemmed cigarette holder held between slender fingers tipped with brilliant red fingernails.

"What'll it be, lover?" she purred.

Jandahl pulled a roll of scrip from his pocket. "Just talk."

The prostitute sighed. "Okay. The hourly rate is the same. Talk ain't cheap here in the House of Shaysanda."

Jandahl chuckled as he peeled off several bills. "That's fine."

"You want me to talk dirty to you, Daddy? Humiliate you? Have you been a bad boy?"

"Nothing like that. I want to have a chat, like two regular people." He stopped counting scrip. "When we're done I want to make sure nobody will find out what we talked about."

The prostitute unfolded herself from the chair and approached him with an exaggerated hip-wiggle.

"Honey, for that amount of money, my lips are sealed forever." She held out her hand, and Jandahl gave her half the scrip. She chewed on her bottom lip in a pouty expression. "What's wrong, baby, don't you trust Shaysanda?"

"Sure I trust you. That's why I gave you half."

Shaysanda sashayed back to her chair and draped herself across it in a casually seductive pose. "What do you want to talk about?"

Jandahl took the other chair. "Tell me about this afternoon with the police and the Space Marines. What happened?"

Shaysanda stiffened and her eyes narrowed. "Baby, Shaysanda doesn't mess with the police. Why would you ask me something like that?"

"I'm an interested bystander, is all."

"Sugar, you're a terrible liar."

Jandahl shrugged but remained silent. He knew he could outlast Shaysanda's greed, and he was right.

Bracelets jangled, and costume jewelry sparkled as Shaysanda waved her hands.

"Look, honey, it was just a thing, okay? There was a big party downstairs with a bunch of these guys. Two of them came upstairs for, you know, whatever. The next thing I know, the cops kicked the door open and dragged them out."

"What about the China Mike?"

"It was on the nightstand. Someone must have tipped off the police because they went straight for it."

"Was it theirs? The Space Marines?"

Shaysanda looked away.

"Was it yours?"

The prostitute locked eyes with the intelligence operator, and Jandahl saw a flash of anger. "Daddy, you're gonna make Shaysanda angry if you keep talking like that." She blinked, and the anger was gone. "I do this because I like it and because it pays better than any job I could get in the plant. I like the drug, but that doesn't mean I'm a junkie."

"Okay. If the China Mike wasn't theirs and it wasn't yours, whose was it?"

"Are you sure you're not a cop?"

Jandahl held up his right hand and smiled. "I'm not a cop. Promise."

Shaysanda reached for her cigarettes and made a show out of inserting a new one into her cigarette holder. Jandahl knew it was a stall tactic, but he played along. He picked up the lighter from the table and lit her cigarette. She gave him a coquettish look as she blew out a long stream of smoke.

"It's a shame that all you want to do is talk, Daddy," she murmured as she ran her hand along her thigh. "A good-looking man like you deserves more than chitchat."

"Let's get back to the China Mike. Whose was it?"

"I don't know."

"It hurts my feelings when you lie to me, Shaysanda. It makes me want to keep the rest of my money."

Jandahl watched her entire physical demeanor change. Her shoulders slumped, and her flirtatious smile faded.

"Shaysanda, listen to me." Jandahl leaned forward in his chair and lowered his voice. It was an effective technique to foster a sense of us-versus-the-world. He had used it to great effect many times in the past. "I don't care what you're into or how you make your living. I want to know how two Space Marines, who haven't been here for a week, got involved with the resistance."

At the mention of the resistance, Shaysanda stiffened.

"The resistance?" She wagged an index finger at him. "I don't know who you are, mister, but you need to get out of here."

Jandahl chuckled. "What happened to 'Daddy'? Don't you want the rest of your money?" He held up the folded scrip, and her eyes tracked it. "C'mon, Shaysanda. I just want to know where the China Mike came from. Whatever else the resistance is into is none of my business. And to tell you the truth, if I had to work in this fucking place, I'd probably join them."

Shaysanda giggled, and the tension between them drained away. She glanced at the door and took a deep breath. "Okay, look. The bouncer, Shag? He gave me the stuff and told me that if any of the Space Marines came upstairs I was to offer them some and then leave it on the nightstand. I thought he was trying to hook them with a free sample. I didn't know the cops would bust in."

"Shag? He's not in the resistance. He's one of the GRC mercenaries." Jandahl unconsciously touched his cheek.

"Why do you keep talking about the resistance? They're not pushing the China Mike."

Jandahl was taken aback. "But the resistance sells China Mike to fund their movement."

The prostitute shook her head. "No, baby. You've got it all wrong. China Mike is one of their main grievances. They don't deal it."

"If not the resistance, then who?"

"All I know is that Shag is the only guy I buy from these days. If he's not resistance, then he's something else." She shrugged and held out her hand. "I've said enough, Daddy. How about my money?"

* * *

One of the colonial policemen directed Fortis to the police headquarters office complex. An officer there escorted him to the chief's office. Chief Schultz greeted him with a tepid handshake and a disapproving look on his fleshy face.

"Lieutenant, I had hoped we would meet under different circumstances."

Fortis nodded and said nothing.

Schultz opened two file folders on the desk in front of him. "Private Marx and Private Landis. Arrested at the Cock and Tail and charged with Possession with Intent to Distribute China Mike."

"That can't be right, Chief. My Marines know better than to get mixed up with that stuff."

"When my men arrested them they discovered the Marines had a substantial amount of China Mike packaged for sale."

"That doesn't make sense. How did they get caught? Were they arrested for making a deal?"

Chief Schultz shook his head. "We received an anonymous tip that warned of illegal drug activity on the second floor of the Cock and Tail. An undercover operative confirmed the report, and we acted."

"Chief, we've only been here for three days. This is the first time any of us have been out. You expect me to believe that somehow, in a bar full of fellow Marines, these two decided to deal drugs? Who were they going to sell to?"

Schultz folded his hands in front of him. "What you believe is not my concern, Lieutenant, and neither are the motives and schemes of drug dealers. My concern is enforcing the law. Your men broke the law, and my men arrested them. When the colonial circuit judge arrives, they will stand trial."

"When will that be?"

Schultz consulted his computer. "The judge will be here eight weeks from tomorrow."

"Eight weeks?"

The chief looked at his screen again. "That's what it says here. Eight weeks. From tomorrow."

"They can't stay here eight weeks. We'll be gone before that, Chief."

Schultz shrugged. "Not Marx and Landis. They have a court date in eight weeks."

"From tomorrow. Yeah, I get it." Fortis sighed and rubbed his face. "There's nothing I can do to get them out?"

"You could talk to the governor, but I don't think that will do much good. He's a stickler for the law."

"Can I see them?"

"Of course." Schultz reached for his communicator and paused. "You won't try to break them out, will you?"

Fortis gave him a blank stare at the clumsy attempt at humor. The chief shrugged again and picked up his handset. A tall, broad-shouldered colonial policeman appeared in response to the call. "Upham" was embroidered on his name patch.

"Officer Upham, take Lieutenant Fortis to see our guests. Let them use Interview Room Two; the room *without* the surveillance system."

Upham gave him a confused look. "Uh, okay, Chief. This way, Lieutenant."

"You make a lot of arrests?" Fortis asked on their way to the holding cells.

"No, heh. Actually, your guys are the second and third people I've seen arrested since I started here."

"How long have you been a policeman?"

"Two years."

Fortis stopped. Upham turned and looked at him.

"In two years, you've seen three arrests?"

"Yep. Right after I started, an electrician went crazy and strangled his manager in Garage Six. That was the first one. Now, two Space Marines; that makes three." He chuckled. "Not a lot of crime here."

Fortis saw a large sign that read HOLDING CELLS over the door at the end of the corridor.

"If there's so little crime, what do you do with your time?"

The officer held the door open for Fortis. "Plow dirt after sifters, mostly."

* * * * *

Chapter Fourteen

Marx and Landis were grim-faced when Upham ushered them into the interview room, but they broke into wide grins when they saw Lieutenant Fortis seated at the table.

"LT, you gotta get us out of here," blurted Marx.

"This is bullshit, sir. We didn't do anything," added Landis.

Fortis put his finger to his lips and pointed to the ceiling. "You two need to understand that I'm not your attorney and I could be compelled to testify to anything you tell me."

The two Marines looked around the room and then nodded.

"In fact," Fortis continued, "it would be best if you didn't say anything to anyone about this. Not even each other. Understand?"

Marx and Landis nodded again.

"Now that we've got that out of the way, tell me, how have you been treated so far? Any trouble?"

The Marines exchanged glances. "Good so far," said Marx. "We've only been here an hour."

Fortis gave a self-conscious chuckle, and his face flushed. His nap had distorted his body clock and he had begun to think it was the following morning.

He didn't know what to say to Marx and Landis. He didn't want to mention anything about the eight-week wait for the judge, at least until he spoke to Governor Czrk. If he couldn't convince the governor to release them, he would have to appeal to Battalion for guidance, which would complicate everything.

Fortis stood up.

"I will do everything I can to get you guys out of here. You've got to do your part to help me, though. Do what you're told and don't cause any trouble."

"DINLI, sir?"

They smiled, and Fortis was glad to see the pair was in good spirits.

* * *

Fortis searched for the rest of the platoon and found them gathered in the cafeteria under the watchful eye of several colonial policemen. Most of the Space Marines were flaked out on the floor, sound asleep. He waved Ystremski away from the group. They leaned in close to converse.

"What the hell happened?" Fortis whispered.

"After you left things got a little crazy," replied Ystremski. "What do you expect when you mix Space Marines and free booze? Marx and Landis decided to satisfy their curiosity about the whole apple and banana thing. I saw them head upstairs and then the place filled up with cops. They lined us all up in the street and hauled those two away. I tried to find out what was going on, but they wouldn't talk to a lowly corporal."

"What a fucking mess."

"Have you seen Marx and Landis? How are they?"

"They're okay. Confused, but okay."

"What did the governor have to say?"

"I haven't talked to him yet. After I get you guys out of here, that's my next stop."

"You know, LT, this smells like a shakedown."

"A shakedown?"

Ystremski looked over his shoulder. "Yeah. Sometimes local cops grab a Space Marine, trump up some charges, and then offer to release them on 'bail.' The hat gets passed and we pay the ransom. If we don't, the Marine gets screwed by the locals and then again by the ISMC for going AWOL."

Fortis groaned. "Fantastic."

"It's kind of weird, though. If this is a shakedown, it's a strange time for it. We can't raise a lot from a single platoon, and we sure as hell can't call Battalion and ask for more."

"Huh. Well, I guess I'll know more after I talk to Governor Czrk."

"One piece of advice, don't ask him how much, let him lead you to it. These pissant bureaucrats don't like to be confronted with their bullshit. In fact, I wouldn't be surprised if one of his underlings makes the demand." Ystremski nodded toward the door, and Fortis saw Chief Schultz approaching them. "Like the chief here."

"Lieutenant Fortis, your men are free to go," the chief puffed. "There won't be any additional charges filed."

"A bargain," muttered the corporal.

"Oh, and the governor would like to see you, Lieutenant."

"Great, thanks," replied Fortis. He turned to Ystremski. "Get them back to the berthing compartment. Nobody leaves this facility without my express permission, and they don't leave berthing without *yours*."

Fortis followed the portly police chief out the door. He heard Ystremski rouse the napping platoon and smiled.

"Let's go, ladies! Time to get up and at 'em. You guys look like you could use some exercise."

* * *

Shultz escorted Fortis to the governor's office, where they were met by the governor, along with Chive, who scowled at the young Space Marine. Fortis took a seat, and, before the governor could speak, he launched into his prepared remarks.

"Governor, please accept my apologies for any trouble my Space Marines have caused. This was no way to repay your gracious hospitality, and I promise you it won't happen again as long as we are here."

Governor Czrk responded with a thin smile. "Lieutenant, I appreciate your apology, and I'm sure that the actions of Marx and Landis do not represent the ISMC or your platoon."

After a long moment of uncomfortable silence, Fortis glanced at Schultz and Chive. "Governor, can we speak in private?"

Governor Czrk wrinkled his nose for a second and then gestured to the chief and head of security. "You can speak freely in front of these men. There are no secrets here on Eros-28."

"Okay." Fortis took a deep breath. "Chief Schultz told me the judge isn't due here for eight weeks."

Czrk nodded but said nothing.

"Governor, I don't think we'll be here for eight weeks, and I can't leave Marx and Landis here when we go."

Czrk's eyebrows went up. "Why not? We'll treat them well as long as they behave. They'll receive a fair trial. Based on what I've been told about their crimes, I expect the judge will sentence them to time served. After that, we will release them to the ISMC. Eight weeks of time served sounds like a fair sentence for dealing drugs."

"It is fair. The problem is that Battalion isn't going to wait that long. We'll be off on the far side of who-knows-where and those two won't be able to catch up with us."

"We can send them back to Terra Earth with a deep-space mission crew. A shuttle heads back there every six months or so."

"That's very generous, sir, except that the ISMC will classify them as AWOL if they don't come back with us. In two months, the ISMC will downgrade their status to deserter. When they get back to Terra Earth, the ISMC will court martial them, and they'll go to military prison."

"Hmm. That would be unfortunate."

"Sir, what if they're acquitted? They will have spent eight weeks waiting on the judge for nothing. Their lives will be destroyed for something they didn't do."

"Lieutenant, they were found in possession of China Mike. That's really not in dispute."

Fortis looked Czrk straight in the eye. "Is there anything we can do to avoid all that?"

"What do you mean, Lieutenant?"

Fortis glanced at Chief Schultz and Director Chive. "When we get on that Fleet transport you will never hear from us again. Even *if* Marx and Landis are guilty—and that's a big if—they'll be out of your hair. One thing I guarantee you; whatever misery they might feel sitting in your jail for eight weeks, Corporal Ystremski can dispense misery tenfold with his special brand of attention." Fortis threw up his hands. "Otherwise, we leave them with you, they do their time served, and then you have to worry about how to get them back to Terra Earth. It hardly seems worth it."

Czrk's eyes flitted to Schultz and then Chive before he answered. "My hands are tied. Marx and Landis were arrested and charged. The rest is up to the judge."

Fortis struggled to hide his disappointment as he stood up. "I'm sorry to hear that, Governor, but I understand." He stuck out his hand and the two men shook. "With your permission, I'd like to visit with them regularly."

"Let Chief Schultz know, and you can visit them whenever you want."

* * * * *

Chapter Fifteen

On the Fleet flagship *Atlas*, Colonel Sobieski examined the art in the office belonging to the aide-de-camp to General Gupta and tried to ignore the intestinal gymnastics taking place in his stomach. Sobieski wasn't the nervous type, but the general's mercurial temper was legendary and the news about Third Platoon was certain to provoke an explosive response.

Captain Nilsen, the general's personal assistant, gave him an apologetic smile. "I'm sure it won't be much longer, Colonel. May I offer you some coffee?"

"No, thank you, Captain."

Under normal circumstances, Sobieski would have accepted her offer and relished the opportunity to sit and enjoy the view. Nilsen was a stunning blonde from the northern regions of Terra Earth, with ice-blue eyes, flawless skin, and a shapely body that was barely disguised by her tailored utilities. He got a faint whiff of an exotic fragrance; ISMC regulations forbade perfume in uniform, but she was the general's aide.

Today, even the stunning Nordic beauty wasn't enough to distract him from the sense of dread that grew with every minute. He was a veteran of many bug hunts and had never shied away from a tough assignment, but for some reason this one had him on edge.

DINLI.

A detailed depiction of the famous Space Marine bug hunt on Bezel Nine caught his eye and he studied the oil painting closely.

Although traditional art forms were still practiced on Terra Earth, Sobieski had become so accustomed to pixelated holographic images that the swirls and strokes that created the stunning contrasts in the almost solid white painting were remarkable. The artist had captured the fight between the Space Marines and the bugs with subtle splashes of red and black. It impressed the colonel, even though he knew the battle had taken place deep underground, far below the frozen surface. When he—

"Colonel. Colonel?"

Captain Nilsen's smooth accent jolted Sobieski from his reverie.

"The general will see you now."

She led him to the door, rapped three times, and opened it.

"General, Colonel Sobieski."

Sobieski gave Nilsen a half-smile as he slipped past her into the general's office.

"Kivak, come in," said General Gupta as he rose and gestured at the seats in front of his desk. "Sit down. Can I offer you something to drink?"

"Thank you, sir, but I'm fine."

Gupta dismissed Nilsen with a wave of his hand, and she pulled the door shut behind her.

"What's on your mind, Colonel?"

Sobieski cleared his throat. "Well, General, I've got an issue with the recall."

"Don't we all." General Gupta gestured to the papers spread out across his desk. "Five thousand Space Marines spread all over hell and back, all of them doing their best to avoid the recall. What's your issue?"

"A platoon from Foxtrot Company was misrouted." As soon as he ended the sentence, Sobieski caught himself. "What I mean, sir, is that they're not on Eros-69."

Gupta's eyebrows furrowed, and Sobieski recognized the sign of an impending eruption. "Where the hell are they?'

"Eros-28, General."

"Eros-28? That place is a goddamned truck stop. How did they get sent to Eros-28?"

"I'm looking into it, sir, but it seems they were bumped from the Eros-69 liberty shuttle and somehow wound up on Eros-28."

The lie came too easily, but Sobieski wanted to protect the rest of his men from the general's wrath. He had relieved Reese and Brickell and ordered them back to Terra Earth for reassignment; that was punishment enough. He didn't want to give the general a minor issue to focus on, even if it was caused by the recalcitrance of the air boss.

"So, get them back."

Sobieski winced. "That's the issue, sir. The air boss won't send a transport to pick them up without your authorization. He's under orders to dedicate all his assets to the recall."

It was the Staff Law of Thermodynamics: If the heat was on the air boss, it wasn't on Sobieski. He hated to use it, but it was the truth.

General Gupta shook his head and let out an exaggerated sigh. "Are you telling me that two full-bird ISMC colonels aren't capable of working together to recover a platoon from some other planet?"

"No, sir. We are more than capable, but your orders were specific. The trip to Eros-28 is a multi-day mission and given our current alert condition we could sortie at a moment's notice and leave behind a shuttle along with the platoon."

134 | P.A. PIATT

After exposing the air boss, Sobieski took the opportunity to give his fellow officer some cover.

"All we need is your permission, sir, and we'll get it done."

"Okay, Colonel. Go down and tell the air boss that you have my authorization to send a shuttle to recover your lost platoon. Is there anything else?"

Sobieski jumped to his feet. "No sir, that was it. Thank you, sir."

As he was reaching for the doorknob, Gupta's voice brought him up short.

"Colonel, I saw the passenger manifest for the transport headed back to Terra Earth and I saw Captain Reese and Captain Brickell from your Battalion. They're headed back for reassignment?"

Dread washed over Sobieski. "Yes, sir. I relieved the captains and made them available for orders."

"I'm not in the business of micromanaging my Battalion commanders, but would you care to explain why?"

"Captain Reese is the officer who signed the orders that sent Third Platoon to Eros-28. Brickell was Foxtrot Company commander and let it happen."

Gupta glared at Sobieski for a long second before he nodded.

"Good decision, Colonel. Carry on."

* * *

After the office door clicked shut behind Fortis, Chief Schultz cleared his throat and Director Chive snorted. "That was a ham-handed attempt at bribery," the scarred man told the governor.

"I don't know. He seemed sincere to me," said Schultz.

Chive sneered. "That's because you're a fat fool." He glared at the chief and dared him to do something about the insult. Schultz stared, open-mouthed.

Governor Czrk held up his hands. "Gentlemen, please. There's no need for that." He looked at Schultz. "Your case against the Space Marines is solid, isn't it Chief?"

Chief Shultz squinted at the governor. "It sure is."

"Tell us about it," interjected Chive. The chief gave him a hurt look, and Governor Czrk nodded.

"That's an excellent idea. Why don't you do that?"

The police chief cocked his head and pulled on an earlobe. "We received an anonymous tip that some of the Space Marines were dealing China Mike upstairs at the Cock and Tail. One of my officers verified the report with a confidential informant and we made the arrests."

"Did your officer make a purchase?"

"Um… no. He verified the report with the confidential informant."

Czrk and Chive traded knowing glances.

"How much China Mike did the Marines have?"

"There was a plastic bag with eighteen grams in it on the nightstand."

Czrk shook his head. "That's not what I asked. How much China Mike did the Marines have in their possession?"

Schultz shrugged. "I don't know. The arresting officers logged eighteen grams."

Governor Czrk exhaled heavily and massaged the bridge of his nose.

"Fuckin' amateurs," muttered Chive.

"Now, look here," protested Schultz, "it was a good bust. We got two dealers and some China Mike off the streets."

"Whose room was it, Chief?" demanded the governor. "Was it rented to either Marx or Landis?"

Chief Shultz's fleshy jowls jiggled, and red blotches bloomed across his face and neck. "I don't know whose room it was, Governor. It's the Cock and Tail. You know how it works, the prostitutes rent rooms by the hour." His voice became an irritating whine, and Chive had the sudden urge to grab a handful of his fleshy cheek and shake him until he squealed.

"Chief, would you mind if I spoke to the governor alone for a minute?" Chive's tone was almost civil, but there was an undercurrent of menace in his voice.

"Ah... ah... about what?" he stuttered. "Me?"

Chive shook his head. "Not about you, Chief. If I wanted to talk about you, I'd do so in front of you." He pointed to the door. "Please, go."

Chief Schultz looked at Governor Czrk, who nodded.

"It's okay, Chief. Director Chive and I need to discuss another matter that doesn't involve the Colonial Police Department."

Chief Schultz slunk from the room like a scolded teenager, and Chive scoffed at his departure.

"What do you want, Chive?"

"We both know there's no way those charges will hold up in court."

"I'm aware of that, thank you. Tomorrow, I will take the time to read through the reports and see if there is anything there. If the situation is as Chief Schultz described, then I'll have no choice but to let those men go."

Chive shook his head. "We shouldn't let this crisis go to waste, Governor. There's a genuine opportunity here."

Czrk's eyebrows arched. "Oh? What opportunity is that?"

"That lieutenant, Fortis, practically begged you to name your price to free his men."

The governor held up his hand. "Stop right there. I will not extort money from Lieutenant Fortis and his men."

"I'm not talking about money. My intelligence sources have identified five members of a resistance cell, and I want to run operations to capture them."

"I've given no approval for you to operate against the resistance. Chief Schultz—"

"Chief Schultz is a fat, corrupt freeloader who sees nothing while his men actively take part in the China Mike trade; the same China Mike trade that funds the resistance." Chive sighed with impatience. "Governor, the GRC sent me here to pacify the situation, and they gave me broad powers to do so. I trade in information to develop actionable intelligence, and my intelligence is time sensitive. If I give it to Schultz or his men, they will compromise it."

"Chive, in case you've forgotten, this facility is in crisis mode. We lost weeks of progress when that garage collapsed, and I can't afford another labor slowdown if your men arrest colonists again."

"It won't be my men, Governor."

Czrk's annoyance became puzzlement. "If you won't work with the colonial police and you're not using your men, then who?"

"Space Marines."

"Space Marines?"

"Yes. Space Marines. We give them the suspect list and tell them where to look. They capture the suspects, and we take custody."

The governor shook his head. "No, Mr. Chive. This is a local problem, and we will handle it locally. The ISMC would never allow Lieutenant Fortis to get involved in a local law enforcement problem."

"You don't have to ask the ISMC, Governor."

"Then how?"

"Leverage."

* * *

The smell of sweat and stale beer hit Fortis like a slap to the face when he opened the door to the gymnasium. The red-faced Space Marines were formed up for physical training, and it was obvious that Corporal Ystremski had pushed them hard. When the corporal saw Fortis, he called the platoon to attention.

"How did it go, sir?" he asked as the lieutenant approached.

Fortis glanced at the platoon. "Let's talk about it somewhere else."

"Yes, sir." Ystremski gestured to the Space Marines. "We're about finished here, anyway. Platoon, fall out and get cleaned up for chow. Dismissed!"

The weary Marines filed out of the gym. Soon Fortis and Ystremski were alone. They walked into the weight room and sat down, side by side, on a weight bench.

"We're fucked," Fortis told the corporal. "The governor won't budge."

"Who did you talk to?"

"The governor, the police chief, and that security guy, Chive."

"What happened?"

"I started out with an apology and then we talked about the situation. The colonial circuit judge isn't due for eight weeks. Until then, they'll sit in their cells."

"Eight weeks? Damn."

"I explained that if we leave Marx and Landis here they'll be screwed for life. It didn't do any good."

"What do they want?"

"That's the strange part. I did everything but ask the governor to name his price and there was no reaction. Maybe this isn't a shakedown."

"Fat chance."

The pair lapsed into a lengthy silence before Fortis sighed and rubbed the back of his neck.

"I'll get court martialed again when we show up without Marx and Landis. You know that, right?"

Ystremski gave him a quizzical look.

"What makes you say that, LT?"

"Sobieski's orders were explicit. 'Be prepared for no-notice extraction.' That doesn't include cutting the guys loose or slapping a half-month's pay down for them to get drunk. I might've slid by if Captain Brickell had responded to my message, but the Battalion commander? No way."

"Have you told Marx and Landis?"

"I checked on them, but I didn't say anything."

"When are you going to tell them?"

"Not until the last minute. I'll keep working on the governor; maybe I can change his mind."

Corporal Ystremski sat silent for a moment before he cleared his throat.

"I owe you an apology, LT. I failed you."

"What are you talking about?"

"Sir, I'm wearing socks that have been in the Space Marines longer than you, and I know better than to violate Sobieski's orders. I'm supposed to be the voice of experience. I should have stopped you."

Fortis swallowed the lump that formed in his throat before he responded. "I just wanted to do something good for the guys. They put up with a lot."

Ystremski shook his head. "You don't have to do that, LT. Space Marines live the life they chose. It's no secret that life in the Corps is tough. Hell, most of these guys joined for the challenge. Remember, it takes heat and pressure…"

"…to make diamonds," Fortis completed his sentence. "I remember."

Those eight words, carved into the stone archway over the gate that led to the International Space Marine Corps training grounds, greeted every fresh recruit, officer, and enlisted. By the time they graduated, *if* they graduated, the heat and pressure of their training seared those words into their memories.

"All right, enough reminiscing." Fortis stood up. "Let's get the platoon to breakfast."

The pair walked toward the door, and Ystremski nudged Fortis with his elbow. "Before we go, take a second and square your rack away. I heard there might be a berthing inspection after chow."

* * * * *

Chapter Sixteen

After they ate and Corporal Ystremski roared through the dormitory like a tornado, Lieutenant Fortis and the Space Marines formed up in the gymnasium to pay in sweat for the berthing inspection.

Security Director Chive entered the room and stood by the door.

"Lieutenant Fortis, the governor wants to see you," said the scarred mercenary.

Fortis looked at Ystremski and shrugged. The platoon hooted and laughed as he walked to the door.

"Don't worry, LT, you'll have plenty of company later to help you pay for that soup sandwich you call your rack," Ystremski called after him.

Fortis was a little annoyed by the interruption. It secretly pleased him that the corporal had held him to the same standard as the men during the inspection, and he had been looking forward to the opportunity to work out with them.

He walked past the security director into the corridor and, without waiting, started down the now-familiar path to the governor's office. By now, he knew Chive would answer questions with non-answers. Instead, he focused on what else he could say to convince the governor to release Marx and Landis.

Governor Czrk greeted them when they arrived.

"Lieutenant Fortis, thank you for coming." Czrk smiled and offered his hand. He turned to Chive. "Director Chive, that's all I have for you for now, thank you."

Chive made a noise in his throat, and his face showed his apparent displeasure, but he left without a word.

Czrk ushered Fortis into his office and closed the door. "Sit down, Lieutenant. Can I offer you a drink?"

"Water would be great, thank you."

The two men sat down with their drinks, and Czrk smiled at Fortis.

"Lieutenant, I've been thinking about our earlier conversation regarding Marx and Landis. After consultation with Chief Schultz and Security Director Chive, I think we've come up with a solution that benefits everyone."

"I'm all ears, Governor."

"Do you recall when we were discussing liberty for your men, Director Chive talked about a resistance movement here on Eros-28?

"Yes, I remember."

"Good." The governor leaned back and made a steeple with his fingers. "The resistance on Eros-28, such as it is, began as a group of employees with the usual complaints about pay, working conditions, and so forth. Over time, they have progressed from filing grievances to organized work slowdowns. In response to the escalating problems, the GRC sent Chive and his men to help me get the situation under control."

Fortis nodded as Czrk spoke, uncertain of where the conversation was headed.

"China Mike has flooded the colony, and we suspect that's how the resistance is funding their activities.

"They have recently escalated their efforts and begun to engage in acts of industrial sabotage. A few days before you and your men arrived, they collapsed one of our garages and set our production back at least two weeks."

"Boston's a small town. It seems like the police should be able to root it out," said Fortis.

"Chief Schultz and his men keep the peace well enough, but they're local. The chief used to be a hydraulic technician, and the rest of the force are also former employees. Any move by the police department against the resistance doesn't stay secret for long."

"What about Chive?"

The governor shook his head. "We tried that. Unfortunately, Mr. Chive and his men were heavy-handed with the colonists in Boston, and I had to restrict their activities to the facility. Frankly, they made the situation worse."

"I appreciate all this information, Governor, but what does this have to do with Marx and Landis?"

Governor Czrk chuckled. "Straight to the point. I like that." He cracked his knuckles. "Okay. Here's the situation: I have a problem that you and your men can help me solve. You have the training and experience to act as an auxiliary force for the Security Directorate and help me deal with the China Mike cartel. We will identify and pinpoint the cartel members, and you will apprehend the suspects and turn them over to us. Once you have eliminated the resistance, or the ISMC sends a transport for you, I will drop all charges and release Marx and Landis to your custody, and they'll be free to go."

The governor's proposal stunned Fortis and he struggled to form a response.

"Sir, my chain of command has to approve something like this. We're not law enforcement; we aren't authorized to arrest civilians."

Czrk dismissed his protests with a wave of his hand. "You don't need approval, Lieutenant. We'll call it training or something like that. I'll have the chief deputize you and your men so all the paperwork is legitimate. I'll even have the machine shop make you badges."

"Governor, this isn't about paperwork and badges. We're a military force. We're trained to support and defend the United Nations of Terra."

The governor slammed his hand down on the desk. "Eros-28 is a critical industrial activity. The UNT government and business interests save trillions of credits every year when they send their equipment here for maintenance and overhaul instead of returning it to Terra Earth. There are over five thousand UNT citizens that live and work on this planet, and they face an enemy which our local security forces cannot cope with. Don't they deserve the protection of the ISMC?"

"Yes sir, they do, and if you had a bug problem or an alien life form threatening the colony, we would step up and fight. What I can't do is commit my platoon to a local law enforcement matter without guidance from my chain of command."

Czrk scowled. "Have it your way, Lieutenant. You came to me and asked if there was anything I could do, and I've done my best to help you. If you don't want my help, then the responsibility for what happens to those men is on you." He stood up, and Fortis followed. "Good day, Lieutenant Fortis."

* * * * *

Chapter Seventeen

"**B**adges? We don't need no stinking badges!"

Fortis and Ystremski were standing on the platform at the top of the periscope that overlooked Boston, out of earshot of the platoon. The lieutenant had just briefed his senior NCO on the governor's offer.

"I told him we couldn't do it without direction from our chain of command. He wasn't happy."

"Shit." Ystremski spat into the dirt street below. "There are no good options, are there?"

"None." There was a long silence. "Tomorrow morning, I'll send a report to Brickell. If he says it's okay, I'll go talk to the governor again."

Ystremski snorted. "Brickell? We might as well just stay here and get jobs washing drill rigs." He spat again. "You know, LT, what if we took the governor up on his offer? What if we ran a couple operations, grabbed a few drug dealers, and got Marx and Landis sprung? What's the worst that could happen?"

"Hmm. Let's see. Some of our Marines could be wounded or killed. Bad for them, and hard for me to explain. We could kill a civilian or two. They wouldn't even have to be innocent bystanders for that to be a problem. Then there's always the chance that news of Space Marines raiding houses on Eros-28 would reach the ISMC. That would also be an issue."

"You're looking at it the wrong way, sir. That's worst-case scenario bullshit. Think positive. We're trained to do this. We won't be up against trained soldiers. Those guys are a bunch of drug dealers who won't know their assholes from their elbows when we hit the door."

"You're serious? You really think we should do this?"

"Well, maybe. I mean, there's nothing wrong with keeping our options open. Why don't you find out exactly what he wants us to do and what's involved?"

Fortis stared at his friend for several long moments.

Maybe he's right. Maybe…

* * *

Security Director Chive burst into the governor's office without knocking.

"Well?" he demanded.

Czrk's face twisted with irritation at the intrusion. "He said no."

"No? How can he say no?"

"He said his men aren't law enforcement, and that he needs permission from his chain of command. I don't think we have much to worry about, though. He didn't sound eager to involve his higher-ups."

"You shouldn't be eager to involve them, either. The GRC won't like you inviting ISMC involvement into a problem they didn't know existed, hmm?"

"That's true, but it's a moot point. If the case is as weak as Schultz made it sound, I might as well dismiss the charges and let Marx and Landis go now."

Chive held up his hands. "Don't be too hasty, Governor. I just returned from Boston, and we've got some new information on the location of some resistance members. If it pans out, we're going to need Fortis and his men."

"Okay, Chive. We'll do it your way, for now. If Fortis doesn't work out, I'll send Chief Schultz and his men. We need to get some results."

"Don't worry. The Space Marines aren't going anywhere for now, so let Fortis stew. Space Marines are nothing if not predictable. He'll come around, because he won't leave Marx and Landis behind."

* * *

That night, Mikel Chive and Shag Wychan stood in their usual meeting spot with their heads together.

"Some guy came to the Cock and Tail and asked a bunch of questions," the bouncer told his boss. "Bartender called him a regular, but I haven't seen him around much."

"Huh. What was he asking about?"

"He didn't talk to me, he went upstairs and talked to the prostitute, Shaysanda."

"Talked? Did you get a recording?"

Wychan grimaced and shook his head. "Something went wrong with the microphone. I can hear voices, but they're muffled. He wasn't up there long, but they talked the whole time. I don't think they did anything else." He handed Chive a picture. "That's what I got from the security camera at the door."

Chive recognized Jandahl, but he shook his head. "Nobody I know."

"What do you want me to do?"

"See if you can find out what she told him," Chive said. "*Without* beating it out of her." He waved the picture. "Leave this one to me."

"Got it."

Wychan slipped out into the dark street. Chive waited and absently patted the pocket where he tucked the picture.

What's your game, Jandahl?

* * *

The following morning, Ystremski set the platoon to cleaning their berthing area while he and Fortis made their way to the governor's office. They sat down in front of the desk and Lieutenant Fortis said, "Governor, I've discussed your proposal with my senior NCO, Corporal Ystremski, and we'd like to know some more details."

"I'm glad to see you here, Lieutenant. The plan is simple. You'd be working with Director Chive and his men. They would provide you with intelligence on China Mike cartel members, your men would apprehend them, and then you'd turn them over to Chive."

"Chive? What about Chief Schultz?"

"Like I told you before, Chief Schultz and the colonial police aren't suitable for this because of their ties to the colonists. Chive and his men would guide you, take custody of any prisoners, and interview them to develop further leads. After the interviews, Chive would turn the prisoners over to the colonial police."

"They'd receive fair trials?"

"I'm hoping trials won't be necessary, but if trials are needed, then yes, they would be tried by the circuit judge. I don't want to fill the jail with colonists who have friends and family members that work for me. I believe that approach will lead to more unhappiness and more unrest within my labor force. It would become a self-perpetuating cycle. Better to expose the cartel and trace the China Mike back to the source and eradicate it. That approach better serves the interests of GRC and our employees, I think."

Fortis and Ystremski traded looks, and the corporal arched his eyebrows.

"Governor, I'm in a tough spot here, but I think you know that." Fortis watched Czrk's face for a reaction, and he thought he saw the shadow of a smile. "My chain of command made it clear that we're to remain ready for a no-notice extraction, and that does not include conducting raids across the city against a drug cartel."

"It didn't include a drunken liberty run to the Cock and Tail, either." The governor's eyes had an amused twinkle, and Fortis was forced to concede the point with a tight grimace.

"That was my mistake."

"So, does my proposal sound like something you'd be interested in?"

"What about gear?" asked Ystremski. "We didn't bring any tactical gear or weapons. Does the cartel have weapons?"

"I don't know what we have for missions like this. There's never been a crime committed here with a weapon as long as I've been governor. They probably have knives, but I'm unaware of any civilian firearms in the colony. The colonial police have an armory you can borrow weapons from, and I'm sure they have radios and whatever else you might need."

Fortis sensed that the detailed questions annoyed the governor, so he knew he would have to talk with Chief Schultz to get an accurate picture of available equipment.

"Chief Schultz has agreed to this?"

"Chief Schultz does what I tell him to do," Governor Czrk replied. "He will provide whatever you need, without complaint. So, you'll do it?"

Fortis and Ystremski stood up. "I think so, Governor, but you need to understand one thing. I can't order my men to do this; it would be an illegal order that contravenes the order we received from Battalion. Corporal Ystremski and I will muster the platoon and explain your offer, but they have to volunteer."

"Very well, Lieutenant, but don't delay too long."

* * *

Jandahl fell into step alongside Spears as the mechanic trudged home after a double shift cleaning and repairing equipment recovered from the collapsed garage. Many of his coworkers stopped at the bars of Dirt Alley to ride the edge of the China Mike they had taken to push through their extended shift, but Shears looked too tired to even acknowledge Jandahl's presence.

"Any news?" asked the intelligence operative.

Spears shook his head as he focused on putting one foot in front of the other. "Digging out Garage Number Seven. Any word on Raisa?"

"Nothing. None of my sources reported anything about her." Technically this was true, but only because Jandahl hadn't asked. He figured that workers would find Raisa's body buried in the garage, the victim of her own sabotage.

"How's the digging going? Much progress?"

"It would be faster if Chive and his men didn't stop us to remove the drugs when we uncover it. We had to stop six times and wait for them to remove China Mike from the equipment on the last shift."

Jandahl stopped him with a hand on his arm. "Wait a second. GRC security is removing it? Not the colonial police?"

"The mercenaries said they're turning it over to the conglomerate, not the colony."

"The GRC doesn't—" Jandahl caught himself. "What I mean is, the word around headquarters is that the resistance is selling China Mike to fund their activities."

Spears shook his head. "No way. Absolutely not. The GRC brings that shit in to keep us working. The resistance is fighting to keep it out. That's why Raisa targeted Garage Number Seven."

Jandahl mentally turned over what Spears was telling him. Spears' information jibed with what Shaysanda had told him about the China Mike cartel, that it was actually the GRC, but he knew that wasn't true. He knew from his mission tasking on Eros-28 that the GRC wasn't behind the drug trade.

Then who?

He looked around and realized Spears had stopped walking.

"Sorry," he stammered. "My mind started to wander for a second there."

Spears gestured to the house where he had stopped. "This is my place."

"Ah, yeah, okay." He turned to leave.

"Hey, Jandahl. One more thing. One of my guys, a mechanic by the name of Glenn Deale, has disappeared. He hasn't been to work for a couple shifts, and he hasn't been home. Anybody talking about him at headquarters?"

Jandahl shook his head. "I haven't heard anything about a missing worker. You sure he's not on a bender? Maybe he's riding the edge somewhere."

Spears shook his head. "Not Deale; he hates China Mike. He's not on a bender. Something's wrong."

"Report it to the colonial police. Maybe they know where he's at."

Spears sighed and put a hand on his door. "Yeah, I guess so. I gotta get some sleep."

"I'll be in touch."

* * * * *

Chapter Eighteen

Third Platoon gathered in a semi-circle in the berthing compartment. Fortis wanted the informal gathering to convey that this was a discussion and not a briefing followed by orders. Every eye was on the young officer who looked from face to face and made eye contact with every one of them. He wanted to pace, but he forced himself to stand still, his hands clasped behind his back.

"I talked with Governor Czrk about Marx and Landis. He won't release them until they've been tried in court, and the circuit court judge won't be here for eight weeks."

Several of the men grumbled while others shook their heads. Fortis waited for several seconds before continuing.

"If we leave without them, the ISMC will declare them AWOL, designate them as deserters, and court martial them when they return to duty."

"That's bullshit!" blurted Private First Class Davis

Fortis nodded. "You're right. It is bullshit. No doubt about it." He punched his fist into his other palm. "However…" He stopped and searched their faces again. "However, the governor has offered a solution. Apparently, there is a resistance movement in the colony that funds their activities by dealing China Mike. The colonial police and security force have been unable to deal with them. Governor Czrk has agreed to drop all the charges against Marx and Landis if we conduct some raids and arrest some suspects for them."

The Space Marines nodded and smiled at each other.

"When do we start, sir?" called Corporal Anderson. Fortis held up his hands, and the group fell silent.

"There are some things you need to understand about this offer. What the governor has proposed violates the orders of Colonel Sobieski, the Battalion commander. He ordered Third Platoon to be prepared for no-notice extraction. If we go into the city and do this, we will be liable for failure to obey a lawful order. What's more, I can't order you to do this, because that would be an illegal order. If something goes wrong, there would only be so much cover I could give you."

Fortis started pacing; he couldn't stand still any longer.

"If you volunteer, and the ISMC finds out, you might face charges." The Space Marines exchanged glances. "I know a little something about facing charges, and it's no picnic."

The veterans laughed, and the cherries looked confused.

"If you're wounded, the ISMC could force you to repay them for your medical care. If you're killed, they could refuse to pay out death benefits to your family." He scanned their faces, but he couldn't read them.

"This is strictly voluntary. What you decide is your choice. You're under no obligation to participate. No man in this room will face penalty or sanction, no matter what he decides. I'll leave the room and let you discuss it among yourselves. Corporal Ystremski, take charge of the platoon. I'll be in the gym."

Ten minutes later, Ystremski joined him.

"How'd it go?"

"Unanimous; first vote. We're in."

Fortis took a deep breath and exhaled as he shook his head. "You know, Gunny Hawkins kicked my ass back on Pada-Pada when I took a vote among Warrant Pell and you sergeants. And here I am doing it again, only this time I'm polling a bunch of privates."

"Gunny Hawkins was one helluva a Space Marine, sir, but this time you did the right thing."

Fortis fought down the lump in the back of his throat. "I hardly knew him, but he died saving my life, you know."

"Yeah."

After a long moment of silence, Ystremski slapped Fortis on the shoulder and laughed. "Let's go, Pig Dog."

Fortis laughed at the hated nickname Captain Reese had tried to adopt when he commanded Foxtrot Company.

"Pig Dog, my ass," he said. "Let's do the deed."

* * *

Shaysanda was wigless when Wychan entered the room without knocking.

"Not so fast, lover…oh. It's you. What do you want?"

"You had a john last night, wanted to ask some questions. What did he want?"

The prostitute stalled for a moment by wiggling her elaborate hairpiece into place.

"Baby, a girl can't kiss and tell in this business, or she won't be in business for long."

Wychan crossed the room in four long strides and grabbed her by the throat. Shaysanda struggled to break his grip, but the mercenary was too strong.

"Listen, freak. I don't have the time or patience for your games. Understand?"

She gurgled and fluttered her eyes. Wychan pushed her away, and Shaysanda collapsed, struggling to get her breath.

"What did he want?" Wychan demanded.

Shaysanda rubbed her injured throat and gave the hulking mercenary a hurt look.

"He asked a bunch of questions about the Space Marines and China Mike. He said something about the resistance, but it didn't make sense. I didn't tell him anything, I swear. I thought he was a nutcase, but his money was good."

Wychan loomed over her and she cringed.

"That's it?"

"That's it, honey. I swear."

The mercenary glared at the prostitute for a long moment before he turned on his heel and strode out of the room. The door slammed shut, and Shaysanda jumped up and locked it behind him.

I need to find a different line of work. All the men here are crazy.

* * *

The governor greeted Lieutenant Fortis and Corporal Ystremski with a friendly smile, which broadened when Fortis gave him the news.

"Excellent!" he said rubbing his hands together. He punched some numbers into the handset on his desk and asked Chief Schultz to report to his office. When the corpulent cop arrived, he gave the Space Marines a suspicious look.

"Chief, Lieutenant Fortis and his men will be conducting some training with Director Chive and the Security Directorate while they wait for their transportation. I want you to provide the Space Marines whatever equipment and weapons they need."

"Weapons? What sort of weapons?"

"Pulse rifles with extended battery packs and infrared tactical sights," Fortis said. He looked at Ystremski, who nodded. "Foldable stocks and forward grips, if you have them. Flash-bangs and smoke grenades."

Chief Schultz stared, open-mouthed at the Space Marine officer. When he didn't answer, Fortis wondered if the chief had heard him.

"Chief? Pulse rifles?"

Schultz blinked and his eyes focused on Fortis. "We don't have pulse rifles, Lieutenant. Nor do we have tactical stocks or infrared grips."

"You mean infrared sights and foldable stocks?"

"Yeah, whatever; we don't have them. We have pistols."

"Pistols?" The Space Marines traded glances. "What kind of pistols?"

Chief Schultz threw up his hands. "I don't know. Just pistols."

Ystremski covered a smile with his hand, and Fortis cleared his throat. Governor Czrk shifted in his seat.

"This isn't a military outpost, Lieutenant. We don't have bugs or aliens or even pirates to contend with. There are over five thousand people who live and work here on Eros-28 and twenty-two colonial police. We have no need for an arsenal of modern weapons."

"Governor, what if the resistance—" Ystremski blurted, but Governor Czrk cut him off with a wave of his hand and a quick head shake.

"The training you will provide to the Training Directorate should be as realistic as possible. If we can't provide realistic weapons to train with, do the best you can with what we have."

Chief Schultz and Corporal Ystremski left for the colonial police armory so the corporal could inspect the weapons and tactical gear available to the Space Marines. When they were gone, Fortis looked at Governor Czrk.

"Can you show me the way to Director Chive's office? We need to figure out how we're going to operate."

"Director Chive doesn't have an office, exactly. He and his men have their own compound several kilometers from here."

"How does he provide security then?"

"Mr. Fortis, don't concern yourself with the inner workings of the facility. Chive and his men fulfill their duties just like Chief Schultz and every other GRC employee here. I suggest you keep that in mind."

"Of course, Governor. Do you have a means of contacting him?"

"Not directly, no. He does tend to appear when I need him, so I expect he will be along shortly."

* * *

Fortis caught up with Ystremski at the colonial police armory. The corporal had selected enough weapons and gear to fill two bulky trunks, and the two men carried them to the berthing compartment.

"I took twelve pistols," Ystremski said. "They're old ballistic technology, and they need a good cleaning, but they were the best of the lot. The ammo is dated, so we'll to need to test fire some of it. I got four crates of ammunition; if we need more than that, we're in the wrong business. I also grabbed twelve sets of ballistic armor and sixteen radios."

Fortis knew that ballistic technology was almost a thousand years old, but the Marines often chose ballistic weapons for their reliability and simplicity of operation. He wasn't surprised to learn that the colonial police force had them.

"Why only twelve pistols?"

"The rest were junk. Half of the weapons I left behind were inoperable and the other half were missing pieces. From what the chief told me about the local architecture, we'll only need a six-man assault team to take down one of those houses. The radios aren't great, but I don't think we'll need much in the way of tactical communications."

"How did the chief react? Is he angry?"

"I don't know. If he's angry, he hides it well. He's curious about what we're doing, but he doesn't buy the training story. Schultz isn't much to look at, but he's a lot more aware of what's going on than people give him credit for."

When the two men returned to their quarters, the platoon fell into ranks, and Corporal Ystremski set them to work.

"First Squad, you've got the armorers, so you strip and clean the pistols and the rest of the gear. Second and Third Squads, you work with me to set up some floor plans. Let's get it done, ladies!"

Fortis helped Ystremski direct the efforts of the two squads tasked with setting up floor plans. The Space Marines moved the bunk beds around until they had two complete mock-ups and hung blankets over the sides to simulate walls.

"The chief told me that the houses in Boston have the same basic layout. A main room where the people live and eat, a small kitchen, and one or two bedrooms in the back." Ystremski gestured at their set-ups. "None of them have windows because of the sifters. The workers build their exterior doors from scraps they recover from the industrial plant, so the doors could be heavy-duty metal, plastic, or fiberglass. We won't know until we hit it.

"He also told me there's a tunnel system under the city called the subway. A bunch of it is collapsed, but some of the people have dug down and connected their houses to sections that didn't collapse. That might complicate things."

"Are you sure you didn't slip up and tell him what we're doing?"

"I didn't say a word, LT. I didn't even have to ask questions, he just started talking. Like I told you, Chief Schultz is smarter than he looks. Before I forget, he told me about a place outside Fenway where we can live-fire the pistols."

"How do you think we should break up the teams?"

"I figure me and Heisen will be assault team leaders. When he's not song-singing drunk or doing the Dance of the Flaming Asshole, he's a good Marine. Five additional Marines per team, with you as the command element for every raid. Durant and Cowher as team medics. That reminds me, we need to get in touch with the medical department and put together a trauma care kit, just in case."

"I'll take care of the medical stuff," said Fortis. "I feel like a third wheel around here, anyway."

Fortis headed down the passageway toward the administration offices in search of the medical department.

"Hey. Hey, Marine."

Fortis turned around and saw a plain-looking man with sandy brown hair. He wore the same coveralls that the GRC employees wore, but his were noticeably cleaner, and his skin didn't have the same pallor as the people that lived and worked underground.

"You're Lieutenant Fortis, aren't you?"

Fortis felt a sudden wave of apprehension as the man approached, but it vanished when he saw the man's hands were empty.

"That's correct, I'm Lieutenant Fortis. What can I do for you?"

"Hi." The brown-haired man extended his hand. "Do you have a minute?"

Fortis shook his hand. "Sure. What's on your mind?"

The other man looked up and down the corridor. "Can we go somewhere a little more… discreet? I have some information that you need to hear, but it's best passed in private."

Fortis examined the other man for a long second. He seemed earnest, and Fortis couldn't detect any threatening vibes. Still, he hesitated.

"Mmm, no. How about we if talk right here? You can start with your name."

The other man shrugged. "Have it your way." He looked up and down the corridor again before he lowered his voice and leaned in conspiratorially. "My name is Jandahl. I work for the GRC."

Fortis gestured to Jandahl's coveralls and something about his furtive demeanor made Fortis feel flippant. He forced himself to keep a straight face. "I guessed as much."

"Don't misunderstand me, Lieutenant. I'm not a mechanic or a welder. I work for GRC corporate. I'm an investigator."

"Mr. Jandahl, I have a lot to do. Can you get to your point?"

"Look," Jandahl whispered urgently and clutched at Fortis' sleeve. "I know what you're doing, but I don't think you do."

Fortis pulled his arm away and took a step backwards. "I don't know what you're talking about, Mr. Jandahl."

"Your work, for Chive, it's not what you think."

"We're training, Mr. Jandahl. It's not unusual for Space Marines to operate with other agencies to exchange ideas and tactics."

Jandahl scoffed. "You're not foolish enough to believe that, Lieutenant Fortis." He fixed Fortis with a steady stare. "Your reputation with the GRC precedes you."

Fortis crossed his arms and tilted his chin up in a skeptical pose. "Okay, Mr. Jandahl. Tell me; what do you think I'm doing, and what don't I know about it?"

Jandahl looked around again. "The operations that you are about to get involved with are not what they seem. You think you'll be operating against the China Mike cartel on behalf of the GRC, but you'll really be working for Chive and the Kuiper Knights."

It was Fortis' turn to scoff. "I don't know what you think you know, but you're wrong. We will conduct some training with the Security Directorate. That's it. Now, if you don't mind..."

Fortis turned to go, and Jandahl grabbed his arm again.

"Chive and his mercenaries are up to something here on Eros-28," he hissed at the lieutenant. "I don't know what their angle is yet, but you need to be wary of them. They're not your friends."

With a last look around, Jandahl strode down the corridor. Fortis watched him go as he rubbed his arm where the other man had grabbed him.

The encounter left Fortis with an uneasy feeling. He'd gotten bad vibes from the security director since the Space Marines had arrived on Eros-28, and now he had unsolicited information that seemed to confirm those feelings. He had no idea who Jandahl was or any way to determine the credibility of his warning, but Fortis couldn't think of a reason someone would feed him misinformation like that.

I wonder what Ystremski will think about this?

* * * * *

Chapter Nineteen

Fortis found the medical department around the corner and down the hall from the sheriff's office, and the technicians there were happy to help him assemble a trauma kit. He described what he wanted and they filled a backpack with splints, bandages, antibiotics, wound-sealing spray and paste, and tight bundles of absorbent material that would expand and immediately stop bleeding when inserted into a puncture wound. Their questions about the kinds of wounds he expected to see were innocent enough, but Fortis sensed that they knew his mission was more than training.

Does everyone on this planet know what we're doing?

"There's someone here around the clock, unless there's an emergency in the plant," the senior medical technician told him. "There's also an emergency alert system throughout Fenway." She pointed to a large red button mounted on the wall near the main door. "Hit that button and alarms will sound in the medical department dormitory."

Fortis thanked the clinic personnel and slung the bulging backpack over his shoulder. When he got back to the berthing compartment, he held it up to show Corporal Ystremski, who laughed.

"I guess they know something we don't."

"Speaking of something we don't know—"

Ystremski's attention was drawn to something behind Fortis. "Ah, shit. Here comes trouble." The lieutenant turned and saw Security Director Chive standing by the door. He walked over and greeted the mercenary.

"Director Chive, I'm glad you stopped by. We're about to run some training scenarios, so this will be an excellent chance for you to see how we operate."

Chive sniffed, but Fortis couldn't tell if it was derision or a runny nose. "I'm sure whatever you do will be adequate, Lieutenant. Especially with so many men."

"We plan to use six-man assault teams, with myself and a medic on standby. Chief Schultz gave us some intel on the houses in Boston, which we're tried to recreate here," Fortis said as he gestured to the maze of racks and blankets.

"Schultz?" Chive demanded. "Why did you involve Schultz? He's supposed to know nothing."

"Governor Czrk sent us to Schultz to draw weapons and equipment," Fortis replied. "Corporal Ystremski talked with him while they were in the armory. He says that the chief doesn't believe the training story."

Chive sneered. "You sent a *corporal* to talk to the chief? Are you that stupid?"

Fortis' cheeks flushed as the blood rushed to his face. He paused for a second to get himself under control before he responded to Chive's insult.

"Chive, I trust Corporal Ystremski with my life. He knows not to speak with anyone about our mission. Whatever suspicions Chief Schultz has he didn't get them from us. I stopped into the medical department to pick up a trauma kit and they also seemed to know a lot about what we're doing. I don't think our secret mission is much of a secret."

Chive's expression softened. "Chief Schultz is a conduit of information straight to the resistance. All the colonists are, one way or another. The success of our mission depends on secrecy and surprise, which is why I'm using you instead of the colonial police."

What he said made sense, but Fortis didn't like how Chive referred to the Space Marines as though they were tools to be used however the director wanted. He wanted to respond but thought better of it and steered the conversation in a new direction.

"We can train up the assault teams, but there are a lot of important details we need to know for specific missions."

"Such as?"

"Daytime or nighttime missions?"

"Both. It depends on the target's shift schedule."

"We don't have night vision, which will affect how we operate. What about movement to and from the target? Are we traveling on foot or by vehicle? If we go by foot, we'll need a guide."

"My men will provide transportation, either by crawler or hovercopter. Anything else?"

"We need to inspect those vehicles and rehearse with them, too."

Chive sighed. "Rehearse? Is that necessary, Lieutenant?"

"Absolutely necessary. We'll be un-assing a hovercopter in the dark, with dirt and sand blowing everywhere, no night vision, and unfamiliar weapons. Plenty of ways for things to go wrong, and that's before we even approach the target building. Rehearsal isn't just necessary, Mr. Chive, it's mandatory."

The director shook his head. "I'm losing confidence in your claim that the Space Marines can complete what should be simple missions. Perhaps the governor was wrong."

Fortis gave the mercenary a piercing look.

"I'm serious. The targets are rabble-rousers and malcontents who have turned to the drug trade to fund their sabotage. They live in mud huts on the edge of nowhere, not in prepared defensive positions. If it was up to me, I wouldn't use your men, but the governor gave me no choice."

"The governor gave me no choice either, so I guess we're stuck with each other."

The two men considered each other for a long moment before Chive nodded.

"Okay, Lieutenant. You're right. Given the importance of speed and discretion to our success, perhaps there is some merit to your preparations. You want to demonstrate?"

Fortis led Chive to a platform the Space Marines had built overlooking their mock-ups. Ystremski and Heisen stood by with their assault teams, armed with the police pistols and dressed in ballistic armor. Fortis waved his arm, and Ystremski ordered the start of the first scenario.

The breacher simulated knocking down the exterior door and the assault team flowed into the dwelling. Fortis narrated the action for Chive.

"The lead man has a flashlight and pistol. His job is to sweep the entire space and spotlight threats. Everyone else has one hand on the shoulder of the man in front of him and his other hand holding his weapon up and at the ready. We train to shoot both strong and weak hand, so the team alternates weapons left and right."

"Why did they stop?" asked Chive when Ystremski called a halt to the exercise and the assault team exited the mock-up. "They didn't search all the rooms."

The assault teams switched places, and Heisen's team conducted the next assault.

"Crawl-walk-run," replied the lieutenant. "First, we have to crawl. We check out the weapons and gear, test communications, and give the assault team members a chance to familiarize themselves with each other during the initial entry.

"Then we walk. We'll dim the lights and the assaults will become more complicated. The assaults will speed up, and the team will break up into smaller elements to hit all the doors in the space. Other Marines will resist the assault or play innocent bystanders, and we'll simulate casualties.

"When the teams are confident in their movement and ability to handle the unexpected, we run. Full mission profile. Everything that can go wrong will go wrong and usually at the worst time."

"How long is all of this going to take?"

"Not long. Two hours, maybe a little longer. We train urban assault as one of our core war-fighting competencies, so crawl and walk will be refresher training because the men know what to do. Chief Schultz provided enough weapons and equipment for two teams, so Corporal Ystremski selected our twelve best Space Marines. They just need some time to get comfortable.

"Once we finish here, I'll take the platoon to a spot outside the facility that Chief Schultz told us about so we can test fire the weapons. After that, we'll be ready to go."

Chive nodded his approval. "Good. My driver parked the crawler in the garage area. Your men are welcome to look it over when you're finished here. The hovercopter is at our compound; you and your men will have time to inspect it well before any mission."

"Thank you."

The training continued at a rapid pace. The assault teams moved with deadly purpose and overwhelming force. Ystremski had the opposing force use every dirty trick and tactic imaginable, but the result was always the same: the Space Marines secured the building and carried the detainees out in restraints.

"LT, I think we're there," the corporal reported to Fortis. "Unless you have something else you want us to try."

Fortis looked at Chive, who shrugged. "Corporal Ystremski, if you're satisfied, I'm satisfied," Fortis replied. "Whenever you're ready, Mr. Chive's crawler is available for us to look at on the way out to test fire the pistols. After that, I'll put Assault Team One on alert."

* * *

Chive's driver met the Space Marines in the garage.

"My name is Dolph, and this is a Multi-Purpose Mining Platform, or Meep-Meep. I call her *Roadrunner*." After a pregnant pause, he continued. "*Roadrunner* is basically a large, battery-powered motor mounted inside a heavy-duty body fitted to accept a variety of mining machinery. She is capable of carrying a plasma-fired deep-drilling bit, a surface excavation blade, and a high-pressure fracking pump, along with a half-dozen other resource exploration and extraction rigs.

"I discovered *Roadrunner* in one of the remote garages, where she'd been abandoned by a failed mining venture. There were two ore cars parked next to her, so we modified her for use as surface transport. We removed the ore chutes, welded benches inside the cars, and sealed the vents against sifters. There is a positive air pressure system inside the cabin and cars for use during high dust conditions to keep the dirt out and protect passengers.

"She was originally configured as a tracked vehicle, but the tracks were so slow and inefficient that we modified the suspension to accept standard axles and knobby tires. She can do seventeen kilometers per hour forward and eight in reverse, and a full battery charge will last eight to nine hours at full speed.

"She can fit through most of the roads in Boston without the ore cars. There are some narrow alleys that she won't fit through, but I know where those are, and we can plan around them. Have a look."

Fortis looked inside the cockpit and saw a bewildering array of levers, switches, and gauges. He counted six gear shifts and five floor pedals. Some things were marked in foreign languages and several lacked any labels at all.

"All of these to drive around?" he asked Dolph, standing at his elbow.

"No, most of those controls are for the detachable equipment. Her main controls are a lot like those on the first-generation heavy battle mechs."

Fortis gave Dolph an inquisitive look, and the mercenary chuckled. "I was a mech driver in the Space Marines a long time ago."

Ystremski and the assault teams rehearsed mounting and dismounting the converted ore cars, first with one team and then both. They determined that the rear car provided the greatest freedom of movement for the assaulters, so Fortis decided that the command element would ride in the first car and leave the second car unobstructed. The rear car would also serve as the casualty collection point, and the medic would ride there with the assault teams. The

Space Marines would load detainees into the first car with Fortis and an armed escort.

Ystremski gave Fortis a thumbs up. "This will work just fine, sir." He turned to Dolph. "How loud is this thing? Will they hear us coming?"

"The crawler operates on battery power, so the motor is virtually silent. There is still some vehicle noise from the couplings and the brakes, though. There are no private vehicles in Boston, so the residents know it's us when they hear us coming. We can mitigate that by stopping short of the target, or perhaps not stopping at all, if your men can dismount while the crawler is moving."

Ystremski nodded. "I think we can manage that, if it becomes necessary."

Satisfied with their inspection of the crawler, Ystremski formed up the platoon and headed out to test fire the pistols. Fortis and Chive met at the garage door.

"I may have underestimated you and your men, Lieutenant," Chive said as he extended his hand. "I had my doubts, but I think this will work out for both our benefits."

"We will do our best to help bring down the drug cartel," replied Fortis as they shook.

Fortis hurried outside to catch up with the platoon, flexed the hand, and tried to shake off the uneasy feeling he got from the mercenary. Chive's attitude towards the Space Marines had done a complete reversal, but it didn't seem genuine. Instead, it was almost as if he had rehearsed it. The quiet warning Jandahl had given about Chive and his men was still fresh in his ears.

"They're not your friends."

* * *

The pistols Chief Schultz issued to the Space Marines were magazine-fed, semi-automatic ballistic weapons.

"These things are three hundred years old, LT."

Ystremski handed one to Lieutenant Fortis. The officer locked the slide back and peered down the barrel.

"The lads did a good job cleaning them up."

"Yes, sir, they did. The actions and triggers are smooth and the magazine springs are strong. The ammunition is a different story."

The corporal gestured to the ammo cans. "When we opened the crates, all the cans were rusty and dented, and a couple had failed seals. We got about a thousand good rounds out of the four crates, so we have plenty to train with."

The platoon set up a simple four-meter firing line and took turns slow-firing the pistols, both to familiarize themselves and to test the weapons. They progressed to double-taps on multiple targets, and then to fire-reload-fire drills. It didn't take them long to develop proficiency with the pistols, so they pushed the targets out to twenty meters.

"It's a good thing we'll be working close-in," quipped Ystremski as round after round impacted the dirt around the targets. "These guys can't hit shit past four meters." The corporal took his place on the firing line and the platoon chuckled as he struggled to hit the longer-range target.

"These pistols are shit," Ystremski growled when he finished. Fortis laughed as he took his place on the firing line, but his results were no better. He wasn't a great shot to begin with, and the old pistol did nothing for his accuracy.

"Should we give them back to the chief?" Fortis asked after he finished firing.

"This is all they have, LT. We can't go in empty handed. Besides, the guns are mostly for show. The governor said there aren't any firearms in Boston, remember?"

"Yeah. All right then." He motioned for the corporal to follow him. "I have something I want to talk to you about while they're shooting."

The pair stood out of earshot of the other Marines.

"Have you met anyone named Jandahl, or heard the name?

"The name doesn't ring a bell, LT. How did you meet him?"

"He approached me in the corridor when I was on the way to medical. He told me he's some kind of investigator for GRC. He warned me about Chive and these missions. Said that Chive has something going on behind the scenes, and he's using us to do it."

"Weird. This guy works for the GRC?"

"That's what he said. I don't know, maybe he's a crackpot who's been out here too long and he's playing some kind of joke. He might be a member of the cartel running a little psyop on us."

"Or he might be telling the truth. You want me to ask the men if he approached any of them?"

"No. Let's keep this between us for now. It's probably nothing, but if he's telling the truth, this thing just got a whole lot more inter-esting." Fortis sighed and rubbed his face. "Either way, we'll hold up our end of the bargain with Governor Czrk. I don't care who's doing what here on Eros-28 as long as we take Marx and Landis with us when we leave."

* * * * *

Chapter Twenty

Three hours later, Chive sent a messenger to alert the Space Marines of an imminent mission, and Fortis led Ystremski and Assault Team One outside to board the crawler. Fortis rode with the assault team and passed around the photographs the messenger had given him.

"There are two targets, a woman and a man. The woman's name is Shelly Baird. She works in the electronics department, and she's an active member of the resistance. The man's name is Chick Root. He's a former welder who quit in protest back when the Security Directorate operated against the resistance in Boston. Baird and Root live together, and the GRC suspects that Root is operating a China Mike laboratory in their home."

Private Redman raised his hand. "Sir, what does a China Mike lab look like?"

Fortis and Ystremski traded glances. "That's a good question, Private. I don't know. For now, treat anything that looks suspicious as drug-related, and we'll sort it out with Chive when we're done."

The assault team committed the images to memory while Fortis peered out through the view port. Outside, the city was black, and he swore under his breath. He had zero awareness of where they were or what the situation was outside the crawler.

Their plan was simple. The crawler driver would pull up in front of the target location and shine a spotlight on the door. The assault team would dismount and conduct the raid. Meanwhile, the medic would move from the front car to the rear and leave the hatches open behind him. When they completed the assault, the team would fall back with the detainees, load up the crawler, and roll away. Radio communications would be kept to a minimum, since the radios were from the colonial police, and the Space Marines didn't know who might be listening.

The crawler lurched to a halt, and the spotlight stabbed the darkness. The hatch banged open and Assault Team One disembarked the crawler and approached the lighted door.

The assault team formed up in a stack and crouched behind the breacher who examined the door. Just then, the door swung open and a sleepy-looking man poked his head out. The breacher pulled the man through the door and tackled him while the rest of the assault team surged forward into the darkened interior. Within seconds, the breacher had the surprised man's arms and legs restrained.

Less than a minute later, three of the assault team members exited the dwelling. Two of them were carrying a figure that struggled in their arms, while the third struggled to get a hood over the prisoner's head. It was obvious that their captive was female, and the Space Marines were firm but not rough. Finally, they got the woman restrained and hooded.

Ystremski's voice crackled over the radio. "All clear. Targets are secure, location search in progress."

Ninety seconds passed before Ystremski and the last member of the assault team emerged from the house. The Space Marines put their prisoners in the first car and mounted up. Fortis climbed in behind them. The crawler jerked into motion and the spotlight was extinguished.

Fortis and the men exchanged nervous smiles and high-fives on the way back to Fenway. Fortis recognized the effects of an adrenaline surge in their flushed faces and shiny eyes, and he felt a twinge of jealousy. Corporal Ystremski, sitting on the bench across from him, slapped him on the knee.

"Fucking clockwork, LT," he blurted. "Just like we rehearsed."

Fortis nodded. "A little too slow, but yeah, it seemed okay to me."

The Marines stared at the lieutenant in shocked silence for a long second before Fortis' face cracked into a wide grin. Ystremski started laughing, and the rest of the men joined in.

"Did you recover any China Mike?"

Ystremski shook his head. "Negative. Nothing obvious, anyway. There might have been a hidden door or something, but we weren't going to find anything like that unless we destroyed the place."

At the mention of China Mike, the male prisoner struggled and tried to sit up. Private Yew jumped on top of him and pinned the prisoner's head to the floor.

"Take it easy, Yew," ordered Ystremski. "There's no need for that."

"Stay down," Yew told the prisoner before he climbed off. He gave Corporal Ystremski a long look after he took his seat, but a second later he was smiling and laughing with the rest of the assault team.

"Where's Cowher?" Ystremski asked Fortis.

Fortis realized all the members of Assault Team One were in the first car except for the medic. "I think he's in the second car, just like we planned."

Fortis laughed along with the other Space Marines at Private Cowher riding alone in the second car, but inside he was angry with himself. He had allowed himself to get caught up in the action instead of remaining above the fray to control the situation. He keyed his radio.

"Cowher, this is Fortis. What's your status?"

The only response was static.

"Cowher, this is Fortis, What's your status?"

Nothing.

"We need to go back!" he exclaimed.

The lieutenant realized they had no communications with the crawler driver. Ystremski tried to open the hatch, but there was an interlock on the latch that prevented passengers from opening it while the crawler was in motion. Several of the Marines shouted and pounded on the sides of the converted ore car, to no avail.

Fortis struggled to control his emotions as he sat, trapped, with the rest of the assault team while the driver guided the crawler back to the GRC compound. As the minutes ticked by, his anxiety doubled, then doubled again.

As soon as the crawler squealed to a halt, Ystremski popped the hatch, and the Space Marines poured out. Lance Corporal Lemm yanked open the hatch to the rear car and looked inside.

"It's empty," he called.

"Damn it!" Fortis turned to Dolph, who was waiting next to the engine car. "We have to go back. We left a guy behind."

Dolph shrugged. "I can't go anywhere unless Mr. Chive okays it."

Fortis clenched his fists and stepped toward the man. "I don't care what Chive said. We left—"

"Hey, LT. LT!" Ystremski called from the back of the crawler. "Look who we found."

Private Cowher was standing next to the corporal. He was covered in a thick layer of dust and his teeth gleamed white in a sheepish grin.

"Where the hell were you, Cowher?" Fortis' relief was clear in his voice.

"Everybody piled into the first car, so I decided I would, too. I ran back to close the hatch in the back, but by the time I got back up front, somebody had closed the hatch and the crawler started rolling. I guess you guys didn't hear me pounding and yelling. I dropped my radio somewhere, and I couldn't call, so I climbed up on the roof and kept my head down."

Just then, Chive came outside, followed by several of his men.

"Lieutenant Fortis, how did your raid go? Did you capture the suspects?"

Fortis gestured to the crawler. "They are restrained in there. Do you—"

Chive turned to his men. "Mount up. We're heading for the site."

Fortis persisted. "Hey, Chive, hang on. There are some things we need to work out."

Chive put up a hand. "After we interview these prisoners, you and I can talk. Right now, I have more important business to attend to."

The mercenary turned on his heel and climbed into the engine car. Fortis stared after the crawler as it disappeared into the dark city.

Corporal Ystremski had sidled up behind Fortis and witnessed the exchange between Fortis and Chive. "What now, LT?"

"Muster the platoon, and let's debrief," replied Fortis. "We'll get it sorted out, and I'll tell Chive later."

* * *

When Jandahl heard about the Space Marine raid, he went straight to the GRC facility and arrived in a nearby alley in time to overhear Chive tell Fortis he was headed for to the site. Jandahl knew it was his opportunity to locate the headquarters of the Kuiper Knights, if he could hitch a ride.

He ducked into the shadows of a nearby doorway as the crawler rolled past and then clambered aboard the second car. He clung to the roof and squinted against the dusty darkness beyond the dim lights of Boston. The GRC facility faded in the background, but after several minutes Jandahl was able to make out a faint glimmer in the distance.

When the crawler was a kilometer away from the site, Jandahl jumped off and scrambled behind a rock outcropping. From this vantage point, he could make out a low dirt wall surrounding a dome, which he guessed was the primary structure. The crawler stopped and waited for several minutes before a gate opened to allow the vehicle to enter.

Jandahl moved closer and watched and listened for a response. There were no guards posted and no one sounded an alarm, so he approached the wall. It was three meters high and constructed of the same mud that the colonists in Boston used for their buildings. There were lights at regular intervals along the wall, but they did little to illuminate the area outside.

I guess they're not expecting visitors.

He found a place where the smooth surface of the wall had cracked and, with some effort, he dug out enough dirt to form a waist-high foothold. He scraped out another at shoulder height and he used them to climb high enough to get a look inside.

The inside of the mercenary compound was unremarkable. The dome was the main structure and there were eight windowless, single-story buildings in two neat rows around it. Jandahl didn't see any building numbers or signs to indicate what the buildings were. He spent a long time searching the wall and buildings for external cameras or sensors but saw none, so he boosted himself onto the wall and dropped into the compound.

The first two doors he tried were locked, but the third doorknob turned in his hand. As Jandahl was about to crack the door and peek inside, a sixth sense screamed *"RETREAT!"* He barely made it around the corner before the door crashed open.

Two men dressed in black uniforms dragged a third man outside. The man hung limp between the mercenaries and his bare feet left ruts in the arid soil.

"I can't believe this fucker died already," remarked one of the men as they hauled the body to the crawler.

"At least he's not beat up too bad," his partner replied. "We can stick a needle in his arm and dump him in town. Just another dead junkie."

The two men laughed as they returned to the door. When they opened it, Jandahl heard the unmistakable sound of a woman screaming.

Jandahl waited several long minutes before he continued his survey of rest of the compound. The doorknob on the first one opened, and the contents stunned the intelligence operative. The entire build-

ing was full of laboratory equipment. He scanned the flasks and barrels stacked on one side and realized it was a China Mike lab. An
industrial-sized China Mike lab.

The Kuiper Knights are making China Mike!

He pulled the door shut, then tried the rest, but they were all
locked.

He decided to leave before he was discovered. Although he and
Chive were nominally on the same side, now that he had discovered
the security director's secret, he knew that if he was found inside the
compound uninvited he would end up "just another dead junkie,"
too.

He saw some barrels and pallets stacked up against the wall near
where the crawler was parked, so he used the junk as a ladder. Once
he was clear of the compound and there was no alarm was raised,
Jandahl began the long walk back to Fenway. His mind raced as he
thought about his discovery and he debated his next step.

* * * * *

Chapter Twenty-One

The Space Marines debriefed their first mission according to standard ISMC practice. The most junior member of the assault team recounted the raid from his perspective, followed by the second most junior, and so on, until it was Fortis' turn. It was a slow and painstaking process, but it ensured that every data point was collected in a way that a top-down debrief could not. It kept all the men engaged as follow-on missions were planned and their ideas were incorporated. Finally, it gave ISMC leaders an opportunity to identify which Space Marines had leadership qualities.

It annoyed Fortis that Chive and Dolph weren't present for the debrief. The platoon was smart enough to recognize the strain in the relationship between their commanding officer and the director of security, but Fortis cut off any criticisms of the Kuiper Knight and his organization.

When it was Fortis' turn to speak, he was open and honest in his assessment of the raid. He took responsibility for his mistakes in a self-deprecating manner without eroding his authority as the platoon commander and an ISMC officer, and Corporal Ystremski nodded his approval when the lieutenant finished and there were no more questions.

The corporal took charge of the men.

"Third Platoon, fall in!"

Fortis, who had expected the corporal to dismiss the men, gave him a quizzical look.

184 | P.A. PIATT

"First things first, LT."

The doors at the far end of the dormitory opened, and Corporal Anderson and Private Lopez entered the space. Each man had a grip on one side of a large metal jug, and Lopez was carrying a sleeve of reusable plastic cups in his free hand.

"What's this?" asked Fortis, as the two Space Marines set up a serving station while the rest of the platoon smiled in anticipation.

"One of the GRC machinists is a former Space Marine, and he has a son who's a crew chief for a hovercopter assigned to Second Division," Ystremski explained. "When he heard there were Space Marines on Eros-28, he introduced himself to some of the boys and offered to help solve our problem."

Fortis grinned as the platoon lined up while Anderson and Lopez doled out the contents of the jug. "And what problem would that be, Corporal?"

The last of the platoon received their cups, and Ystremski handed one to Fortis and took one himself. The raw alcohol fumes burned Fortis' nose, confirming the contents of his cup.

DINLI.

"We didn't have a way to toast a successful mission. Until now."

Fortis raised his cup. "To the dead and the living." He tipped his cup until a splash of the fiery brew spilled onto the deck. The platoon did the same and then returned the traditional toast response.

"DINLI!"

Corporal Ystremski quaffed his cup, took the cup from the lieutenant, and tossed it back.

"Sorry, sir. Doctor's orders."

* * *

Lieutenant Fortis and Corporal Ystremski kept Third Platoon busy with a full schedule of training built on their experience from the first mission. The Space Marines ran multiple scenarios in their berthing compartment mock-up. They didn't hear from Chive again until late in the afternoon.

The security director appeared at the door to their dormitory and waited until the lieutenant called an end to the exercise.

"Still practicing, Lieutenant?" Chive said as Fortis and Ystremski approached.

"Always," replied Fortis. "We're rotating in the Space Marines who aren't assigned to Assault Team One or Two. It's good training, and it gives us a reserve of troops in case we need them."

Corporal Ystremski followed the two men as they walked out into the corridor.

"Did you get any useful intel from Baird or Root?"

"Hmm, not yet," replied Chive. "These things take time. I do have a new target for this evening." He handed Fortis a file. "Pai Choon. She's an electronics technician and a member of the same China Mike cartel cell as Baird."

Fortis scanned the folder. "I thought you didn't get any useful intel from Baird and Root yet."

Chive only hesitated for a split second, but it was enough to confirm his deception. He cracked a self-conscious smirk.

"I have other sources, Lieutenant."

"Sure, of course." Fortis passed the folder to Ystremski. "We're going to incorporate our lessons learned from last night's mission. Is your crawler driver available?"

Chive shook his head. "Sorry, no. He's back at the site and won't be available until later tonight."

Fortis thought for a second. "Huh. Okay, I guess we can brief him up before we take off."

"That's fine. We'll be here at the same time tonight. Should be another easy breather."

"We'll be ready."

Fortis and Ystremski watched as Chive disappeared around the corner at the end of the corridor.

"I don't like that guy," Ystremski said in a low voice. "There's something not right about him."

"Yeah, I agree. I don't know whether to trust the info from that Jandahl fellow, but the vibes I get from Chive are all bad."

* * *

After the training session, Fortis visited Marx and Landis. The pair greeted him with anxious smiles.

"What's the word, LT? When are we getting out of here?"

"Soon; that's all I can tell you. I tried to negotiate with the governor for your release, but he insisted that you remain in custody until we're evac'd. The Fleet is still on alert in orbit around Eros-69, but I expect them to pick us up any time now."

Their smiles turned to frowns, and the two Space Marines slumped into their seats. Fortis shook his head.

"You two should be happy. You're damned lucky the governor has agreed to let you leave with us. What the hell was going through your minds, messing around with China Mike after you were warned not to?"

"Hey, LT, we didn't do anything. That was a total set up."

Fortis held up his hands. "That's not what the police say. Lucky for you, you won't have to convince the judge."

"What about the ISMC?" asked Marx.

"I don't know that the Corps will ever know about it. That's up to you, I guess. I don't plan on reporting it unless it's absolutely necessary. Corporal Ystremski said he'll handle the justice on our end as long as you don't do anything stupid between now and our departure."

The pair smiled again, and the relief on their faces was evident.

"LT, we'll do whatever you say. Just don't forget about us."

Fortis laughed as he stood up. "No chance of that happening. Ystremski won't let me." He paused at the door. "Be patient. We'll be back aboard *Atlas* before you know it."

Fortis hated to lie, but Marx and Landis didn't need to know about the missions their fellow Marines were involved in with the Security Directorate. He also knew that anything he told the pair would likely reach Chief Schultz through microphones in the ceiling, and he didn't want to reveal what they were up to.

* * *

Fortis and Assault Team Two linked up with Chive and Dolph outside Fenway. As the assault team passed around the photos of Pai Choon, Fortis briefed the mercenaries on their new procedures.

"I'll ride in the cockpit with Dolph," he said. "On our first mission, I had zero situational awareness in the ore car. As the mission commander, I need complete visibility on everything that's happening during the mission.

"The assault team, led by Corporal Heisen, and the team medic, Private Durant, will all ride in the second car. After the mission is complete, we won't leave until I get a positive head count from the assault team leader.

"My men don't know what a China Mike lab looks like, so any information you can provide would be helpful," he told the mercenaries. "I expect this raid will take longer than the first one, because they'll conduct a thorough search for tunnels and hidden doors."

"Whatever you think is best, Lieutenant. We're here to support you," said Chive.

Dolph nodded his agreement, and Fortis gave the order to mount up.

The crawler lumbered along, and Fortis conducted a radio check with Corporal Heisen. In addition to the radios carried by each team member, they decided to leave one in the cockpit and the two converted ore cars. It was probably an unnecessary redundancy, but it didn't cost them anything, and if they needed it, it would be worth the effort.

The set up for the second mission was identical to the first. Dolph piloted the crawler to a halt in front of a house and illuminated it with the searchlight. The assault team formed a stack, breached the door, and poured inside. Seconds later, two of them dragged a hooded figure outside and dumped her in the second car.

Fortis listened as Heisen directed his team through the house. The long periods of silence on the radio unnerved him, but he knew it would take time for the assault team to thoroughly probe every inch of the building in search of drug-related materials and tunnels.

Finally, Heisen called all clear and the assault team exited the house and made for the crawler. After he confirmed the head count,

Fortis gave Dolph the okay to head back to Fenway. As the crawler jerked into motion, Fortis checked his watch. The entire mission had taken nine minutes. *Nine minutes? It felt like forever.*

When they arrived back at Fenway, Chive and his mercenaries were waiting on Fortis and the Space Marines. The assault team dismounted and brought their captive out. Corporal Ystremski and the rest of Third Platoon came out of Fenway to meet the assault team. The two groups unconsciously faced off.

"That's Choon?" asked Chive.

"It is," replied Fortis. "She was the only person there, but there was no evidence of drugs or lab equipment."

"Good job." Chive waved at his men to take custody of the prisoner, but the Space Marines didn't budge.

"What's the news on Baird and Root?" Fortis asked. "Have you made any progress with them?"

At the mention of the first two prisoners, Choon twisted in her restraints.

Chive gave Fortis a long look. "It turns out my information from earlier was inaccurate. We released Root earlier today; he isn't involved with the drug cartel. We're still questioning Baird. Satisfied?"

Fortis looked back at Ystremski, who shrugged.

"Yeah. Yeah, I'm satisfied." Fortis nodded, and the Space Marines stepped back to allow the mercenaries to take custody of Choon. "I just want to make sure we're doing the right thing, and that the prisoners are treated properly."

"Don't worry, Lieutenant," Chive said. "We're on the same team, remember?"

190 | P.A. PIATT

As the crawler rolled off into the darkness, the Space Marines filed inside Fenway. Fortis and Ystremski stood silently until the lights of the crawler had disappeared in the distance.

"I trust that guy less and less every time I see him," Ystremski said. "I think he's full of shit."

"And you're right to think so."

The two Space Marines whirled around at the strange voice. A man wearing GRC coveralls emerged from the darkness. Fortis recognized him as the man who had approached him before.

"Jandahl?"

"Yes, it's me."

Ystremski rested his hand on the butt of his pistol, and the GRC intelligence operative kept his hands open and by his sides as he approached the two men.

"Have you had a chance to think about our discussion the other day?" Jandahl asked.

Fortis nodded. "I have, and I've discussed it with Corporal Ystremski, too."

"And?"

"And it's too early for us to tell whether you're credible or not. We have no way to corroborate your information."

"Here's some information you can corroborate. Chick Root is dead."

"Dead? How?"

"Chive and his men tortured him to death."

"How do you know that?

"I was at the Kuiper Knights compound when they dragged Root's body outside and stuffed him in the crawler. My guess is that they'll dump him somewhere in Boston and make it look like an overdose."

"Prove it."

Jandahl shook his head. "I can't. Talk to Chief Schultz and ask him if there's any news about Root. By midday tomorrow, I predict he'll have another OD on his hands. There's something else; the Kuiper Knights—"

The door banged open and Corporal Heisen stuck his head out. "Hey, Corporal—" He saw Jandahl talking with the two Marines. "Ah, sorry."

The man abruptly turned and strode off into the darkness. "I'll be in touch, Lieutenant," he threw over his shoulder. "Watch your back."

Ystremski elbowed Fortis. "C'mon, sir. The lads are waiting."

Fortis shook his head as he followed the corporal.

"Everybody in this place is nuts."

* * * * *

Chapter Twenty-Two

The second mission debrief was much shorter than the first. The rough spots encountered by Assault Team One had been smoothed over, so the list of issues was much shorter.

Insertion and extraction had gone as planned. Apprehending their target had been quick and efficient, but the Space Marines expressed a familiar concern.

"We searched the entire place, LT, but we still don't know what we were looking for," said Heisen. The rest of the men nodded their agreement. "I saw a bunch of glassware in the kitchen, but it looked like regular dishes to me, so I left it."

"You're right, we can't be expected to do the mission if we don't know what to look for," replied Fortis. "I've asked Chive a couple times and gotten no answers. I'm going to see Chief Schultz first thing tomorrow morning, and I'll try to get an answer for you."

Later, Fortis and Ystremski discussed their situation while they lifted weights.

"What do you think of Jandahl?" Fortis said as he lowered a heavy weight bar to his chest and pushed it back up.

"He's as sketchy as anyone else we've met here," replied the corporal as he guided the bar. "Let's go, don't quit. Two more."

Fortis grunted and lowered the bar again. "I guess we'll know after I talk to Schultz." His arms trembled as he pressed the bar up.

"Last one. Come on, don't be a pussy." Ystremski wrapped his hands around the bar and steered it down to Fortis' chest. "Everything you've got. Push!"

All thoughts of Jandahl and Chive disappeared as Fortis focused his mind on the heavy bar. The burn in his pectoral muscles faded, and he felt a surge of strength as he pushed the weight all the way up, but he resisted when Ystremski tried to guide the bar to the rest.

"One more," he spat through gritted teeth. Fortis let the weight drop slowly to his chest and then shoved it up with a final mighty effort. The bar clanged onto the rack, and the young officer let his arms fall to his sides as his heart thundered, and he gasped for breath.

"Not bad, for an officer," the corporal commented with a smile of approval. "A private would have gotten two more, though."

Fortis sat up with a groan. "You'd know more about being a private than I would."

The corporal chuckled as he added fat plates to both sides of the bars. "Slide out of the way and let this two-time private show you how it's done."

* * *

Chive rode next to Dolph. "That kid is becoming a pain in my ass," he told the driver. "He's asking a lot of questions. Did he say anything to you?"

Dolph's shoulder itched where he had a tattoo of DINLI, the unofficial Space Marine mascot, removed. He got it as a cherry private during his first liberty run on Terra Earth. He had it removed two years later, after he was dishonorably discharged and joined the Kuiper Knights.

"He didn't say much at all," Dolph replied. "He's like every other second lieutenant I've ever known. Long on enthusiasm and short on smarts."

"I hope he can curb his enthusiasm for a while longer. Baird and Root have gotten us a lot closer to Finkle." He gestured to the converted ore car where the rest of his men were riding with their new captive. "There's no telling what Choon can do for us."

"Do we really need Finkle? I mean, once your plan starts to roll, the resistance will become a loose end, won't it?"

"Loose ends have a bad way of becoming snags, Dolph. My plan, and this place, are too important to the Knights for us to leave anything to chance. The arrival of the Space Marines was a fortuitous turn of events, and I believe we are best served by using them to pursue the resistance. The colonists and the resistance both have to believe the UNT sent them to support the GRC, which will drive the wedge between them and Governor Czrk a little deeper."

* * *

The following morning, Lieutenant Fortis found Chief Shultz in his office. The portly cop waved him into a chair and offered the Space Marine a steaming cup of coffee.

"What brings you here this morning, Lieutenant? Besides the best coffee on Eros-28, I mean."

"I didn't get a chance to thank you for the loan of weapons and gear for our training with the Security Directorate," Fortis replied. "I meant no offense when we talked about weapons earlier; it never occurred to me that you don't need much to maintain law and order here." He gave a self-conscious grin. "This is the first time I've been somewhere like the Eros Cluster."

Schultz smiled in return. "We're in a unique situation here, and I didn't take any offense. We're able to keep the peace here with community engagement; we don't need an arsenal. We stay close to the people and they appreciate that."

Fortis nodded while the two men sipped their coffee in silence.

Finally, Fortis said, "What can you tell me about China Mike, Chief? Marx and Landis got mixed up with it, but I still don't know much about it."

Schultz considered him for a long second before he responded.

"China Mike is a synthetic stimulant, originally developed by a deep-space mining company contracted to the Senegalese government on Terra Earth. That was before your time, back when individual countries still competed for resources out here. Workers used China Mike to work double shifts, which made the companies happy. The workers got eight hours of regular time and eight hours of overtime for every day worked, which made them happy come payday."

"If the workers take it voluntarily and everybody is happy, what's the problem?"

"For starters, China Mike is highly addictive. Chronic users need frequent boosts to maintain their high and it's easy to overdose. The effects of the drug are cumulative, as well. The higher users go, the farther they crash.

"If they don't kick the habit, they spend all their overtime pay on the drug and work even more hours so they can earn more overtime pay. Eventually, most addicts lose their jobs and turn to crime to pay for the drug. Not too long ago there was a group of asteroid wranglers who murdered their GRC project foreman and hijacked the company transport to go to Eros-69 in search of more China Mike."

"What happened to them?"

"They were tried, convicted, and purged from an airlock."

"Damn."

Schultz shrugged. "It's a vicious cycle that usually ends in trage-dy. Some users experience psychological effects that result in aggressive behavior. If they are predisposed to violence, China Mike makes it worse. Some colonies don't care about the health and safety of their workers; we do."

"If China Mike is that bad, why not outlaw it?"

Chief Schultz chuckled.

"Lieutenant, this isn't Terra Earth, with a government to enact laws and the law enforcement to see to it that those laws are obeyed. This isn't a deep-space asteroid grab, where the crews know they're going home rich in three or four years. The people who work here are out here for decades, sometimes for life. They've all got their reasons for living this lifestyle, but they're not typically the kind of people you can just order around."

"So you let it go."

Schultz's smile became a scowl.

"No, we don't just let it go. We rely on the workforce to self-regulate. The governor granted their request to add an automatic, voluntary four-hour overtime work period to every shift. The workers don't feel the need to get amped up to make it through a twelve-hour shift like they would for a sixteen-hour shift. In return, shop supervisors agreed to keep their coworkers in line. It's not perfect, but it worked for a long time."

"What happened?"

"China Mike happened."

Fortis couldn't disguise his confusion at the chief's answer. Schultz picked up on it immediately.

"Look, there was always a little bit of it around. Some people use it recreationally, but they keep it under control We get all kinds of crews through here and there's always someone willing to supply it. It came and went, but it wasn't a big problem. Then we had a series of strikes and vandalism and the GRC sent Chive and his men here to deal with the labor unrest, which they call 'the resistance.'" The chief made air quotes. "Suddenly the drug was everywhere, and the price was so low nobody could resist." He gestured to the ceiling. "Corporate claims the workers manufacture it to finance some kind of half-assed resistance."

"They don't?"

Schultz snorted. "There's no resistance here. What the hell do they have to revolt about? The work is hard, but the pay is the best in the industry, and the working conditions are good. The only real complaint is the lack of family housing, and that's a budgetary issue. Governor Czrk just sent a plan to corporate to make some modifications to existing dormitories to allow familial living inside Fenway, but the wheels turn slow at headquarters.

"Meanwhile, Chive built a compound for himself and his guys out in the desert, doing whatever it is they do out there. I haven't seen much of them around here since they cracked down on the workers after the entire facility went on strike. Czrk put them on a leash, and they don't appear to do much anymore. Except train with Space Marines."

Fortis grinned self-consciously. "Chief, you know as well as anyone that we're not training."

The chief nodded. "At least you're man enough to admit it."

Fortis had an urge to confide in the corpulent cop.

"If I had a choice, we wouldn't be involved in this," replied Fortis. "But the governor didn't give me any good options. I can't leave here without Marx and Landis."

"I understand. Even though the colonial circuit judge will probably dismiss the case, you can't take the chance, can you?"

Before Fortis could respond, Officer Upham appeared in the door.

"Chief, we've got trouble. Chick Root—" He stopped when he recognized Fortis.

"What it is, Upham?"

"Uh, well…the morning patrol just found him. Dead. OD'd."

"Damnit!" Chief Schultz jumped up and grabbed his hat. "Sorry, Lieutenant, duty calls."

Fortis struggled to conceal his surprise at the news as he followed the chief into the corridor. "Mind if I ride along, Chief?"

Schultz paused for a second, considered Fortis through narrowed eyes, then nodded.

"Sure. Come on."

* * *

Mandel Spears turned the torque wrench until he felt it *click* and then straightened up. His back protested, but he felt a surge of satisfaction. After five shifts digging and cleaning the equipment buried by Raisa's attack on Garage Number Seven, he was finally back to the work he loved.

Raisa.

He wiped his hands and fought back the emotions that welled up in his chest.

As the excavation of Garage Seven proceeded, his mood soared as each shovelful of dirt failed to uncover her body. Then he plunged into deep despair when he realized that if she wasn't buried in the garage, she was in the hands of the Colonial Police or worse, the Security Directorate.

Even though their marriage was essentially over, they had remained bonded by their son. Her disappearance had hit Mandel hard, and he hadn't figured out how to tell his son that his mommy wasn't coming home. He saw Raisa in his son's face, and it was so painful that he had sent his son to live with friends until her disappearance was solved.

"Spears!"

Mandel turned to his shift manager and he saw two men in black uniforms standing at the shop door. The manager waved at him, and Spears walked across the shop on wooden legs.

"The director of security wants to talk to you," said one of the uniforms. They escorted him into the passageway.

"What's this about?" asked Spears as the two men propelled him along. "Is this about my wife?"

They remained silent, and Spears began to panic. By the time he worked up the courage to fight them off and run away, they had stopped at a door in the passageway.

B-Level Utilities B-149A6
Authorized Personnel Only

They shoved Spears inside, and he ended up face to face with the fearsome mercenary Chive.

"What do you want? What's this about?"

Chive showed Spears a photograph, and the mechanic's heart stopped.

"This is your son," Chive told him. "I know where he is. I have a man watching over him."

"M-my son." Spears lunged forward, and his face twisted with rage. "Leave him alone, you bastard!"

Chive sidestepped the clumsy attack and slapped the mechanic across the face.

"He's safe, as long as you do what you're told," he told the stunned man.

Spears rubbed his stinging cheek and glared at the mercenary.

"What do you want me to do?"

"Set up a meeting with Dask Finkle."

"Dask Finkle? I don't know a Dask Finkle."

Chive sighed and backhanded the mechanic on the other side of his face. Spears staggered back, and Chive's men grabbed his arms.

"Don't lie to me, Spears. Don't ever lie to me. You're the leader of a resistance cell and you know Dask Finkle."

Defeated, Spears could only hang his head.

"You're going to set up a meeting with Dask Finkle for tonight. You will go to that meeting, and my men will arrest you and Finkle, but you'll be released."

"What do you want with Finkle?"

Chive poked him in the chest. "That's not your concern. Your concern is your son, who will remain safe as long as you do exactly what I tell you to do. Do you understand?"

He nodded slowly.

Chive shoved him toward the door. "Your shift is over. Go set up the meeting."

Spears left Fenway and trudged along the dirt street toward his house. He didn't know what excuse he could use for a face-to-face meeting with Finkle, but the image of Chive holding a picture of his son drove him forward.

* * * * *

Chapter Twenty-Three

Jandahl paused by the door to Fenway and looked around. The streets of Boston were deserted, and the only sounds came from a group of Space Marines training on a flat spot beyond the wall. Satisfied he wasn't being followed, Jandahl slipped inside.

He went down the corridor to the utility room where he'd met Chive before, stopped to collect himself, and entered the room. He wiped his hands on his coveralls and wished his palms would stop sweating. What Jandahl had witnessed at the Kuiper Knight compound had shocked him. Now that he was back inside the safety of Fenway, his shock had transformed into righteous anger.

The doorknob clicked as the door closed behind him, and he saw Chive and two of his men waiting.

"What do you want, Jandahl?"

Chive's dismissive attitude infuriated Jandahl further, and he grabbed the bigger man by the front of his uniform.

"You son of a bitch! You murdered Chick Root, and you're manufacturing China Mike at the site!" he hissed.

Chive stumbled back a couple steps before he caught himself. He gripped Jandahl's wrists and twisted so Jandahl was forced to let go as pain shot up his arms.

"You've forgotten who you're dealing with, Jandahl." He shoved the intelligence agent away, and Jandahl slammed into the wall behind him. "I don't know what you think you know, but you're wrong."

"I was at the site, you bastard. I saw your men stuff Root into the crawler after you killed him, and I heard Baird screaming."

Chive flinched. Jandahl continued.

"I looked inside a couple of your other buildings, too, and I saw your lab. You're manufacturing China Mike and using your position as security director to eliminate your competition under the guise of prosecuting the resistance. When the governor hears what I have to tell him, you're finished."

Suddenly, Jandahl looked around for an escape route, but Chive was looming over him. He rushed past the mercenary and headed for the door.

Too late, he sensed Chive behind him. A fist hammered the back of his neck and stars exploded in his head. His legs gave out.

Chive caught him before he collapsed onto the deck.

"Wrong, little man," the mercenary leader said as he tucked Jandahl's head under the crook of his arm. "I'm taking over the entire colony."

The last thing Jandahl heard was a *crack*.

* * *

Corporal Ystremski watched Jandahl lurking near the door to Fenway before he disappeared inside. Something about the intelligence operative's furtive actions piqued Ystremski's curiosity, so he turned the training session over to Heisen. He trotted to the door, cracked it, and followed Jandahl inside.

Ystremski glimpsed Jandahl as he disappeared around the corner at the end of the corridor. He hurried after the man. He chanced a look and saw Jandahl glance around before entering a room halfway down the corridor.

Damn it! Did he see me?

He waited several seconds before he crouched and risked another glimpse, but the corridor stayed empty.

Ystremski didn't know where the door led, but his curiosity rooted him in his spot. He wanted to take a look, but he would be completely exposed if the GRC operative came out. Instead, he watched and waited.

After several long minutes, the door opened again, and Ystremski ducked behind the corner. He strained his ears for the sound of approaching footsteps, but when he didn't hear any he checked around the corner in time to see Security Director Chive and two of his men moving away from him down the corridor.

What the hell?

Ystremski couldn't wait any longer. Once the three men were out of sight, he went to the door, stopping to read the sign.

B-Level Utilities B-149A6
Authorized Personnel Only

He turned the doorknob and entered.

The utility room was a maze of pipes and wiring runs. Mechanical equipment hummed and lights flashed on control panels. At first glance the space appeared to be empty, so he quickly stepped into the room and closed the door. Finally, he saw Jandahl sprawled on the deck. Jandahl's head was twisted at an impossible angle and his tongue protruded from between purple-blue lips. Ystremski knew at first glance that the other man was dead.

He had seen plenty of death in his ISMC career, but this discovery rattled him. There was no question Chive murdered Jandahl, and the callous way he left the body told the corporal that he didn't care if or when the body was discovered.

The corporal cracked the door, looked up and down the corridor, and jogged toward the exit to rejoin the platoon. Lieutenant Fortis was somewhere with Chief Schultz, and, until he talked to his platoon leader, Ystremski wasn't sure who to trust with his discovery.

* * *

There wasn't much to the crime scene where Chick Root's body was dumped. The dead man was flat on his back with his arms spread wide, his sightless eyes staring at the sky. His shoes and shirt were missing, and Fortis saw distinct bruises across his ribs. Old surgical scars crisscrossed his chest. A syringe in his arm looked like a lazy and cynical attempt to make his death look like an overdose.

Chief Schultz and his team processed what little evidence they could find. No one had witnessed the body dump, and the ground around the body was too hard to obtain useable shoe impressions. From what Fortis could tell, there was no reason why a China Mike user would choose that particular alley to shoot up.

After the body was zipped in a body bag and placed on one of the police carts, Schultz turned to Fortis.

"Have you seen enough, Lieutenant?"

Fortis cleared his throat. "Yes, sir, I certainly have." He felt shocked and guilty at the pitiable sight of Root's body and his unwitting role in his death.

The two men climbed back into the chief's cart and rode in silence back to Fenway. Finally, Fortis couldn't stand it any longer.

"Chief, I have a confession to make. We took Chick Root into custody two nights ago and turned him over to Security Director Chive and his men."

Chief Schultz stabbed the brakes, and the cart skidded to a stop. He turned sideways in his seat, and Fortis saw his face was dark and twisted.

"What did you say?"

"Two nights ago; we took Root into custody, along with Shelly Baird, and turned them over to Chive."

"Why did you do that?"

"Chive identified Root and Baird as members of the resistance, so we raided their house. Chive was supposed to turn them over to you for prosecution after he interviewed them."

Schultz glared at Fortis. "Chick Root and I arrived here on Eros-28 on the same transport, back when the GRC thought this dusty rock had minerals worth mining. That was thirty years ago. In all that time, I never once knew him to be involved with China Mike or a labor slowdown, much less the resistance."

"We were told he quit his job and joined the drug cartel in protest of the Security Directorate."

Schultz squeezed his eyes shut and shook his head. "Chick Root quit because he had a heart attack. He stayed on as a freeloader because his wife, Shelly Baird, has two years left on her contract. You say Chive has Baird, too?"

Fortis nodded, too numb to speak. He wanted to apologize, but he couldn't form the words. He doubted anything he could say would suffice, so he sat in silence.

"He probably has her at the site," said the chief.

"I'm sure you're right." Fortis didn't know what Chief Schultz knew about Jandahl and his activities, and he wasn't sure what he could reveal. "What do you want to do?"

Schultz hit the accelerator and the cart lurched forward. "I have to report this to Governor Czrk and find out how he wants to proceed. It's going to be a tough sell without any evidence."

"Do you want me to go with you?"

Chief Schultz stopped the cart next to the door into Fenway. "No, I think you've done enough, Lieutenant. This isn't your problem anymore."

* * * * *

Chapter Twenty-Four

Fortis caught up with Ystremski and the platoon in their dormitory. He motioned for the corporal to follow him, and the two men crossed the hall into the weight room.

"Remember Jandahl told us that the Kuiper Knights killed Chick Root, and they would make it look like an OD? He was right. I just came back from the crime scene with Schultz. Chick Root *is* dead and they *did try* to make it look like an OD. I guess Jandahl's got some credibility now."

"Uh, yeah. About Jandahl…"

Ystremski told him about the meeting between the intelligence operative and Chive and his subsequent discovery of Jandahl's body.

"You're sure Chive killed him?"

"There's only one access to that utility room, sir. He went in and a few minutes later Chive and his goons came out. Unless Jandahl figured out a way to break his own neck like that, Chive murdered him."

"Did you tell anyone?"

Ystremski shook his head. "You were out with the chief, and I didn't know who else I could trust."

"Shit." Fortis rubbed his face with both hands.

"What do you want to do, sir?"

"Let's find Chief Schultz. We'll tell him everything we know about Jandahl and show him the body. Maybe that will be enough to get the governor to move against Chive."

Ten minutes later the two Space Marines were standing in front of Schultz's desk.

"Chief, do you know a man named Jandahl?"

Shultz shook his head. "Not one of ours. Who is he?"

"He told me he worked for GRC corporate. The day before our first mission with Chive, he approached me in the corridor and warned me about Chive and the Kuiper Knights. Jandahl claimed they were up to something here on Eros-28, but he didn't say what it was."

"It's wise to be wary of mercenaries. Especially the ones you aren't paying."

Fortis continued. "I didn't think much of his information until he returned last night. He told me Chive and his men tortured Root to death at their site, and his body would probably be dumped in Boston and made to look like an OD."

"You knew that last night, and you didn't say anything this morning?"

"What was I going to say, Chief? Would you have believed me if I had told you?"

"You went to the crime scene with me, and you didn't say a word."

Fortis felt his face redden. "I'm not proud of it."

Schultz steepled his fingers under his chin. "Okay. Why are you telling me this now?"

Fortis gestured to Ystremski. "Tell him."

"I saw Jandahl sneaking around, and I got curious, so I followed him. He went into a utility room, and I waited for him to come out. Instead, Chive and two of his guys came out, and when I looked in the room I found Jandahl dead."

"You say Chive killed this GRC intelligence operative…uh…"

"Jandahl, sir. That's exactly what I'm saying. I watched Jandahl go into that utility room, then I saw Chive leave. Afterward, I found Jandahl with his neck broken."

Chief Schultz heaved himself to his feet.

"Let's go take a look at this body."

A few minutes later, Fortis, Ystremski, and Schultz entered the utility room. Jandahl's body was gone.

"It was here, I swear!" protested Ystremski.

"Nobody's calling you a liar, Corporal." Fortis turned to Schultz. "I bet Chive and his men moved the body."

"They probably took it out of here and loaded it into their crawler. Maybe they'll dump it in Boston, make it look like another OD," said the chief.

"What do we do now? Go to Governor Czrk?"

The chief stroked his fleshy chins. "And tell him what? Do you think Governor Czrk is going to believe your tale about a GRC corporate operative sent here to spy on Eros-28? Where's your evidence? Czrk is a company man, and he's going to need more than the word of a couple Space Marines whose troops were arrested for their involvement in the China Mike trade."

"Look, Chief. When we got here, the last thing I wanted to do was get mixed up in the internal politics of Eros-28. I don't know the players, I don't know the issues, and I don't know who to trust." He took a deep breath. "I fucked up. I let my men go on liberty against orders. Everything that happened after that is my responsibility. I only agreed to the raids because the governor left me no choice, but I didn't agree to torture and murder. If there's a price to be paid when we get back to *Atlas*, I'll pay it, but I wasn't about to leave Marx and Landis here."

Fortis felt Ystremski's hand on his arm, and he realized how close he was to the chief. He took a deep breath, forced himself to relax, and took a step back.

Chief Schultz's eyes flicked from the lieutenant to the corporal and back before he spoke.

"I believe you, Lieutenant. Sending a corporate spy to investigate what's going on here sounds exactly like something the GRC would do."

"It does?"

"Czrk is our third governor in two years," said the chief. "Appleton was the governor for years, but, when the subway collapsed, she was replaced by Warren. That's when the entire facility went on strike. And then they sent Czrk. He got the place under control. Now China Mike is everywhere, and productivity is slumping again."

"Maybe Jandahl was onto something."

"Could be." Schultz stroked his chins again. "I guess we'll never know."

They stood in silence for a long second until Corporal Ystremski shuffled his feet and said, "Sir, I need to get back to the platoon."

"Yes, by all means, you two should get on with your duties," replied Chief Schultz.

"What do we do now?" asked Fortis as they walked to the door.

"You should do what you have to do for your men," said Schultz as they exited the utility room. "I need to think about how to proceed with the information you've given me. Chive and his men might be dangerous, but they don't run this facility."

* * *

Three hours later, Chive waved to Fortis from the door of the Space Marine dorm. Fortis followed him into the passageway, and the security director handed him a now-familiar target folder.

"Ben West. Electronics technician. We believe he constructed the timers used in the explosive charges that destroyed Garage Number Seven, as well as being a member of the resistance."

Fortis examined the photographs. "What's the source of your intel?"

"That's not your concern. I develop the targets, and you execute the raids. That's how this works, remember?"

After a long moment, Fortis closed the folder. "What time do we execute?"

"As soon as you can get your men together, I think," said Chive. "My source indicated that West finished a night shift early this morning, so he should be home asleep."

"A daylight mission. Hmm."

"The streets around the target location are too narrow for the crawler, so you'll have to debark the crawler a couple blocks away and proceed on foot. Dolph will guide you to the location. He's waiting outside with the crawler."

"Okay. I'll have Corporal Ystremski get an assault team together, and we'll meet you outside."

"We have a new target," Fortis told the corporal. "Daytime mission. And we make the final approach on foot. Which team do you think we should send?'

"I'll take it with Assault Team One, LT. Who's the target?"

"Guy named West." Fortis handed him the folder. "Chive said this guy is the electronics technician who built the timers for the charges that blew up their garage."

"Huh. At least we're going after a bad guy and not just some alleged 'resistance' member."

"If you believe Chive, sure. He said this guy should be asleep after working a night shift, and we have to go in on foot because the streets are too narrow for the crawler."

"We'll need to move fast. If he sees us coming, he'll rabbit."

"Good point. Get the men ready, and let's move out. Chive and Dolph are waiting."

Ten minutes later, Assault Team One was loaded, and Dolph was steering the crawler into the duty streets of Boston. Fortis sat in the copilot's seat, and they discussed the mission details with the mercenary driver.

"I'll park two blocks away and lead you the rest of the way," Dolph said. "After I point out the house, I'll return to the crawler and let you guys to do your thing. After you cuff him and stuff him, we'll haul ass."

"Why don't you stay?"

Dolph laughed. "The locals know who the crawler belongs to. If I let it sit for too long they'll steal it or torch it."

"Do you know anything about the target location? Is there a China Mike lab, or a tunnel?"

"I don't know, LT. I didn't get any details from Chive except the location. I didn't have time to scout, either. At least it's not dark."

"There's that, but I still don't like it."

"DINLI."

Fortis gave Dolph a strange look, and the Kuiper Knight shrugged.

"Old habits die hard."

The lieutenant nodded. "DINLI."

Dolph stopped the crawler at the entrance to a narrow alley and shut off the engine. "We walk from here."

The Space Marines formed up single-file with Dolph in the lead, followed by Ystremski and his assault team. Fortis and Cowher brought up the rear. When they arrived at the target, the corporal waved Fortis forward, and he crouched with Dolph.

"It's the third house from the left," the mercenary told them. "Green metal door."

The corporal took a quick look around the corner and spotted the door. "Got it."

"Good luck." Dolph turned and jogged back to the crawler.

Assault Team One formed up, the breacher in front followed by Corporal Ystremski and the other team members behind him.

"Go, go, go!"

The assault team ran across the street and spread out along the front wall. The breacher tried the door and signaled that it was unlocked. The assault team poured inside.

Fortis listened to the chorus of "Clear" over the radio as the team moved through the dwelling.

Finally, Ystremski announced, "All clear." The corporal emerged and jogged over to Fortis and Cowher.

"The place is empty, but somebody was definitely in there, LT. The boys found a tunnel in a bedroom closet. They're checking it out now."

Three doors down, a figure burst outside, turned a corner, and sprinted down the alley.

"Shit!"

Ystremski took off in pursuit, followed closely by Fortis and Cowher.

"We've got a runner!" Ystremski shouted into his radio.

The man had a head start, but he was no match for the speed-enhanced corporal, and Ystremski tackled him less than a block away. He struggled to escape, but the trio of Space Marines subdued him without much trouble. They confirmed his identity as Ben West and dragged him back to the target location.

The assault team was waiting in the street when they returned, but they weren't alone. A group of civilians was gathered in the alley a short distance away, shouting and cursing at the Space Marines. The crowd was growing quickly.

"What's going on?" Fortis asked.

"We came outside to find you, and these people showed up. They started yelling at us, and then their friends showed up."

"You didn't respond or point weapons at them or anything like that?"

"No, sir. They're over there shouting, that's all."

A fist-sized rock flew toward the group and bounced along the dusty street.

"Let him go, you bastards!"

Ystremski gestured. "LT, we're ready to move out to the crawler. Let's get the hell out of here."

"Mercenaries go home!"

More rocks pelted the group.

"Lead the way, Corporal."

Four Space Marines grabbed West by his arms and legs and the Space Marines withdrew toward the crawler. Fortis brought up the rear, and the crowd gave chase. The shouts continued and more rocks landed around the them, but there were no injuries.

They arrived at the crawler and Fortis saw the engine cowling up with Dolph deep inside.

"What's going on?"

Dolph stuck his head out. "Fucker won't start."

The crowd rounded the last corner twenty meters away and stopped at the sight of the crawler. A couple stones landed near the vehicle and a large one bounced off the crawler with a *clang.*

They waved their fists and chanted, "Let him go! Let him go!"

Ystremski instructed the men to lean West on the front of the crawler. "If they want to throw stones, they'll hit their own guy," he told Fortis.

Fortis shook his head. "It's our duty to protect him while he's in our custody not use him as a shield. Get him into the back and out of sight." He leaned under open engine cowling. "How's it looking, Dolph?"

"I think I got it." The mercenary slid out and wiped his hands on his uniform. He jumped behind the wheel, the motor whined, and the crawler lurched. "Get in!"

Fortis scrambled into the front while the assault team and Cowher climbed into the back. Rocks rained down on the crawler as the Space Marines jumped in and the crowd surged forward. Several of them ran alongside and pounded on the crawler, but fell back as they picked up speed when the streets widened.

"That was close!" Fortis exclaimed.

"They get pretty pissed off when the crawler rolls up. The first time we went out, Chive butt-stroked one of them, and the guys beat down a few more. That got them so riled up that they went on strike. That's when the governor ordered us to stay out of Boston."

The crawler rolled to a stop at Fenway, and Fortis and the assault team debarked as the waiting Kuiper Knights climbed aboard.

"Wait here, I've got some business to attend to," the mercenary leader told Dolph. He turned to Fortis. "How did it go, Lieutenant?"

"Not bad. West ducked out through a tunnel, but we caught him down the street. A crowd of civilians showed up and things started to get ugly, so we got the hell out of there." He pointed to a large dent in the crawler caused by one of the rocks. "We're not doing anymore daylight missions. If that had hit one of my guys…"

"Huh." Chive examined the damage. "At least you got him."

The Space Marines filed inside and turned toward their dormitory while Chive headed for the governor's office.

Lance Corporal White met Fortis and Ystremski in the corridor. He held up a piece of folded paper.

"The communications center sent down a message from Battalion, sir."

"Bad news, corporal?"

From: Commander, Second Battalion, 1st of the 9th
To: Platoon Leader, 3rd Platoon, Foxtrot Company

Extraction time confirmed for 132:41:87:2 Galactic Standard Time. Fleet transport will contact the spaceport on the standard hailing frequency on final approach.

Ninth Division remains at Alert Condition Bravo.

Sobieski sends

Fortis passed the message to Ystremski and consulted his watch.

"That's fourteen hours from now. Form the platoon, and I'll brief them. Then I'll go tell the governor and get Marx and Landis released."

* * *

L ieutenant Fortis met with Governor Czrk, Chief Schultz, and Security Director Chive in the governor's office.

"Fourteen hours," said Governor Czrk.

"That's correct, sir.

"I guess that's it then. Chief, release Marx and Landis—"

"Just a moment, Governor," interrupted Chive. "There's been a development in our fight against the China Mike dealers that I haven't had a chance to share with you."

Governor Czrk spread his hands wide. "Well, go ahead Mr. Chive. What have you got?"

Chive shot a look at Chief Schultz. "My information is best kept in strict confidence, Governor. I'd rather the resistance not know."

"You're out of line, Chive!" Schultz shouted, getting close to Chive's face. "I've had enough of your innuendoes. I'm the chief law enforcement officer on Eros-28, and I'll be damned if some two-bit mercenary is going to insult me." He pointed a meaty finger at Chive. "If it wasn't for you and your men there wouldn't *be* a drug problem *or* a resistance. In fact—"

Chive's hand flew up and slapped the chief's fleshy cheek with a resounding *smack!* Before anyone could react, Chive shoved Schultz against the wall and pressed a forearm against his throat.

"You fat piece of shit, I should kill you right now," he snarled into the astonished policeman's face.

"Chive! Stand down!"

The governor's order snapped Fortis out of his shock, and he lunged forward. It took all of his strength to peel the mercenary off the chief, and when Chive finally relented, the two men stood toe-to-toe and glared at each other.

"Chive! Stand down! That's an order!"

Chief Schultz choked and clutched at his throat as he sank into a chair. Chive straightened his tunic with exaggerated motions and looked at the governor.

"When you've got some free time, we need to talk. Before you release the Space Marines."

The mercenary leader spun on his heel and strode out of the office before the governor could reply.

"Chief, what the hell was that?" demanded Governor Czrk.

Shultz cleared his throat and heaved himself to his feet. "Chive and his mercenaries are up to no good, Governor," he growled through his damaged throat. "Haven't you noticed that every time something happens around here he's involved?"

"Director Chive is a corporate employee, Chief. There's no reason why he would involve himself except as a matter of maintaining security."

Schultz shook his head. "You're a good governor, but you're a damned fool."

Czrk and Fortis only stared as the chubby cop stormed out of the office.

* * * * *

Chapter Twenty-Five

"And that's where we left it," Fortis told Ystremski as they ate supper. "The governor told me we had to wait to get Marx and Landis until he talked to Chive about this 'development,' whatever the hell that might be."

"Another hot tip he tortured out of somebody, probably." The corporal nodded toward the door. "Speaking of torture, here comes trouble."

Fortis turned and saw Security Director Chive and two of his men standing at the door. When Chive saw him look, he waved to the lieutenant.

"I'll be right back."

Chive and his men led Fortis into the corridor.

"Sorry to interrupt your meal, Lieutenant, but I've got a high priority target with a short fuse. Are your Marines up to the task?"

"What's the source of your intel, Baird or Root? Maybe West?"

Chive cocked an eyebrow at Fortis' question.

"What are you implying?"

"I'm not implying anything. But Root's dead, and nobody's seen Baird since we turned her over to you two days ago. I'm beginning to wonder what happened to Choon since we gave you custody last night."

"I heard Chick Root died of a China Mike overdose. Like the drug dealers say, 'Don't get high on your own supply.' I guess he didn't take his own advice."

"I saw his body. It didn't look much like an overdose. Too many bruises."

"I wouldn't know." Chive studied Fortis for a long second and then shrugged. "Is there something going on that I don't know about? If you want to pass on this one, we should go and tell Governor Czrk." He took two steps down the corridor and stopped. "Coming?"

Fortis felt his anger rise, and he struggled to control his temper. If he refused the mission, the governor might renege on their agreement regarding Marx and Landis.

An image of Chive snapping Jandahl's neck flashed in his mind.

"I'm not refusing the mission, Chive," Fortis said carefully. "I just want to know what we're doing and why. People seem to disappear after you get them out to your site."

Chive smiled and patted Fortis on the shoulder. "Tell you what, Lieutenant, tomorrow I'll take you out to the site, and you can see for yourself. Frankly, if you succeed tonight, I doubt we'll have any reason to hold Baird or Choon any longer."

"There is no tomorrow, Chive. We're due to leave in fourteen hours, remember?"

"Ah, I forgot. What a shame. I would have enjoyed having you out there." He held out his hand, and one of his men passed him a target folder.

"Tonight's target is rumored to be the leader of the cartel as well as a leader of the resistance." He handed Fortis the file. "Meet Dask Finkle."

Fortis flipped open the folder and saw a blurry picture of a dark-haired man taken from a distance. He had a squarish head and wavy black hair that clung to his scalp. His profile was sharp and a jaw that jutted out as if in challenge to anyone who spoke to him. Fortis couldn't tell if the man had a neck as his head seemed to start where his thick shoulders ended.

"Not much to work with. This man is the China Mike cartel leader?"

"We believe Dask Finkle is an alias," said Chive. "We don't know much about him, and this is the only photograph we have of him. He's something of a mystery. My information is that Finkle arrived here about two years ago and that the real labor unrest started shortly afterward. For such a small place, he's been very successful in evading law enforcement."

"Until tonight. You know where he is?"

"We know where he'll be tonight. He's scheduled to meet with one of my sources. That's where you come in."

"I'll alert the men."

Chive held up a hand. "There's an issue we should discuss. Speed is of the essence, so you'll be inserting by hovercopter."

Fifteen minutes later, the Space Marines were standing on the landing platform and examining the aircraft parked there.

"This is our hovercopter," Chive announced to the group. "Dolph is the pilot, and Rentz is the flight engineer."

The two men raised their hands in turn, then Dolph stepped forward.

"This is an older variant of the standard hovercopter configuration you're probably familiar with during your time in the ISMC. This craft has not been militarized; there are no armor plates or bulkhead between the flight deck and the crew compartment. There are no hard points to mount weapons, and the wing tanks have been removed. When we insert, I'll put her into a hover and you guys fast-rope out the ramp." He patted the squat craft. "She's just a big taxi."

Ystremski and several other Marines walked up the ramp into the craft while Fortis inspected the outside. There were several rough patches and large dents, and shiny metal glittered through a scrape along the belly.

"She's seen some hard service," he said to nobody in particular.

"Yeah, the terrain can be pretty unforgiving here," said Dolph from behind him. "I hadn't flown in a while and it took me a few tries to knock off the rust."

Fortis turned and looked Dolph in the eye. "Where did you learn to fly hovercopters?"

Dolph smiled. "The International Space Marine Corps."

Before Fortis could respond, Chive sidled up.

"Questions, Lieutenant?"

"I was just about to ask Dolph why we're using the hovercopter tonight instead of the crawler."

"That's easy enough to explain. The crawler is reliable but slow on these streets, and whenever it leaves the compound word spreads quickly. We've used it three times now, so it's time to mix up our tactics." He leaned in and lowered his voice to a whisper. "The target location tonight is in an area we call Old Boston, on the far edge of the city. The streets out there are too narrow for the crawler, so you will insert by fast-rope directly in front of the target. Your men can fast-rope, can't they?"

Fortis wanted to snap back at the insult, but he smiled instead. "We certainly can, as long as Dolph can hold a hover."

"No sweat, LT. I'll hold her steady as a rock." Dolph clapped Fortis on the shoulder. "We'll be so low you could jump, anyway."

"Lieutenant Fortis." Ystremski's voice from inside the hover-copter interrupted the conversation.

Fortis gestured at the ramp. "Excuse me, I need to see what Corporal Ystremski wants."

He climbed the ramp into the dark interior and found Ystremski near the cockpit.

"What's up?"

"This heap isn't much to look at on the outside, but everything in here looks pretty well maintained. I'm going to take this one with Assault Team One. Fast-roping isn't something we've trained on lately." He tipped his head at the open ramp and lowered his voice. "You think we should do this mission?"

"What choice do we have?" Fortis shook his head. "If we get this Finkle character, maybe that will be enough to satisfy the governor and we can get Marx and Landis back."

"If I get a chance, I'm going to shiv that Chive motherfucker."

"Get in line."

"DINLI, sir."

"Damn right."

* * *

Two hours later, Fortis, Ystremski, and Assault Team One loaded into the hovercopter. Dolph lifted off and piloted the craft in a wide circle around the outskirts of Boston. He and Fortis had agreed that they would approach the target location from the desert to avoid alerting the city.

The hovercraft relied on engine power and not aerodynamics to fly, and the result was a rough ride. The Space Marines frequently trained with hovercopters, but the herky-jerky motion of the aircraft was unsettling.

Fortis watched through the open cockpit door as Dolph and Rentz brought the hovercopter in, guided by a pulsing red locator on the navigation screen. When the pilot held up two fingers, Fortis keyed his radio.

"Two mikes. Stand by the ramp."

The assault team lined up in two columns at the ramp door. At their feet, two coils of thick rope waited. The ramp opened with a hydraulic whine and the interior of the hovercraft became a maelstrom of sand and noise. Rentz clambered through the crowded compartment and hooked up his safety harness above the open ramp.

The indicator light next to the ramp switched from red to green.

"Go, go, go!" ordered Fortis, and the head of each line kicked out the coils and practically dove down the ropes. Fortis and Cowher were the last out the door, and Fortis barely had time to get a grip on the rope before his boots hit the ground.

That wasn't even five meters.

Cowher grabbed his sleeve and pulled him clear just before Rentz unshackled the heavy ropes and they dropped free of the hovercraft. Fortis thumped the medic on the shoulder, and the two men dashed across the street to their assigned positions.

The aircraft engines howled as Dolph pulled up in a steep climb and headed back out over the desert to orbit and wait for Fortis and his men. A giant cloud of dust filled the air, but the target area was quiet.

Corporal Ystremski led the assault team to the door of the target house. After a brief pause, the breacher hammered the door down, and the Space Marines ran inside. After several long minutes, the assault team emerged, empty handed. They took up positions crouching along the wall of the house, and Ystremski ran to where Fortis and Cowher waited.

"Nothing there, LT," reported the corporal. "Nobody home, and the place looks like it's been empty for a long time. You sure this is the right place?"

"Yeah, this is it." Fortis thought for a second. "No point hanging around. Grab the ropes and let's haul ass to the extraction point."

Twenty minutes later, Dolph brought the hovercraft down to the desert floor, and Fortis and the Space Marines climbed up the ramp. They dumped the fast ropes on the deck and slumped into their seats. Fortis took a head count and gave Dolph a thumbs up. The ramp closed, and the hovercraft lifted off.

The ride back to the GRC base was quiet. Even though their intelligence had been faulty, the Space Marines felt responsible for the failure of the mission. Even the antics of Private Queen couldn't elicit more than half-hearted smiles.

Chive met the Space Marines when the aircraft touched down back at Fenway.

"What happened, Lieutenant?"

Fortis shook his head as the Space Marines filed off the hovercopter and headed inside.

"The target location was empty. The assault team reported that the place looked like nobody had been there for a long time."

"Huh. That's odd. My source is usually reliable."

"Not this time."

"There was always a chance we'd miss him. Don't go too far; I'll contact my source to see if there's more recent information."

* * *

C hive waited until the door closed behind the Space Marines before he whirled and faced his men.

"It's time to play hard ball with Spears," he spat. "Grab the kid and find his father."

Forty minutes later, two mercenaries shoved Spears into an abandoned house in Boston. Chive waited inside with a small, tear-streaked boy at his side. When Spears saw the child, he fell to his knees and hugged him.

"You bastard! You said he'd be safe."

"I said he'd be safe as long as you did exactly what you were told."

"I did what you wanted. I set up the meeting, just like you said."

"Finkle wasn't there."

"That's not my fault. Finkle does that all the time. He skips meetings, he shows up out of nowhere. He's paranoid."

"Where is he now?"

"I don't know. Nobody knows."

Chive grabbed the boy by the arm. The child screamed and clung to his father as the mercenary leader pulled him away.

"Please, stop!" cried Spears. "I might know where he is. There's a safe house…"

* * * * *

Chapter Twenty-Six

"My source says that Dask Finkle and others were at the target location, but they fled into the desert as soon as they heard the hovercopter. He gave me a location he says will be good for the next thirty minutes or so. Are your Marines ready?"

"We're ready to go," affirmed Fortis. "What's your intel?"

Chive unfolded a rough map of Boston. "The target is a house located on the edge of Old Boston. If you can get on the ground fast enough, you ought to be able to catch him before he can get out into the desert."

"Getting on the ground isn't the problem. The problem is clearing the house. It takes time, and even a two- or three-minute delay gives Finkle a big head start."

"LT, how about if we use both assault teams?" Ystremski traced a wide arc over the desert on the map and tapped a spot outside the city limits. "Drop me and my guys four klicks out, far enough to not alert the target. Then Dolph orbits the city with Assault Team Two for a few minutes while we approach on foot to set up a blocking position. Then Team Two drops in on the front door like before, and if Finkle scoots for the desert, we grab him."

Fortis, Chive, and Dolph nodded.

"That's a good idea, Corporal. What about blue-on-blue? It's pretty dark out there."

Ystremski shrugged. "Tell Team Two not to go out into the desert until they get the all clear unless they're in hot pursuit, and I don't mean chasing noises in the dark, either. If they don't have eyes on the target, don't come out into the sand."

"Can you execute a plan like this on short notice?" asked Chive.

"The assault teams are standing by, Mr. Chive. What Corporal Ystremski is proposing is a pretty straightforward plan. Honestly, I should have thought of it myself." He turned to the pilot. "Dolph, we'll meet you at the hovercopter in eight minutes. Wheels up in ten?"

Dolph nodded and gave two thumbs up. "Can do."

Eleven minutes later, the hovercopter was roaring into the night sky and headed out over the desert. The aircraft bucked and bounced more than it had before, and Dolph's voice crackled in Fortis' headset.

"Hey, LT, the tower just reported a sifter starting to blow up on Dirt Mountain. They said it shouldn't be a problem, but they've been wrong before."

"Is the mission still a go?"

"Yes, sir. As the hovercopter commander, I'm okay with flying through a light sifter. You're the ground commander; are you okay with operating in a little dust storm?"

Fortis looked at Ystremski, sitting on the jump seat next to his. The corporal nodded and gave a thumbs up.

"We're good to go, Dolph. If it looks like the sifter is going to shut us down, give us a heads up and we can exfil."

"Roger."

Dolph brought the hovercraft down with a gentle *thump*, and Corporal Ystremski and Assault Team One raced down the ramp. A gust of wind buffeted the hovercopter as it climbed back out over the desert and it lurched sideways.

"Whoa!" exclaimed Dolph over an open mic.

"Are we good?" asked Fortis.

"Yeah. Yeah, we're okay." The pilot's voice sounded like he was speaking through gritted teeth. "I might have to drop you guys in sooner than planned, though. Conditions are worse out here over the desert; let's see how they are over the city."

The weather seemed to settle down as the aircraft orbited over Boston, but the wait was interminable. Fortis stared at the darkened indicator lamps by the ramp and willed them to light up. They finally glowed red and when he looked toward the cockpit, he saw Rentz hold up two fingers.

"Two minutes!" he shouted over the whine of the engines.

Assault Team Two stood up and braced themselves on the overhead handrails as the ramp went down and a blizzard of sand roared into the compartment. Fortis felt Dolph bring the aircraft to a hover and the lights turned green.

"Go, go, go!"

The Space Marines poured down the ramp and dropped to the ground below. Fortis and Dolph had agreed to forego the fast ropes, and the pilot held the hovercopter rock steady two meters above the ground. As soon as the last Marine was off the ramp, the engines howled, and the aircraft moved off.

The assault team took their positions at the target building. On command, the breacher hammered the door open, and they charged inside. Once again, Fortis and the medic Durant could only listen as the team swept through the house. When they finished the sweep, they mustered out front with Fortis.

232 | P.A. PIATT

"There's no one inside, but somebody was just here. The stove is still hot," reported Heisen. "There's a hole in the back wall. Maybe they went out that way."

Fortis tried to reach Ystremski, but the blowing sand interfered with the high frequency line-of-sight radio.

"Form a skirmish line and let's move to the edge of the city," he told Heisen. "Maybe we'll get comms there. Make damn sure nobody heads out into the desert."

The assault team spread out and moved through the few remaining houses until they reached the edge of the city. The wind stiffened as they left the cover of the buildings, and when Fortis hailed Ystremski again, he got static in response.

A twinge of panic hit him in the gut. Their plan was simple and should have been easy to execute, even in the dark with limited communications. Now, Assault Team One was somewhere in the darkness, and he had lost comms with them. The wind and blowing sand played tricks with his hearing, and he heard invisible hovercraft engines in the sky all around him. The unexpected sifter added a level of difficulty to every aspect of the operation, and Fortis mentally kicked himself for not considering the weather.

Suddenly, his earpiece came to life.

"Fortis, this is Dolph, do you copy?"

"This is Fortis, go ahead."

"Ystremski has been calling. They are fifty meters straight ahead of your position with the package. Advance and link up with them, and I'll drop in for pickup."

"Roger, wilco."

Fortis leaned close to Heisen. "Get another head count and then we're moving out," he shouted at the assault team leader. "We're moving to meet Team One and our ride fifty meters out."

Fortis and the Space Marines advanced slowly as the sifter whirled and blasted them with sand from every direction. Fortis estimated each of his steps was about half a meter, and a figure loomed at him out of the darkness when he got to ninety-seven.

It was Ystremski.

"My whole team is here, and we've got a guest," the corporal reported. "Dask Finkle."

"Outstanding." The lieutenant thumped him on the shoulder and then keyed his mike.

"Dolph, this is Fortis, we are standing by for extraction with one pax."

The hovercopter settled to the surface, and the Space Marines raced up the ramp. After the assault team leaders reported all their troops were aboard, Fortis climbed the ramp and belted into a seat next to their restrained and hooded prisoner.

"Dolph, this is Fortis, all Marines are onboard. Let's get the hell out of here."

The aircraft made climbed uncertainly from the desert floor and banked toward Fenway. The craft lurched suddenly to the left and shook violently. The lurch became a roll as thousands of rocks pummeled the body of the craft.

"Hang on!" shouted Dolph from the cockpit. "Shit—"

The hovercraft slammed the ground, rolled once, and came to rest on its left side. The howl of the engines was replaced by shrieking wind, and what sounded like shrapnel rattled the stricken craft.

By the light of the battery-powered emergency lighting, the Space Marines tumbled from their seats and hauled their prisoner to his feet.

"We're taking fire!" Heisen shouted.

"That's not incoming, that's rocks," replied Ystremski. He turned to Fortis. "What's our move, sir?"

"Check the cockpit for Dolph and Rentz."

The corporal jerked his head toward the cockpit, and Heisen clambered forward. The hooded prisoner twisted and shook his head. Fortis yanked the hood off.

"That's not a sifter blowing out there, it's an Eolian Blast! We need to get under cover!" Finkle shouted.

"A what?"

A boulder slammed into the hovercraft and everyone ducked.

"An Eolian Blast! A fucking tornado made out of rocks. If we stay here, we're dead."

Just then, Heisen returned.

"Windshield is smashed, sir. Rentz is dead and there's no sign of Dolph."

"Take off these restraints, and I'll lead you to safety," urged Finkle. More large rocks pelted the craft. "We need to go now, before it gets worse."

"Hey! There's fuel leaking in here. This fucker's gonna blow!" shouted one of the Space Marines.

Fortis looked at Ystremski.

"Fuck it."

The corporal stepped forward and cut the restraints off Finkle's wrists. The resistance leader motioned behind him.

"Grab the back of my belt and form a chain. Make damn sure you've got a good grip, because if you get lost out there right now, it's over. How do we get off this thing?"

Fortis pointed forward. "The ramp's no good. Go out the windshield."

Ystremski grabbed his arm. "LT, grab the prisoner and everyone will line up behind you. I'll bring up the rear and make sure everyone gets out."

"Are you sure? You should—"

"No time to argue! We have to go *now!*" Finkle shouted.

Fortis latched onto Finkle and someone grabbed his belt.

"Go, go, go!" shouted Ystremski, and Finkle led the chain of Space Marines through the gore-covered cockpit of the wrecked hovercopter and into the storm.

The wind tore at Fortis and a sudden spray of gravel almost made him lose his grip. He tried to watch where they were going, but driving sand stung his eyes and clogged his nostrils. The line of Space Marines accordioned as they clung together and stumbled through the maelstrom.

After what seemed like hours, Finkle stopped at a small building and kicked the door open. He staggered inside with Fortis, the Space Marines following close behind. Fortis was able to breathe again, and he sank to his knees and coughed up the dirt that filled his mouth and throat. Through slitted eyes he saw Finkle stride across the room and point to low arch set in the wall.

"We can't stop here," he told Fortis. "Follow me, we'll be safe in the subway."

Finkle disappeared through the arch, and Fortis stumbled after him, trailed by the rest of the Space Marines. A set of stone steps wound down another five meters and ended in a dark, cavernous space. Fortis lost track of the resistance leader in the confusion of their flight from the storm until lanterns threw dim light around the room. Finkle moved from sconce to sconce and sparked them to life, and Fortis was finally able to get a look at his surroundings.

All around him, Space Marines hacked and coughed as they struggled to clear their airways from the choking dust driven by the storm winds. Water splashed across his face and when Fortis looked up Finkle pushed a plastic bowl into his hands.

"The tap's over there." Finkle pointed to a bent pipe sticking out from the wall. "Get your men cleaned up before the dust dries and turns to concrete."

"Over here," Fortis croaked, and grabbed the nearest men. "Water."

The troops gathered around the tap and took turns scrubbing the dust from their nostrils, mouths, and ears. Fortis tried to take a head-count, but the dim lanterns made it difficult.

Corporal Ystremski loomed out of the shadows. "All present or accounted for," he rasped. "Four walking wounded, one head injury that requires a litter."

Fortis stared at Ystremski for a long second before he comprehended what he had been told. He'd been so focused on surviving the Eolian Blast that he hadn't considered injuries.

"Head injury? Who?"

"Redman. A big rock hit him behind the left ear and knocked him out cold. Doc Cowher took a look, but he won't know much until Redman wakes up."

"The others?"

"Bumps and bruises, mostly. Lemm might have a broken arm. Just another day in the Corps, sir."

"DINLI."

Ystremski laughed and then doubled over into a coughing spell. When it was over, he hawked and spat.

"DINLI."

* * * * *

Chapter Twenty-Seven

At Fenway, Dolph squeezed his eyes shut against the blast of air that blew the sifter dust from his uniform and waited while the vacuum sucked it out of the airlock. Mikel Chive and two Kuiper Knights watched from behind the glass. When the decontamination procedure was completed, Chive met Dolph at the door.

"Well? What happened? Where is Finkle?" the mercenary leader demanded.

Dolph ran his tongue across his gritty teeth and spat before he answered.

"That little sifter turned into an Eolian Blast that blew my hovercopter out of the sky," the pilot replied. "We went down and rolled upside-down, and I was thrown out the windshield. When I came to, I was under a pile of rubble and the Space Marines and the prisoner were gone." He hawked and spat again.

"Gone? Where did they go? Do they still have Finkle?"

"How the fuck should I know, Chive? I was unconscious."

"Damn it!" Chive whirled on his heel and strode away, followed by the two mercenaries.

Dolph rolled his head and rubbed the back of his neck. "It was a long walk back here, but I'm okay, thanks for asking," he said to the empty room. "Oh, and Rentz is dead." He shook his head and spat again. "Prick."

* * *

239

After the Space Marines had flushed away the worst of the dust, Fortis stuck his head under the tap and scraped at the dried dirt in his ears. The water was warm and tasted like shit, but the lieutenant didn't care. He flushed his nostrils and mouth, and, when he was done, Fortis felt vaguely human again.

The lieutenant moved around the room, exchanging nods or brief comments with his men gathered along the walls. He found Redman sitting up and conscious, a dirty bandage wrapped around his head. Doc Cowher was hovering close by.

"I stopped the bleeding and bound the wound," the corpsman reported. "His pupils are responsive, and he's not babbling any more than usual."

"Fuck you, Doc," growled Redman. He groaned and clutched his head. "I'm good to go, LT. Just a little headache."

Fortis chuckled and patted the injured Space Marine on the shoulder. "Good to go."

He continued around the room and found Dask Finkle seated next to a dark door that appeared to lead deeper underground. Fortis leaned against the wall and slid down until he was seated next to the resistance leader. The two men exchanged glances.

"Thank you for leading us out of the storm," Fortis said.

Finkle shrugged. "You might be mercenaries, but you're still human."

"We're not mercenaries. We're Space Marines."

"You work for Chive and the Kuiper Knights; that makes you a mercenary."

"You've got it all wrong. I don't work for Chive."

Finkle shrugged again. "It's your story. Tell it any way you want to."

"I'm serious!" Fortis' voice drew looks from nearby Space Marines and he lowered his voice. "I'm serious. We're not mercenaries, and we don't work for Chive. The governor—" He stopped himself.

Why am I explaining things to this guy?

"Look, Lieutenant. You kidnap citizens and turn them over to Chive to be tortured and murdered. I'm surprised the UNT decided to back the Kuiper Knights. I figured they would support the GRC."

"The UNT? The UNT isn't involved in this. At least, not that I know of. And the Kuiper Knights work for the GRC."

Finkle snorted. "Then why are Space Marines here?"

"We got sent here by accident. We were supposed to go on liberty on Eros-69 with the rest of Ninth Division, but our orders got screwed up and we ended up here."

"And while you're here, you decided to hook up with the Kuiper Knights to kidnap some locals. Just for fun."

"No! We're not doing this because we want to. We're doing it because we have to."

"DINLI. That's what you guys say, right?"

"Exactly. DINLI. Two of my Marines were arrested on charges of dealing China Mike, and the colonial circuit judge won't be here to hear their case until long after we're gone. The governor and I agreed that we would help his Security Directorate clear out the drug cartel so he would release my men when our transport showed up. That's what we're doing."

Finkle chuckled, which turned into a belly laugh that ended in a phlegmy cough. He hawked and spat a gooey brown globule that rolled up against the wall.

"If you want to clear out the China Mike cartel, Lieutenant, you're going after the wrong people. Chive and his men are who you should be after. We're trying to stop him."

The information stunned the Space Marine officer. "The GRC is manufacturing the drug?"

Finkle shook his head. "No, not the GRC, the Kuiper Knights. They're manufacturing China Mike and shipping it out all over the place."

"I don't understand. Why would the GRC permit them to do that?"

"They don't know about it. For some stupid reason, the GRC contracted with the mercenaries to run facility security here. Eros-28 didn't even have a Security Directorate until Chive showed up. Before that, it was just Chief Schultz."

"What's their play? Why come here to manufacture the drug?"

"I think it's because they can ship the stuff all over the sector by hiding it in the heavy equipment that leaves this facility. Nobody checks it, and it brings a good price in the mining colonies. Most of the other colonies are privately owned, so they don't care what their workers are on as long as they produce."

"What about Eros-28? Chief Schultz said the workers self-regulate here."

"We do. It helps to have a governor that understands the labor force. When he negotiated the four-hour overtime rule, it eliminated the reason most people used the drug. There are still some people who like to ride the edge, but not like it used to be. Right before you arrived, we collapsed a garage full of equipment that was full of China Mike waiting to be sent out around the sector. They captured Raisa Shears and tortured her to death."

The two men lapsed into silence in the flickering light.

"So, what's next?" Finkle asked.

Fortis looked at his watch and shrugged. "We've got a transport to catch in seven hours. As soon as this storm passes, point us in the right direction and you'll never see us again."

The resistance leader blinked in surprise. "You're letting me go?"

"You're crazy if you think I'm going to hand you over to Chive now."

"What about your men? What about your deal with Governor Czrk?"

"We took you into custody, the storm knocked down the hover-copter, and you disappeared in the chaos. We got lucky and found a place to ride it out."

The two men locked eyes, and Finkle stuck out his hand. The two men shook hands. "Thank you, Lieutenant."

"Thank you for getting us out of that storm, and good luck in your fight."

Finkle nodded to a doorway on the other side of the room. "Behind that door is a set of steps that will take you to the surface. When you get outside, look to the right and you'll see one of the Fenway periscopes." He climbed to his feet. "It sounds like the wind has died down, so you should be safe." He gestured to another door a few feet away and chuckled. "I wish you had said something sooner. I've been working up the courage to run into the subway since we got in here."

Fortis stood and walked to the door. "Here, let me help you." He pulled it open and gestured.

Dask Finkle clapped his hand on Fortis' shoulder and then, without a word, disappeared into the dark passage.

Corporal Ystremski had watched from a discreet distance and approached Fortis after the resistance leader had left.

"What's going on, sir? Why'd you let him go?"

"We've been on the wrong side, Corporal. Get the men ready to go; we've got a transport to catch."

* * *

"Chive and the Kuiper Knights are manufacturing China Mike at their facility out in the desert," Fortis told Ystremski as they led the Space Marines on a fast-march through the dust-choked streets of Boston. "They're shipping it all over the sector hidden in refurbished mining equipment."

"Sounds like a job for the governor and Chief Schultz," the corporal replied.

"Yeah, it does, but there must be something more to the story. I just can't put my finger on it."

"That's what I told her," Ystremski said deadpan.

Fortis slowed and stared at the other man for a long second before his face split into a dusty grin.

"I'm trying to be serious here, Corporal, and you're cracking jokes."

"It's my duty to maintain a cheerful attitude in the face of adversity, sir. According to the ISMC Platoon Leader Manual, the Bible for young officers—"

"Yeah, I've read it once or twice, dickhead."

Fortis threw a look over his shoulder at the assault team medics supporting Redman, who refused to ride in a litter.

"Good to go?" he called to them.

Private Durant waved. "He's okay, LT."

Fortis took a quick count of the rest of the platoon and continued toward Fenway.

"As I was saying, before you interrupted me with your wet dream fantasy, there's something more to the story here."

"Like what? It sounds pretty straightforward to me."

"Like why would the GRC send a guy like Jandahl here to spy on their own facility?"

"Beats me, sir. Maybe they don't trust the governor."

"Huh."

The Space Marines marched on in silence for several blocks.

"Eros-28 isn't a stable colony," Fortis panted. "Schultz said as much. Three governors in two years is a lot of turmoil. From what I can tell, Czrk has the place under control. Even Finkle seems to like him. If it wasn't for Chive and his guys, the resistance wouldn't exist. It's almost like they *want* the resistance to act out."

"Makes sense. Stir up trouble, drop the hammer—"

"And seize control."

They rounded a corner and spotted the walls of Fenway two blocks ahead.

"Home sweet home, sir."

Fortis looked at his watch. "Only for another six hours."

* * * * *

Chapter Twenty-Eight

Governor Czrk and Director Chive met Fortis and his men after they completed decontamination.

"Where's Finkle?" Chive demanded as soon as the door opened.

"We lost him," Fortis retorted. "The hovercopter flipped over and crashed in the middle of a rock storm—"

"An Eolian Blast," interjected Czrk.

"Yeah, an Eolian Blast. We went down, hard. Your guy Rentz is dead, and Dolph is missing. I've got a man with a head injury and a couple others who require medical attention."

"What happened to Finkle?"

Fortis threw up his hands. "Mr. Chive, didn't you hear what I said?" He felt the blood rising in his face. "The hovercopter crashed upside-down. One of your men is dead, and the other one is missing. I don't know where Finkle is; he might be dead, too."

"Dolph is here. He said Finkle was with you."

"Dolph is here?"

"He returned shortly after the storm subsided. He was thrown clear of the wreck. When he came to, you and your men were gone, along with the prisoner. Where were you?"

The lieutenant shook his head. "The storm was tearing the hovercopter apart, so we hauled ass and found a building to hide out in. Rentz is still in the wreckage, without his head."

"So, you don't know what happened to Finkle?" Chive stabbed an accusatory finger at Fortis and scowled. "Are you sure?"

Fortis took a step toward the mercenary leader, and Ystremski threw an arm across his chest to hold him back.

"Director Chive, if you want to accuse me of something, then accuse me. What the fuck do you think was happening out there? Have you ever been in an Eolian Blast?"

Governor Czrk stepped between the two men. "Gentlemen, please. There's no need for this. Lieutenant, we're all happy that you survived the crash and the storm. If your men need medical attention my staff will do our best to patch them up. As for the prisoner—" he looked at Chive, "—there will be other opportunities to apprehend him."

"You'll have to put in your own work," Fortis said as he stared at Chive. "Our transport is due soon, and I won't put any more of my men at risk this close to our extraction."

"That's understandable," agreed Czrk. "I'll arrange with Chief Schultz to have Marx and Landis transferred to your custody."

"Thank you, Governor. There's another matter I'd like to speak with you about in private, if you have a moment."

"Of course. Follow me to my office."

Fortis turned to Ystremski. "Take the men down to the dormitory and get them ready for extraction."

"Yes, sir."

Fortis and Chive followed Czrk to the governor's office. Fortis resisted the urge to glance at the mercenary as they walked, but he didn't want to acknowledge Chive's presence. When they arrived, he stopped and blocked the mercenary from entering.

"In private."

Chive looked past him to Governor Czrk, but the governor just waved.

"It's okay, Director Chive. I'll contact you later. Come on in, Lieutenant."

Fortis entered the office and closed the door behind him before he accepted the offered seat. The governor settled into his own chair and folded his hands on his desk.

"What's on your mind, Mr. Fortis?"

"Mikel Chive and the Kuiper Knights are manufacturing China Mike at their compound outside Boston. They hide the drug in the refurbished equipment the GRC sends to mining colonies throughout the sector. They do some local trafficking to lend credence to the idea that there is an active labor resistance movement and to foment instability here on Eros-28."

Governor Czrk stared at Fortis for a long moment, and the Space Marine started wondering if he'd even heard what Fortis had said.

Finally, he said, "How do you know all this? Did Director Chive admit it to you?"

"No, sir, not Chive. Have you ever heard of a man named Jandahl?"

"No, the name's not familiar. Should it be?"

"Jandahl is—or was—a GRC intelligence operative sent by corporate to investigate what was going on here. You've had some recent problems with production?"

Czrk nodded. "Yes. We had a work slowdown, and then the resistance blew up a garage full of equipment that was ready for transportation."

"Jandahl approached me a couple days ago. He told me that he suspected Chive and the Kuiper Knights were up to something, but he wasn't sure what it was. He also told me that they had murdered Chick Root at their compound and that they would likely dispose of his body to make it look like an overdose.

"The next day some colonists found Root's body in Boston. I went to the scene with Chief Schultz, Governor. Someone did try to make it look like an overdose, but it wasn't. That same day, Corporal Ystremski witnessed Jandahl and Chive meet in a utility room off the main passage. Immediately after that meeting, he found Jandahl dead."

"Chive killed Jandahl?"

"It looks that way. The corporal didn't see Chive do it, but he entered the utility room immediately after Chive left and found Jandahl's body."

"I've received no reports about a body discovered here in Fenway."

Fortis grimaced and shook his head. "Unfortunately, Corporal Ystremski didn't report it right away. He waited until Chief Schultz and I returned from the Chick Root crime scene, and by the time we got to the utility room Jandahl's body was gone."

"A corporate intelligence operative I've never heard of tells you that Chive and his men are 'up to something,' but he doesn't know what. Then your corporal reports that Chive murdered him, but when he took you to the body it's disappeared. Is that a fair summary of your story?" The skepticism in the governor's voice was thick.

"Sir, Jandahl talked to me and Corporal Ystremski. Ystremski has no reason to lie about finding Jandahl's body. There's more, too. Dask Finkle, the resistance leader, is the one who told me that they collapsed the garage because the Kuiper Knights stuffed the equipment full of China Mike."

"You talked to Finkle?"

"After the hovercopter crashed, Finkle led me and my men to safety in the subway. We talked while we were down there. That's when he told me about the resistance and the reason they bombed the garage."

"Where is Finkle now? How did he escape?"

"He didn't. He saved my men, so I let him go."

"You lied to Chive."

"Damn right I did, and I'd do it again. I'm not turning anyone else over to Chive and his men. All the resistance members that we've turned over are dead or missing."

Czrk shrugged but said nothing.

"He's torturing and murdering them."

"You're sure about that? Why would he do it?"

"To ratchet up the pressure on the resistance and force them to act out. To ratchet up the pressure on *you* and destabilize Eros-28."

Governor Czrk leaned back and steepled his fingers on his chin. "To what purpose, Mr. Fortis? What reason would Chive have to want to destabilize this colony? If he needs this place as a safe haven to manufacture his drugs, it doesn't make sense to draw attention to it."

Fortis took a deep breath before he answered. "He wants control of the colony, Governor. I can't prove it, but I believe he's attempting to take over Eros-28, either for himself or for the Kuiper Knights. I think Jandahl discovered what Chive is up to, so Chive murdered him."

"You've spoken to Chief Schultz about this." It wasn't a question, but Fortis nodded.

"Some. Not since I put this all together."

"The chief made some pointed remarks in that meeting with me and Director Chive."

Fortis scoffed. "I'll say." He leaned forward in his chair. "Chief Schultz has a complex job, sir. He's a corporate officer with deep local roots, but I think he sees what's happening. You need to as well."

"Chive and his men are here at the direction of the GRC, Lieutenant Fortis. My name appears in a box above his on the organizational chart, but he operates independently."

"If you don't stop him, your name won't be on the organizational chart for much longer. Governor, please, listen to me. You're popular with the workers here. Dask Finkle told me as much, but the resistance is not going to stand by and let your director of security turn their colony into a narco-state.

"If Chive and the Kuiper Knights seize control of Eros-28, they'll be reinforced in large numbers, and it will be impossible to get them out. I don't think the UNT will get involved in a hostile business takeover. The GRC will be forced to negotiate with the Knights to continue Fenway operations or lose trillions of credits. Resource extraction in this sector will stop without somewhere to repair and refurbish the equipment."

By the time he finished, the enormity of his accusations against Chive and the scope of the plot against Governor Czrk and Eros-28 astounded Fortis. When he put the pieces together, it sounded more like the plot of a blockbuster film than real life.

* * *

C hive signaled to his men to follow him as he made for the colonial police complex. They burst through the doors and rushed into the space with their weapons at the ready.

"It's time we take control of the leverage."

"What the hell's going on here?" demanded Officer Upham. "You can't do that—"

One of the black-clad mercenaries butt-stroked the burly policeman and he crashed to the deck in a heap.

Chief Schultz heard the commotion and emerged from his office.

"Chive, what the hell are you doing here?"

"We've come for Marx and Landis," Chive replied. "I'm taking them with me."

"You can't do that—"

"Do you all read from the same script?" Chive drew his dueling sword and thrust it deep into Schultz's chest. The chief made a surprised face, looked down at the red stain blooming across his chest, and collapsed. Three spurts of blood marked the final beats of his heart, then he was dead. Chive pointed to the sign that read HOLDING CELLS.

"Go get them."

Even with four men per cell, the Kuiper Knights had difficulty subduing the two strength-enhanced Space Marines.

Marx knocked his first attacker out cold with a straight right, but the other three crowded too close to generate more full-power punches. Eventually, he went down under a flurry of kicks, punches, and pulse rifle jabs.

In the next cell, Landis managed to tear the leg off his chair and used it to fend off his attackers. Instead of rushing him, one of the mercenaries deployed pepper spray and then tackled him before he could land more than a couple strikes with his improvised weapon. Landis was beaten unconscious before he was dragged from his cell and dumped on the office floor.

Chive led his men to the garage, where they met Dolph at the crawler. The Space Marines were dumped into the back, the mercenaries mounted up, and the vehicle was driven out of the facility.

* * *

Back in the governor's office, Czrk and Fortis were still deep in conversation, oblivious to the action taking place down the hall. Governor Czrk remained expressionless as Fortis talked. Finally, he sat up and placed his hands flat on his desk. "Lieutenant, I'm—"

The door slammed open, and Officer Upham staggered in with his hands clutched to his head. Blood flowed between his fingers, and he would have fallen to the floor if Fortis hadn't caught him.

"What happened?" Czrk and Fortis demanded simultaneously.

"Chief Schultz…dead…Chive…"

"*Chive?* Chive what?"

"Stabbed…we fought…prisoners…" Upham's head rolled on his shoulders as he collapsed in Fortis' arms, unconscious.

Czrk helped Fortis lower the injured man to the carpet and Fortis inspected his wounds. He had two long gashes under his hairline that were bleeding profusely.

"Head wounds bleed a lot," he told the governor as he wrapped Upham's head in a towel Czrk handed to him. "Call your medics. I'll go check on the chief and Marx and Landis."

Fortis found Chief Schultz on the floor in front of his desk with a bloody wound in his chest. He raced to the holding cells.

The overturned and broken furniture and a bloody handprint smeared along one wall was testament to the ferocity of the battle. The faint smell of pepper spray still hung in the air. Marx and Landis were gone.

He found the governor in the passageway as medical technicians wheeled Officer Upham toward the infirmary.

"Chief Schultz is dead; Marx and Landis are gone."

"Chive probably took them to his compound," replied the governor. "What can we do?"

Fortis consulted his watch. "I've got three hours and a platoon of Space Marines. I'm going to get Marx and Landis back. And then I'm going to kill that sonofabitch."

* * * * *

Chapter Twenty-Nine

"What the hell is going on?" Dolph asked Chive as he piloted the crawler.

Chive wiped his bloody hands with a rag and threw it to the floor. "We went to take custody of the Space Marines and Fat Schultz got in the way."

"You killed Chief Schultz?"

"Maybe. Probably. The last time I saw him he was bleeding from a hole in his chest."

"Fuck, Chive, are you out of your mind? You can't just kill the chief of police."

"Who's going to stop me? *We* are the law here, not some obese freeloader and his band of half-witted plow drivers."

"What about the Space Marines? Why did you have to grab them? You think Lieutenant Fortis is going to just forget about his men?"

"Leverage, Dolph. Forget about Fortis and the Space Marines. They won't do a damn thing because they don't have time. Their transport's due to arrive, and they'll go back where they came from and make up a story to cover their asses."

"You're making a mistake, Chive. Don't underestimate them."

"Underestimate *them*? You're underestimating me."

Dolph looked down at the bloody rag. "Obviously."

"Remember, you're the one who said the lieutenant was long on enthusiasm and short on smarts. Now you're warning me not to underestimate him?"

They rode in silence as the crawler bumped over the rocky track that led to the Kuiper Knight compound.

"I think you're moving too fast, Chive. Killing the chief is a pretty drastic step. I thought the plan was to run Czrk out of the colony and get you appointed governor."

"It still is. Schultz had to go, anyway. I just improvised and eliminated one of our problems a little early." Chive stared at Dolph in the lights of the console. "It sounds like you're going soft on me. Whose side are you on, anyway?"

Dolph shook his head. "You're in command; I just do what I'm told. All I'm saying is that picking a fight with the ISMC isn't a good move."

* * *

Fortis burst into the dormitory and found Ystremski and the Space Marines with their bags packed and the space gleaming.

"Get both assault teams ready to go," Fortis ordered. "Everybody else grab our gear and head to the landing pad airlock."

The platoon gathered around the two men.

"What's going on, LT?"

"I met with the governor. I laid out everything we knew about Chive, the Kuiper Knights, the China Mike, and the resistance. I think I had him convinced when one of the cops came in, all bloodied up. Chive and some of his mercenaries beat this guy down, murdered Schultz, and kidnapped Marx and Landis."

"*What?* Where did they go?"

"Beats me, but I'd bet they went to their compound."

"Saddle up, lads," Ystremski ordered the Space Marines. "I want two full assault teams; substitutes for the guys who got hurt in the crash. Move!" He turned back to Fortis. "Where's the compound?"

Fortis waved the keys to Chief Schultz's police cart. "I have no idea, but I think I know who does."

The lieutenant steered the cart through Boston in search of the wrecked hovercraft. He kept the Fenway periscope behind his right shoulder as he wound his way through narrow alleys and side streets, eventually ending up at the wrecked hovercopter. The neighborhood was dark and quiet. It was hard to believe a deadly storm had raged there just hours earlier.

He flipped a switch marked Siren and turned on the flashing lights. After a few seconds he turned them off.

"Dask Finkle!" he shouted. "I need to talk to Dask Finkle."

His voice echoed through the deserted streets.

"Dask Finkle!"

"Fuck off!" someone shouted in the distance, and several other voices laughed.

Fortis hit the siren again and let it wail for a full minute before he turned it off.

"I need to talk to Dask Finkle!"

A shadowy figure detached from a building down the street. As it approached, Fortis recognized the resistance leader.

"Take it easy, Lieutenant. I'm right here. Why have you come here?"

"Chive murdered Chief Schultz and kidnapped my men from the holding cells in Fenway. I think he's taken them to the Kuiper

Knights' compound. I'm going to get them back, and I need your help."

"My help? What do you want from me? I'm not a fighter, LT. I don't have a gun."

"You know where their compound is, and I'm pretty sure you *do* have something I need."

"What's that?"

"Explosives."

Finkle was quiet for a long second.

"Let me get dressed."

* * *

The two men heaved the crate of explosives out of the subway and loaded it onto the police cart. Despite Fortis' strength enhancements, the crate was heavy and awkward, and the effort left him out of breath. Dask Finkle didn't seem fazed by it.

"A lot of years in the engine shop," he said. "You know, you can't take this cart on the track to the compound. It won't make it."

"Then we'll break open the crate and carry it on foot," Fortis replied. He pointed to the passenger seat. "Hop in; we have to link up with the platoon."

Fortis and Finkle met Ystremski and the assault teams outside the door to Fenway. The sky was perceptibly lighter, so Fortis knew dawn was imminent.

"The other lads are helping the cops lock the facility down, then they'll muster with our gear in the space port area," the corporal reported to Fortis. He looked at Finkle and then back to Fortis. "What's the plan, LT?"

"Finkle has agreed to lead us to the Kuiper Knights' compound, and he donated a crate of explosives to the mission. We'll have to hump it; there are no vehicles here that can make the trip. When we get there, we get Marx and Landis back and kill all the mercenaries. We'll use the explosives to destroy their compound and hotfoot it back here in time to meet the transport."

"How far is the compound?"

"Seven kilometers, give or take. The track is pretty rough," answered Finkle.

Ystremski looked at his watch. "Run seven kilometers, kill some bad guys, make boom-boom, and run back, all in under two hours. Sounds like an easy day." He turned to the Space Marines. "There's a box of explosives on the back of this cart that's coming with us. Break it down and spread it around. Cowher, Durant, grab a couple litters." He looked at Fortis and shrugged. "We might need them."

As they were about to move out, the door slammed open and Governor Czrk and Bob Drager came outside.

"Lieutenant Fortis! We just heard from your transport. They're inbound and will be at the spaceport in just over ninety minutes."

Drager pointed at Finkle. "Hey, isn't that—"

"Yeah, it is," Fortis replied. "Dask Finkle. He agreed to lead us to the Kuiper Knight compound." Fortis consulted his watch and exchanged looks with Ystremski. "Ninety minutes. It's going to be close."

* * *

While they ran, Fortis and Ystremski peppered Finkle with questions about the mercenary compound, but there was little the resistance leader could tell them.

"I snooped around while they were building it, but I don't know what any of the buildings are for. I haven't been inside since they finished it. The wall is about three meters tall, and there's one gate. I don't remember any guard towers."

"They have twelve men, plus Chive," Fortis stated.

"Eleven guys, plus that prick Chive," Ystremski corrected him. "Unless Rentz figured out how to reattach his head."

"Touché. Still, they have pulse rifles."

"C'mon, LT," Ystremski laughed breathlessly. "We'll be victorious because we're pure of heart."

Finkle gestured at Ystremski. "Lieutenant, do all of you have rocks in your heads, or just him?"

The Space Marines laughed but continued running.

The resistance leader also gave the Space Marines an impromptu lesson on the explosives they'd be using.

"It's not the military-grade stuff you're used to," he told them. "It's pliable so it can be shaped into cutting charges to blast rock formations. All you have to do is form the charge, stick a chemical fuse in it, and break the glass ampule inside. Once the chemicals inside mix enough the fuse turns bright green and boom!"

"What's the time delay on the fuses?" asked Corporal Ystremski.

"Fifteen seconds, give or take."

"Give or take?"

"Yeah. It could be five seconds or it could be forty-five seconds. It could be never."

"That reliable, huh?"

"This stuff has been around since construction crews began building the colony. The fuses are even older. So yeah, probably."

Ystremski snorted in disbelief, and Finkle shrugged.

"If you don't want to use it, don't."

Fortis and Ystremski traded glances.

"DINLI," they said in unison.

Thirty minutes later, Finkle waved the column to a halt and bent over, his hands on his knees.

"I gotta stop," he panted. "It's another klick, maybe a klick and a half. Just follow the road over that rise. You can't miss it."

"Hey, LT, look at this." A knot of Space Marines was gathered on the side of the track. Fortis and Ystremski saw several bodies crumpled face-down in the dirt. The first body was clad in familiar GRC coveralls and when they rolled it over Fortis saw it was Jandahl. They examined two more; Fortis recognized the remains of Pai Choon, but the other one was unfamiliar to him.

"That's Glenn Deale," said Finkle. "He's a mechanic. Was."

"I guess we know what Chive's been doing with our prisoners," Ystremski said wryly.

Anger rose in Fortis' chest and his resolve to punish the mercenary leader doubled.

"Mark the spot, and let's go. We're running out of time."

Five minutes later, Fortis and Ystremski raised their heads over the sand berm concealing the assault teams and stared at the Kuiper Knights' compound.

"Not much to it, LT. One gate, no towers."

"I don't see any cameras, either, though they'd be hard to spot from here." Fortis looked at his watch. "It doesn't matter, we don't have time to be sneaky. What do you think?"

"We need to get a peek over that wall, but it looks like a version of what we've been raiding for the last week."

The pair slid back down the berm and rejoined the men.

"Not much to it," Fortis told the men. "Straight run for half a klick to the wall. After we get a look over the wall, we'll attack. Questions?"

Nobody responded.

"Let's move."

Fortis felt naked as they dashed to the base of the compound wall. With every step he expected a salvo of plasma bolts from the mercenaries' pulse rifles, but they never came. He made it to the relative safety of the wall unscathed and joined Ystremski.

The corporal crouched down and laced his fingers together.

"Alley-oop, sir."

Ystremski boosted Fortis high enough to get his head and shoulders over the wall. The lieutenant had a moment of panic when he cleared the safety of the wall, but no alarm was raised. Two sentries were lounging on makeshift chairs near the front building, but they appeared to be asleep. Fortis noted a domed main building surrounded by two rows of smaller buildings and the crawler parked near the gate. The buildings were featureless and there was no indication what might be inside any of them. He didn't see any other mercenaries besides the sentries. Satisfied, Fortis dropped back down.

"Eight buildings in two rows," he said as he scratched the layout in the dirt. "The crawler is parked over here next to the gate, and there's a bunch of pallets and stuff along this wall. There are two guards sitting in chairs here and here, but I think they're asleep. I didn't see any other mercenaries. No idea where Marx and Landis are."

"We don't have time to hit one building at a time, sir. If they hear us coming, we lose the element of surprise."

Fortis thought for a second. "Okay, how about this? Assault Team One takes these four buildings and Team Two takes these four. Team One handles the sentries, quietly. After they eliminate the sentries, I'll post up at the gate and put a charge on it. When it blows, the mercs should come running, and we shoot them as they come outside. Keep an eye out for Marx and Landis."

The Space Marines scrambled over the wall and took their positions. Two members of Team One slipped up behind the dozing sentries and simultaneously slit their throats. They dragged the lifeless bodies around the corner and out of sight, then took their positions.

Fortis dashed to the gate and inspected the lock. He broke off a fist-sized piece of explosive, flattened it into pancake, and stuck it to the gate just above the lock. He jammed two fuses into the charge to make sure at least one of them went off and waited. When Ystremski and Heisen signaled that their teams were ready, he cracked the ampules inside the fuses. One of the fuses immediately turned bright green and his memory flashed to Dask Finkle's words: *"...the fuse will turn bright green and boom!"*

Oh, fuck!

Fortis lunged away from the gate a millisecond before a thunderclap exploded over his head. A wave of superheated air engulfed him and a giant invisible hand slammed him on the ground and pelted him with rocks. Blinded by dirt and deafened by the explosion, Fortis fought back as invisible assailants slapped him on the head. He heard popcorn popping while he grappled with his enemies, and he felt a satisfying *crunch* when his elbow made contact with his attacker's face. His ears finally cleared with a *POP!* and the popcorn sound became small arms fire.

"Stop fighting!" a familiar voice shouted above the sounds of battle. Rough hands grabbed his arms and dragged him across the rocky ground. A pulse rifle round hit the wall above him and sprayed the area with bits of rock.

Fortis regained his senses and recognized Space Marine boots as they heaved him the last few meters to safety behind a stack of barrels.

Private Durant tore open a hydration back and squirted the contents into the lieutenant's face.

"LT, can you see?"

"Yeah," Fortis sputtered and blinked. His eyes focused on Private Cowher, who was leaning against the wall next to him with bloody hands pressed to his face. "What happened to him?"

Durant laughed. "You happened to him, sir. Your head was on fire, and when he slapped out the flames you elbowed him in the face."

At the mention of fire, Fortis' scalp and neck began to sting. He reached for his head, but Durant stopped him.

"Don't touch it, sir. Let me get some flash cream on those burns."

The gunfire sputtered until there were only scattered shots and then nothing.

"What's happening?" Fortis struggled to sit up to see for himself, but Cowher and Durant pressed him back down.

"Take it easy, LT, we're almost done. A quick bandage to keep this clean and you can go see for yourself."

* * * * *

Chapter Thirty

Ystremski watched Lieutenant Fortis disappear in a flash of fire and thunder and then reappear as a flaming rag doll tumbling across the hard-packed dirt. His first instinct was to run to the injured man's aid, but he fought it back. The door he was stationed at slammed open, and two Kuiper Knights ran out.

The corporal fired twice, and both mercenaries went down. He waited, but no one followed. He aimed carefully and delivered a kill shot to the head of each of the fallen mercenaries. He peeked inside the building, but it appeared empty.

Most of the gunfire he heard was pistols, but a stray plasma bolt sizzled past and told him there were still some live mercenaries. Ystremski holstered his pistol and retrieved one of fallen mercenary's pulse rifles, checked the charge, and went in search of more Kuiper Knights to kill.

* * *

The massive blast saved Chive's life.

He had finished showering when the entire compound shook. Five minutes later and he would have been dressed and gathered with the other mercenaries in the lounge area. Instead, they raced outside to investigate while Chive struggled into his clothes to the unmistakable sound of gunfire outside. One of them burst back inside as Chive was shrugging into his tunic and fastening his equipment belt.

"The colonial police are attacking!" The mercenary fumbled with the rack of pulse rifles on the wall next to the door. "There's a hundred of them!"

"Get back out there! Go!" Chive grabbed his own rifle and pushed the man toward the door. "We have to stop them."

A ragged fusillade of bullets tore into the mercenary, and Chive pulled up before he stepped outside. From the sound of the gunfire there were at least two shooters covering the door. He saw a shadow cross the doorway and heard a whispered conversation.

They're coming in.

Without hesitating, Chive quietly set his rifle down and sprawled on the floor next to the dead mercenary. He swiped at the man's blood and smeared it on his face and then turned his head in what he hoped looked like an unnatural angle. Through slitted eyes, he watched as two figures advanced into the room with their weapons at the ready. The two men moved with practiced confidence as they cleared the lounge, the bunkroom, and the showers. Chive considered making a break when they were occupied in the back of the barracks but thought better of it when he heard more shots outside.

When they finished clearing the building, one of the men prodded Chive with the toe of his boot, but the mercenary leader didn't move.

Satisfied, the two men ran back out into the morning light.

* * *

When the Kuiper Knights had arrived at the compound, they'd dragged their Space Marine captives to the interrogation building. Dolph hung back and crawled into one of the converted ore cars. He wanted no part of whatever Chive had planned for Marx and Landis, and he'd long since lost any lingering feelings of fraternity toward his fellow mercenaries. Events had begun to swirl out of control, and the driver just wanted out.

Dolph was asleep in the back of the crawler when the massive explosion tipped the heavy vehicle, and it almost flipped before it slammed back down. The mercenary was thrown face-first against the metal benches, and the impact left him stunned. Pain exploded across his face and snapped him back to reality when his tongue probed the jagged remains of his front teeth.

He heard the familiar *pop-pop-pop* of gunfire, and when he lifted himself up to look out the window, he saw armed men moving from building to building and engaging the occupants.

Space Marines.

He cracked the hatch and dropped to the ground. After a quick look around, Dolph scrambled under the crawler to hide.

* * *

When the medics finished treating Fortis, he climbed to his feet and stood on wobbly legs to survey the compound. He couldn't tell if the bodies scattered around were mercenaries or Space Marines. He was relieved when Corporal Ystremski emerged from the nearest building. He waved, and the corporal jogged over.

"Target is secure, LT. We have a hostile body count of eight, plus two prisoners. We shot one of them through the legs. The driver, Dolph, and that fucker Chive are unaccounted for, but we're still looking."

"Our guys?" croaked Fortis.

"No KIAs and no major injuries. Modell smashed his fingers in a door and Harrigan got hit by a pulse ricochet. They're both on their feet."

"Marx and Landis?"

"They're beat up but okay. The mercenaries knocked them around pretty good when they grabbed them. It's a good thing we got here before those bastards could start working them over for real. There's a regular fingernail factory set up in one of the buildings. We found West in there, too. He's in rough shape." Ystremski motioned to his head. "What's your status, LT? You look like you've been smoking a dynamite cigar."

"Goddamn fuse was a lot less than fifteen seconds. It wasn't even five."

Ystremski chuckled. "*Probably*. Nice job on the gate, by the way." They looked at the gaping hole where the gate once stood. "I bet you blew that sonofabitch fifty meters into the desert."

The Space Marines arranged the bodies of the dead mercenaries in a rough line and Fortis felt a twinge of guilty satisfaction at the sight of the bouncer from the Cock and Tale.

Lance Corporal Head ran up to the two men. "Hey, LT, Corporal, we found the China Mike lab. There's a warehouse, too, and it's full of that shit."

"Let's go take a look."

* * *

As soon as he was alone, Chive rolled to his feet and retrieved his rifle. He checked that his dueling sword was still snug in the scabbard and chanced a look out the door. The compound appeared deserted, so he dashed toward some pallets and other junk the slovenly mercenaries had piled next to the wall. He breathed a silent prayer of thanks for their laziness as he boosted himself up to vault over the wall.

He rolled over the top and dropped down outside the compound, but he lost his grip on the rifle and it fell back inside the wall.

"Shit!"

Chive landed in a crouch and searched the surrounding desert for any threats. The suddenness of the attack and the loss of his rifle left him feeling vulnerable, and he was certain the attackers were not colonial police.

Space Marines.

He weighed his options as he hunkered down next to the wall. He knew his current hiding place was temporary. If the Space Marines took a body count they would realize they were one body short and Fortis would know he was the missing mercenary.

His long-term prospects on Eros-28 weren't good. Even after the Space Marines departed, he couldn't return to Fenway, and he couldn't stay out in the desert forever.

In retrospect, murdering Chief Schultz had been a foolish and impulsive act. Had Chive not killed the corpulent cop, he could have hidden out until the Space Marines departed and then emerged from the desert with a plausible—if not entirely believable—story. Czrk would accept almost anything to avoid a controversy that could reflected badly on him.

Now, if he turned himself over to Governor Czrk and the colonial police, he'd be fortunate to survive the eight weeks to face the colonial circuit judge. He wouldn't find any help in the dusty streets of Boston. Even if he somehow succeeded sneaking into Fenway, it was impossible to stow away on one of the supply shuttles that visited Eros-28.

A sudden crazed fantasy flashed through his imagination. He would return to Fenway, assassinate Czrk, and seize control of the colony. As quickly as the idea came to him, he shook it off. Without his brother Kuiper Knights, Chive was powerless.

He was cornered, and that made him dangerous.

The sound of raised voices floated over the wall to his hiding place.

* * * * *

Chapter Thirty-One

"You asked what a China Mike lab looked like, there's your answer."

Head opened the door and stepped aside. Fortis and the Space Marines crowded around to peer inside. Rows of shiny tanks, tubes, burners, and a bank of blinking control equipment filled the space.

"This is an industrial operation," said Fortis. "They were making it by the ton."

"You ain't seen nothing, sir. Take a look at this."

Head led the group to the neighboring building and opened the door. "Anybody want to get high?"

Fortis gaped.

Rows of shelves stretched the length of the building, and every shelf overflowed with taped-up bundles, all of them about the size of an old-fashioned loaf of bread.

"Kilos, packed up and ready to ship."

"That's all China Mike?"

"We don't have a drug testing kit, but based on the lab next door, I'd say yes."

"How much is there?"

"No idea, sir, and we don't have time to count." Corporal Ystremski tapped his watch. "We're gonna miss our ride if we don't get moving."

"We can't just leave it here."

Ystremski looked at the Space Marines. "Get all the boom-boom we have left and bring it here. We'll blow these buildings and then haul ass."

While they prepared the explosives, Fortis went into the domed building in the center of the compound. It was an austere room with four rows of benches facing a pulpit on the far end. Ystremski had told the lieutenant that the Kuiper Knights were some kind of cult, but there weren't any conspicuous religious artifacts or regalia. After a quick look around, he pulled the door shut and joined Ystremski by the gate.

Some of the Space Marines worked quickly to fashion charges as Ystremski directed them to demolish the lab and warehouse. The result was a long string of explosives woven through ropes that were then wrapped around the China Mike lab and storage building. Another string ran to the front of the compound where the Marines waited. Fuses dotted the explosive ropes throughout.

While Ystremski led the explosives preparation, Corporal Heisen had the other Marines collect all the pulse rifles and chargers they could find.

"The colonial police are going to get a major upgrade to their armory," he explained to Fortis.

"When you finish with that, have them check out the crawler. Maybe we can ride back to Fenway."

"Once we get everyone outside the wall, I'll break these two fuses and run," Ystremski explained to Fortis pointing to the nearest rope. "With any luck, the explosion will travel down the rope break more fuses, and the whole thing will go up in a long series of bangs."

Fortis wanted to believe in the plan, but he was skeptical. "And if it doesn't?"

The corporal shrugged. "It will work because it *has* to work, sir. If it doesn't the governor can bring his cops out here and burn the place to the ground or let a sifter bury it. Either way, we've gotta go."

"Hey, LT! No keys in the crawler but look who we found hiding underneath."

Childers and Boudreaux dragged a dusty figure forward and dumped him next to the other two prisoners. The new prisoner sat up, and Fortis recognized Dolph, the mercenary driver. The Space Marines zip-tied his hands and ankles and yanked a hood over his head.

"Search that guy for the crawler keys," Ystremski ordered. The guards turned his pockets out but didn't find any keys.

"Where are the keys?" the corporal demanded. He prodded the mercenary with his boot, but Dolph shrugged and said nothing. Ystremski turned to Lieutenant Fortis.

"What do you want to do with these guys, LT?"

"Take them with us, I guess. Turn them over to the governor."

Ystremski shook his head. "Sir, they're not gonna make it back to Fenway. The guy we shot through both legs can't walk, much less run. We'll never make the extraction if we have to carry him."

"What do you want to do, leave them out here?"

"No way, sir. We policed up all the weapons in the compound, but there's no telling if these pricks have more hidden or cached out in the desert somewhere. We don't have time to fuck around with these guys."

"Then what?"

Ystremski shrugged. "Shoot them."

"What? We can't shoot prisoners! They need to stand trial."

"Let's have a trial right here." He whipped off Dolph's hood and pressed his pulse rifle to the mercenary's head. "Dolph, you piece of garbage, you're charged with murder, kidnapping, and drug distribution. How do you plead?"

Dolph twisted away from Ystremski. "What the fuck is this?" he slurred through his damaged mouth.

Fortis stared in shock as the corporal straddled the driver and prodded him with his rifle.

"Never mind your plea. I find you guilty as charged and sentence you to death by one-man firing squad. You have three seconds to pray."

"Hey! Hey, man!" Dolph tried to wriggle away, but the corporal was right on top of him.

"One...two..."

Fortis found his voice. *"Corporal!"*

Ystremski shoved the rifle barrel under Dolph's chin. "Drive and live; refuse and die. Choose. Now."

"Okay. Okay! I'll drive!"

"What?"

All the energy drained out of Dolph's body, and he collapsed to the ground. "The crawler. I'll drive. Just don't kill me."

Ystremski smiled at the astounded Fortis as he shouldered the rifle. "Court's adjourned, LT. All aboard!"

* * *

Chive remained hidden while the Space Marines loaded the prisoners and captured weapons into the crawler. His plan required split-second timing and some luck, but he was determined to get some small degree of revenge on the Space Marines before he died.

Chive moved around the corner and positioned himself by the gaping hole in the wall when the crawler engines fire up. As the ponderous machine rolled out of the compound, he ran at a crouch, grabbed a handhold, and scrambled onto the second car. He lay flat and waited for someone to shout the alarm, but it never came.

The crawler stopped thirty meters from the compound and waited. Chive looked up and saw Corporal Ystremski running for the vehicle. The hatch opened, the Space Marine dove in, and the crawler lurched into motion.

Boom! Boom! KA-BOOM!

A series of explosions rocked the former Kuiper Knights' headquarters. The final blast sent a cloud of dust and rocks a hundred meters into the sky and the shockwave buffeted the crawler. Chive buried his head in his arms as small rocks rained down in all directions, but the crawler continued to roll toward Fenway. A few seconds later, the vehicle stopped, and Chive watched as Dask Finkle emerged and climbed aboard. The engine whined, and the Space Marines and the Kuiper Knight rumbled toward their destiny.

* * *

Lieutenant Fortis rode in the copilot's seat, pistol in hand, and watched as Dolph piloted the crawler along the rocky track that led to Boston and Fenway.

"What was Chive's plan? Did he really believe the GRC and UNT would stand by and let him take over the colony?"

"I don't know, LT. The Knights are always coming up with crazy ideas like this. The original plan was to generate enough upheaval that the GRC would make him the governor in place of Czrk. We were sent to crack a few heads and piss off the workforce to drive down production. Once Chive was governor, the Knighthood was supposed to show up, take over operations, and force the GRC to negotiate. All this drug shit was part of a plan I didn't agree to."

"Are there more mercenaries on the way or standing by somewhere close?"

Dolph shook his head. "Not that I know of, but Chive didn't share a lot of details with anyone but that psychopath Wychan. Drive here, fly there, that's about all he ever told me."

"Do you have any idea where he might be?"

Dolph shook his head again. "No idea. When you blew the gate, I was asleep in the crawler. He must have hidden somewhere."

"I'd feel better if he was accounted for."

"I wouldn't worry too much about Chive if I were you. If he's not dead yet, he will be soon. He won't last long out there. He's got nowhere to go."

The driver pointed out the windshield at a massive cloud of dust billowing up in the direction of Boston.

"Don't look now, but that's your transport."

* * * * *

Chapter Thirty-Two

Dolph brought the crawler to a stop around the corner from the landing pad where the transport was waiting, its engines whining. The ore car hatches slammed open, and the Space Marines poured out. They deposited armloads of pulse rifles, chargers, and the borrowed pistols in a pile next to the wall where the other Marines had stacked their gear.

Corporal Anderson, the Marine Ystremski had left in charge in Fenway, came outside, accompanied by Governor Czrk and several colonial policemen. The Space Marines turned over custody of the captive Kuiper Knights, grabbed their gear, and headed for the Fleet transport.

"Mission accomplished, Governor," reported Fortis as the two men shook hands. "We located and destroyed the China Mike lab and a large cache of the drug. We killed eight mercenaries and captured three; along with Rentz, that's all twelve accounted for."

"And Chive?"

Fortis frowned. "We didn't find him. He might be out in the desert, but he wasn't in the compound." He gestured to the pile of weapons. "We captured some pulse rifles and chargers for your police force, in case the Kuiper Knights decide to return."

"Thank you, Lieutenant. You've done a great service for the citizens of Eros-28."

Dask Finkle walked up, a pulse rifle slung over his shoulder.

"Thank this guy, too, Governor. He gave us the explosives and led us there."

Finkle and the governor eyed each other.

"You're the resistance leader. Why should I trust you?"

"Governor, if you promise me that these three mercenaries will be tried by the colonial circuit judge and there will be no future reprisals against the workers, then you've got nothing to worry about from us." He patted the rifle sling. "I'd like to keep this, just in case."

After a long second, the governor smiled. "Deal."

"LT, the platoon is loaded, and we're ready to take off," shouted Ystremski. "Grab your gear and let's go!"

Fortis gave a brief wave and bent over to grab his gear. As he straightened up, he heard the governor and Finkle shout. He whirled around in time to see Chive, lips peeled back in a dusty snarl, lunge forward with his dueling sword at eye level.

The lieutenant twisted away and the point of the sword burned across his right cheek instead of plunging into his skull. Fortis stumbled away from the attack and his hand closed around the handle of his kukri. He ripped it from its scabbard as Chive pressed the attack. Fortis was forced to retreat further.

The glittering point of Chive's sword seemed to be everywhere at once—in Fortis' eyes, aimed at his chest, poking at his flanks. It was all Fortis could do to avoid the killing blows, which he warded off with his left arm.

The speed of Chive's attacks overwhelmed Fortis' ability to defend himself, and another lightning lunge opened a searing cut on his left cheek. Chive laughed at his distress and the sight of blood propelled him to redouble his attacks.

Fortis knew he was doomed if he tried to outduel the skilled Kuiper Knight. His kukri was a brutal weapon designed for close-in chopping attacks, not long-range parrying.

Everybody bleeds in a knife fight. The winner bleeds the least.

The words of Fortis' hand-to-hand combat instructor rang in his ears as he screwed up his courage to meet Chive's next lunge with an attack of his own. He parried Chive's thrust with his arm instead of his kukri, ducked under the strike, and delivered three quick slashes to Chive's lead leg before the mercenary could retreat. Fortis' arm tingled, and he felt blood leak down his sleeve, but he knew he'd done some damage to the mercenary.

Like most duelists, Chive adopted a sideways stance with one leg forward, the same side as his sword arm. His back leg propelled him forward to attack, but his front leg drove him back, away from counterstrikes. With an injured lead leg, he wouldn't be able to retreat out of Fortis' range.

Blood spilled down Chive's leg, and he gave a crazed laugh. A second later, he sprang forward and aimed his next jab at Fortis' chest, but the lieutenant was ready for it. He slipped the thrust and spun low. As he whirled, Fortis hacked at Chive's rear leg. The kukri twisted in his hand when the blade glanced off bone.

Chive yelped and almost dropped his sword as his hands reached for the grievous wound. The blow had struck a major blood vessel and thick crimson rivulets spurted onto the dusty ground.

Fortis waited, kukri at the ready, as the Kuiper Knight gathered himself.

"Surrender!" Fortis shouted. "Surrender and stand trial or die!"

Fortis locked eyes with the wounded mercenary. He knew Chive would never surrender, and he wouldn't stop until he was dead. He focused his entire being on the mercenary, and, finally, Chive attacked.

Instead of using a traditional dueling form, Chive attacked with his sword held overhead to plunge downward into his target. At the last second, Fortis sidestepped and crouched low, with his kukri held by his feet. His legs drove him upward in a massive slash, and the kukri ripped up into Chive's groin and abdomen. The blade skidded along the Kuiper Knight's ribs and caught the mercenary under the chin, splitting his throat wide open. Blood sprayed Fortis in a hot, choking mask of gore.

Chive collapsed in a pile of blood and purple-gray viscera. He struggled to gather his intestines and push them back into his body cavity, but his body spasmed as his nerves struggled to come to terms with what his brain already knew: he was dead.

Fortis sank to his knees next to the quivering pile of Chive, exhausted and dripping with the mercenary's blood. His cheeks burned, and his left arm hung limp. He became aware of shouts from somewhere behind him as blowing sand stung his eyes.

"LT, let's go!"

Rough hands grabbed Fortis by the shoulders and dragged him toward the transport. He smiled at Ystremski as the corporal half-carried, half-dragged him up the ramp.

"I told the governor I was gonna kill that sonofabitch."

Corporal Ystremski chuckled as he dumped Fortis into one of the aluminum-frame jump seats and strapped him in.

"You should have let Finkle shoot him, you crazy son of a bitch."

The transport lurched as it clawed its way into the sky for the long ride back to *Atlas*.

* * * * *

Chapter Thirty-Three

The fifty-hour journey to catch up with the flagship was a blessing in disguise for Third Platoon. The transport was configured to carry cargo, and the only creature comforts were canvas and metal jump seats welded to each bulkhead. There was a tiny berthing compartment for the crew, but no troop accommodations. Without racks to sleep on, the Space Marines sacked out on the deck with their packs as pillows. There was a single head—almost big enough to turn around in—with a dented metal sink that dribbled tepid water. Someone had thought to send a pallet of hydration packs and a pallet of pig squares, or the Space Marines would have gone hungry for the two-day-plus trip.

The transport crew consisted of two pilots, a flight engineer, a communicator, and two loadmasters. Once they were free to move about the vessel, the senior pilot came back and introduced herself to Fortis.

"Captain Shelly Hampton," she said extending her hand.

"Lieutenant Abner Fortis."

She motioned to her cheeks. "What's all that about, Lieutenant? You guys were supposed to be on liberty."

"It was a friendly exhibition that got out of hand." Fortis looked at Ystremski hovering nearby and saw the corporal look away to hide a smile.

"Exhibition? You cut that guy in half!"

"Yeah. Like I said, it got out of hand. What can you tell me about Alert Condition Bravo?"

Hampton shrugged. "Nobody's talking. Division ordered the re-call, and I've been flying loads of pissed-off Marines from Eros-69 back to the flagship. Then I got orders to come out here to get you."

With no more information to offer each other, their conversation dwindled into an awkward silence. She was curious about his fear-some appearance, but he was reluctant to give her more than short answers to her questions about his injuries. Finally, Hampton ex-cused herself to check on things in the cockpit. He didn't see her again for the duration of their trip.

The transport loadmasters finally left the Space Marines alone af-ter Private Queen subjected them to a torrent of deeply insulting jokes and harassment, and the platoon was grateful for the privacy so they could talk. When Marx and Landis heard what their brother Marines had done to free them, they were astounded.

Cowher and Durant did the best they could to treat Fortis' wounds. The medics cleaned the worst of the dirt from the slashes on his cheeks, pulled them shut with butterflies, and slathered them with generous dollops of antibacterial cream. Still, he would require surgery to repair the damage from Chive's sword. They shaved the rest of his head to treat his burns from the explosive charge with a blue-green burn cream that smelled like peppermint and stung like hell. The lieutenant also had four puncture wounds in his left arm that required deep antibiotic injections that burned as the medicine penetrated his flesh.

Fortis was an awful patient. He chafed at the attention, and Ystremski finally threatened to physically restrain the lieutenant so the medics could finish their work.

"LT, how's it going to look if you're hogtied when we get back to *Atlas*. Just relax, would you? DINLI, you fucking crybaby."

When Cowher and Durant were finished, Ystremski chuckled as he handed Fortis a small signal mirror to inspect the results. "LT, you look like you've been shaving with a chainsaw and trimming your hair with a blowtorch."

"Fuck," Fortis mumbled.

Random tufts of hair that had resisted the razor stuck up at wild angles, and the burn cream was thick and greasy. The flesh of his face felt heavy, and, when he tried to make a face, his expression didn't change.

"We had to give you a powerful muscle relaxer to numb your facial muscles so you don't smile or wince and tear the wounds open," explained Durant.

Fortis' injured left arm was supported by a sling that was stained with dirt and blood. All of this added to his torn and dirty uniform to give him an absurdly bedraggled appearance.

"Sorry we can't wash you up any better, sir. There's not much to work with. But don't worry, LT, when we get back to *Atlas*, you'll have all the time in the world to get cleaned up and squared away," Ystremski told him.

"Forget about me. What about our guys? Marx and Landis and the others."

"They're okay. Marx is concussed and Landis has a broken hand, but nothing worse than they might get from a good game of Calcio Fiorentino. Harrington's wound will heal cleanly, and Modell's fingers are just bruised."

Fortis laid back with a groan. "Great."

Ystremski looked over his shoulder, then leaned in close and lowered his voice. "What are you gonna tell them back at Battalion?"

Fortis didn't hesitate. "The truth. All of it."

Ystremski's eyebrows went up in surprise. "Are you sure?"

"I have to."

"You know you'll catch a lot of shit for this, sir."

"At this point, I don't care. I'm not going to ask these guys to lie for me; they deserve better than that. I let this go way beyond a bull-shit arrest and shakedown when I agreed to the governor's offer."

"What the hell were you supposed to do, leave Marx and Landis to rot in jail?" The corporal shook his head emphatically. "No, sir. No way. We don't leave ours behind, no matter what. There's no way they'll bust your balls for this."

"Here's hoping Colonel Sobieski feels the same way."

"LT, I'll let you in on a little secret. If you hadn't done what you did for Marx and Landis, none of these other guys would have ever followed you again. Oh, they'd obey orders, but someday you would have found yourself all alone in a bug hole, you know?"

"Yeah, I guess you're right."

"Damn right I'm right. They might be a bunch of ignorant knuckle-draggers, but they know who's got their backs."

The two men sat in silence for a moment.

"If there's a part of the story that you want to, you know, *nuance*, say the word. These animals will go along with whatever you say."

"I appreciate the offer, but I'm not going to lie, and I don't want anyone else to, either." Fortis closed his eyes. "Captain Hampton watched me chop Chive in half."

Ystremski chuckled. "Yeah, there's really no way to nuance that."

Fortis sighed. "Right now, I just want some sleep."

Ystremski waited until Fortis' breathing became deep and regular before he stood up and looked around the cargo bay. The rest of the platoon was spread out to grab some shuteye, so he moved carefully. The corporal returned to where the lieutenant had begun to snore softly and removed the officer's kukri from his scabbard. Fortis didn't stir as Ystremski walked to his own pack, dug out a length of crimson paracord, and went to work.

* * *

everal hours later, Lieutenant Fortis woke with a start. He opened his eyes and discovered his kukri on his chest.

"What's this?" Lieutenant Fortis held up the weapon and examined the crimson paracord wound around the handle. "Why did you rewrap the handle with red paracord?"

Corporal Ystremski, who had been asleep next to the officer, sat up and considered Fortis through bleary eyes.

"It's not red, it's crimson, as you should know from the striping on your dress uniform, sir." The corporal laid extra emphasis on "sir" and made it sound like an insult. "Space Marines earn their kukris after they fight in combat. They earn the crimson handle when they kill an enemy with it." He pointed to his own kukri, with its olive-drab handle. "Most of us haven't had that honor yet."

Fortis shook his head. "Come on, that's not necessary. Switch it back."

"Can't do it, LT. It's a tradition. Practically a regulation."

The rest of the platoon gathered around them with broad smiles and eyes that gleamed with anticipation.

"Here's another tradition that's practically a regulation." Heisen passed a canteen to Ystremski, who unscrewed the cap and presented it to Fortis.

"What the hell is this?" asked Fortis before he sniffed the open canteen. The raw alcohol burned his nostrils. "Whew!"

Several of the Space Marines laughed and Ystremski motioned for the lieutenant to drink. "The lads we left in charge of our gear had the good sense to bring along some of Eros-28's finest. This seems like as good a time as any for a toast. DINLI, sir."

Fortis held up the canteen and then lowered it and looked at Corporal Ystremski.

"Go ahead, LT. If that strength enhancement hasn't taken by now, it never will."

Fortis nodded and raised it again.

"To the dead and the living."

He tipped a splash onto the deck as was the custom and then took a pull from the canteen. Tears stung his eyes, and he struggled to swallow without choking as the lethal homebrew stole his breath.

"DINLI!" the platoon roared in unison.

* * *

Fortis and Ystremski debriefed the platoon in turns, and Fortis took extensive notes for the report he planned to submit when they returned to the flagship. The task took several hours, and it was several more before Fortis finished writing. When he was done, Ystremski assembled the men so Fortis could address them.

"I think it's important that all of you know and understand what's in here," the lieutenant said as he held the report over his head. "What happened back there was a failure of leadership. My leadership." His eyes flicked from face to face and he saw a lot of puzzled looks. "None of this would have happened if I hadn't violated the colonel's orders and allowed all of you to go on liberty in Boston. Whatever happened after that is my responsibility."

He gestured to Marx and Landis. "I don't know what you were doing with that prostitute, but I'm sure it wasn't drug-related." Guffaws greeted this remark.

"First time for everything," a voice called from the back, and even Ystremski chuckled.

Fortis waited for the merriment to die down before he continued.

"Based on everything we learned during our time on Eros-28, I believe that Chive and the Kuiper Knights were involved in a coup against Governor Czrk. I don't know why he chose to involve us; I guess it was an opportunity he felt he couldn't pass up. Either way, the decision to accept the governor's offer to conduct the raids was mine."

Several Space Marines opened their mouths as if to protest, but Fortis held up his hand.

"I know you think you volunteered, but the simple fact is that there was no way you were *not* going to agree to the raids, and I knew that. I can't share the responsibility for my decisions with you, vote or no vote. I never should have let it come to a vote. That's not how the ISMC works.

"But legal or not, we did the right thing. I'm convinced that the destruction of the China Mike lab and that warehouse saved lives. Maybe not mercenary lives, but the lives of people that matter."

More smiles and chortles greeted this line, and he smiled with them.

"In about twelve hours, we'll be back aboard *Atlas*. When we get there, I imagine there will be all kinds of rumors and stories flying around. You've all heard the truth, and I encourage all of you to stick to it. If there's a price to be paid for what we did, it's mine to pay. All of you conducted yourselves with courage and professionalism, and I'm grateful that there were no serious injuries—"

"Except your hair!" Private Queen quipped. The Space Marines howled with laughter, and Fortis knew he'd set the right tone with them. He could have ordered them not to say anything, but he knew the story would eventually leak, and he felt it was better to get the truth out first. The lads were smart enough to understand that wild rumors wouldn't do anyone any good.

"Third Platoon, lock it up!" Corporal Ystremski roared over the merriment and the entire platoon came to attention. "You've had your kumbaya moment with the lieutenant. Now it's time to get back to being Space Marines. We have twelve hours before we get back to the flagship, which gives us plenty of time to square away those uni-forms. Some of your boots look like you polished them with a warm chocolate bar. Uniform inspection in two hours. Move!"

* * * * *

Chapter Thirty-Four

The transport docked with *Atlas* and Lieutenant Fortis led Third Platoon down the ramp and into the hangar. They were as clean and presentable as they could get after surviving the hovercopter crash, the Eolian Blast, and the battle at the mercenary compound. Fortis felt a surge of pride at their appearance. They were field Marines, not headquarters ceremonial types, and it showed.

Captain Hampton approached Fortis as Ystremski got the Space Marines formed up.

"Fortis, I don't want you to be blindsided, but I have to report what I witnessed at the landing pad on Eros-28."

"Yes, ma'am, I know." Fortis patted the pocket where he'd tucked his report. "I've got the whole thing detailed right here."

She nodded and stuck out her hand. "Good. And good luck to you. That was one hell of an exhibition."

The officers shook, exchanged salutes, and Hampton disappeared back into the transport. Corporal Ystremski posted up in front of Fortis and saluted.

"Third Platoon, all present or accounted for, sir."

"Very well. Dismiss the men."

Fortis got strange looks from everyone he encountered as he headed for the hatch leading to his stateroom in officer's country. He had fixed the worst of his hair and wiped off the excess burn cream, but it had left behind a bluish-green cast. The medics had urged him to leave his cheek wounds uncovered to dry and the damage was conspicuous.

"Lieutenant Fortis. Lieutenant Fortis!"

Fortis turned to see who was calling him, and an unfamiliar staff sergeant approached. The Space Marine's eyes widened when he got a look at the officer's injuries. His nametape read "Willis."

"Lieutenant Fortis, Colonel Sobieski wants to see you, on the double."

"Now?" Fortis looked down at his shabby uniform. "Can I take a minute to get squared away?"

"'Get his ass up here, now.' His words, sir." Willis smiled an apology. "I'm sorry, Lieutenant; the colonel's patience is wearing thin these days."

"What about Captain Brickell? Shouldn't I report to him first?"

"There is no Captain Brickell, sir. The colonel got a little pissed when he heard you were on Eros-28. He fired Brickell and Captain Reese, too."

Shit.

Fortis sighed. "Lead the way, Willis."

The strange looks continued as Fortis followed Willis through the maze of gleaming passageways deep into the command suite. Finally, the staff sergeant paused at a door with a large eagle insignia painted on it. An engraved plate hung below the eagle.

Colonel K. R. Sobieski
2nd Battalion/1st Regiment

Willis looked at Fortis as if to ask if he was ready, and Fortis nodded. The staff sergeant rapped three times and opened the door.

"Colonel Sobieski, Lieutenant Fortis is here."

Fortis approached the colonel's desk, stopped three paces in front, and rendered his sharpest salute.

"Lieutenant Fortis, reporting as ordered, sir."

The colonel, a tall man with swarthy skin and a tight buzzcut flecked with gray, looked up from a chart that was spread across his desk.

"What happened to your face, Fortis?" He leaned in for a closer look. "Have you been dueling?"

"Not exactly, sir. A Kuiper Knight attacked me with his dueling blade."

"A Kuiper Knight? Where did you run into a Kuiper Knight?"

"Liberty on Eros-28, colonel."

"Why is your head blue?"

"It's burn cream, sir. An explosive fuse detonated prematurely and burned my hair off."

"Explosives?"

"It's hard to explain, sir. It's all right here, in my report." Fortis held up the document.

"Never mind that right now, Fortis. General Gupta received a private communique from the governor of Eros-28 yesterday, and he's been anxious to talk to you."

Fortis froze. "General Gupta?"

"Yeah. General Gupta. The only general we have. Come on."

Fortis' heart sank. He'd lost the initiative, and now he'd be playing defense.

"Sir, I can explain—"

"Not to me, you won't." The colonel walked around his desk to the door. "Let's go. The general is waiting."

The lieutenant forced his legs to carry him up the ladder behind Colonel Sobieski to the flag deck. The first time he'd encountered General Gupta had been the day Fortis was both court martialed for Failure to Obey an Order and awarded the *L'Ordre de la Galanterie* by direction of the president of the UNT.

Maybe he forgot?

When they arrived at the general's office, the shapely flag aide nodded and waved them to the general's door. Sobieski rapped three times and entered with Fortis in tow.

"Sobieski and Fortis, sir."

The general was engrossed by a holograph of a planet hovering over his desk. Fortis recognized symbols for various Fleet vessels in orbit around it, including *Atlas*. When he finally looked up, his eyes widened in surprise.

"What happened to your face, Fortis? Have you been dueling?"

This time, Fortis was ready for the question. "A Kuiper Knight attacked me with his dueling blade while I was on Eros-28, General," he replied. "I killed him with my kukri."

Gupta cocked an eyebrow at him. "With your kukri?"

"Yes, sir. It was the only weapon I had available."

"Hmm." General Gupta stared at him for a long moment. "I received a private message from the governor of Eros-28 yesterday."

"Sir, I detailed the entire situation here, in my report."

"The governor tells me that my Space Marines got involved in a local law enforcement matter without my authorization."

"Sir, I can explain."

The general retrieved a sheet of paper from his desk and began to read.

"'When he learned of the situation, Lieutenant Fortis volunteered his platoon to assist GRC security in a mission to eliminate a powerful Kuiper Knight China Mike cartel operating on Eros-28.' The Kuiper Knights? What the hell is that about, Fortis?"

Fortis felt a twinge of panic. He didn't know what else the governor had told the general, so he was unsure how to respond. He decided a non-answer was the best course of action.

"The colonial police force was unable to deal with the cartel by themselves so we assisted them."

"Assisted them? The governor said you killed or captured the entire cartel and destroyed their lab. Is that true?"

"Yes, sir."

General Gupta shook his head and scowled as he studied the message.

"Lieutenant, did you know that after the United Nations of Terra was formed there were several member nations that objected to the formation of the ISMC?"

"No, sir."

"They were concerned about a military force operating far beyond the reaches of UNT authority on behalf of one member or another, perhaps even against one another. Now do you understand why the ISMC isn't authorized to get involved in local law enforcement matters?"

"I do, sir, but there are five thousand UNT citizens who live and work on Eros-28, and they deserve our protection, too."

"Why didn't you request guidance from your chain of command?"

"Given the significance of the industrial operation there and the exigency of the situation, I felt it necessary to act without delay. I mistakenly assumed that with the division on liberty on Eros-69 the necessary authorization might arrive too late."

"You assumed."

Fortis felt his blood rushing to his face, and his wounded cheeks stung.

"General, the Kuiper Knights planned to destabilize Eros-28 to get their man appointed governor. Once they had control, they'd be free to do what they wanted.

"The China Mike lab might have begun as a local law enforcement matter, but we destroyed an entire warehouse full of the drug, bundled up into kilos and ready for transportation. Several metric tons, at least. They manufactured the drug and smuggled it out hidden in heavy equipment all over the sector. It wasn't going to stay a local law enforcement matter for long."

"That bad?"

"Yes, sir, it was."

Gupta stroked his chin. "Any injuries?"

"Mostly scrapes and bruises, sir." He motioned to his cheeks. "And this, of course."

Gupta leaned forward and studied Fortis. "Why is your head blue?"

Fortis felt the skin on his face tighten as he struggled not to grin. "Faulty fuse on an explosive charge went off prematurely. Burned off my hair."

The general shook his head and looked at Colonel Sobieski. "You have any questions, Colonel?"

The Battalion commander looked visibly relieved. "None, sir."

"Well, Fortis, if the governor of a critical GRC operation like Eros-28 is happy that you helped him, then so am I. It sounds like you made the right decision, but you got lucky. If one of your men had been seriously wounded or killed, all the governors in the galaxy wouldn't have been able to save your ass.

"We operate out here without any oversight from the UNT, and we can't afford to take sides. The decision to get involved has to be made at my level, not yours. Understand?"

"Yes, sir."

"Good. Now, get out of here. I've got an invasion to plan."

# # # # #

About P.A. Piatt

P.A. Piatt was born and raised in western Pennsylvania. After his first attempt at college, he joined the Navy to see the world. He started writing as a hobby when he retired in 2005 and published his first novel in 2018.

His published works include the Abner Fortis, International Space Marine Corps mil-sf series, the Walter Bailey Misadventures urban fantasy trilogy, and other full-length novels in both science fiction and horror.

All of his novels and various published short stories can be found on Amazon. Visit his website at www.papiattauthor.com.

* * * * *

For More Information:

Meet the authors of CKP on the Factory Floor:

https://www.facebook.com/groups/461794864654198

* * * * *

Get the free Four Horsemen prelude story "Shattered Crucible"

and discover other titles by Theogony Books at:

http://chriskennedypublishing.com/

* * * * *

Did you like this book?
Please write a review!

* * * * *

The following is an

Excerpt from Book One of the Lunar Free State:

The Moon and Beyond

John E. Siers

Available from Theogony Books

eBook and Paperback

Excerpt from "The Moon and Beyond:"

"So, what have we got?" The chief had no patience for inter-agency squabbles.

The FBI man turned to him with a scowl. "We've got some abandoned buildings, a lot of abandoned stuff—none of which has anything to do with spaceships—and about a hundred and sixty scientists, maintenance people, and dependents left behind, all of whom claim they knew nothing at all about what was really going on until today. Oh, yeah, and we have some stripped computer hardware with all memory and processor sections removed. I mean physically taken out, not a chip left, nothing for the techies to work with. And not a scrap of paper around that will give us any more information…at least, not that we've found so far. My people are still looking."

"What about that underground complex on the other side of the hill?"

"That place is wiped out. It looks like somebody set off a *nuke* in there. The concrete walls are partly fused! The floor is still too hot to walk on. Our people say they aren't sure how you could even *do* something like that. They're working on it, but I doubt they're going to find anything."

"What about our man inside, the guy who set up the computer tap?"

"Not a trace, chief," one of the NSA men said. "Either he managed to keep his cover and stayed with them, or they're holding him prisoner, or else…" The agent shrugged.

"You think they terminated him?" The chief lifted an eyebrow. "A bunch of rocket scientists?"

"Wouldn't put it past them. Look at what Homeland Security ran into. Those motion-sensing chain guns are *nasty*, and the area between the inner and outer perimeter fence is mined! Of course, they posted warning signs, even marked the fire zones for the guns. No-

305

body would have gotten hurt if the troops had taken the signs seriously."

The Homeland Security colonel favored the NSA man with an icy look. "That's bullshit. How did we know they weren't bluffing? You'd feel pretty stupid if we'd played it safe and then found out there were no defenses, just a bunch of signs!"

"Forget it!" snarled the chief. "Their whole purpose was to delay us, and it worked. What about the Air Force?"

"It might as well have been a UFO sighting as far as they're concerned. Two of their F-25s went after that spaceship, or whatever it was we saw leaving. The damned thing went straight up, over eighty thousand meters per minute, they say. That's nearly Mach Two, in a *vertical climb*. No aircraft in *anybody's* arsenal can sustain a climb like that. Thirty seconds after they picked it up, it was well above their service ceiling and still accelerating. Ordinary ground radar couldn't find it, but NORAD *thinks* they might have caught a short glimpse with one of their satellite-watch systems, a hundred miles up and still going."

"So where did they go?"

"Well, chief, if we believe what those leftover scientists are telling us, I guess they went to the Moon."

* * * * *

Get "The Moon and Beyond" here:
https://www.amazon.com/dp/B097QMN7PJ.

Find out more about John E. Siers at:
https://chriskennedypublishing.com.

* * * * *

The following is an

Excerpt from Book One of Murphy's Lawless:

Shakes

Mike Massa

Available from Beyond Terra Press

eBook and Paperback

Excerpt from "Shakes:"

"My name is Volo of the House Zobulakos," the SpinDog announced haughtily. Harry watched as his slender ally found his feet and made a show of brushing imaginary dust from his shoulder where the lance had rested.

Volo was defiant even in the face of drawn weapons; Harry had to give him points for style.

"I am here representing the esteemed friend to all Sarmatchani, my father, Arko Primus Heraklis Zobulakos. This is a mission of great importance. What honorless prole names my brother a liar and interferes with the will of the Primus? Tell me, that I might inform your chief of this insolence."

Harry tensed as two of the newcomers surged forward in angry reaction to the word "honorless," but the tall man interposed his lance, barring their way.

"Father!" the shorter one objected, throwing back her hood, revealing a sharp featured young woman. She'd drawn her blade and balefully eyed the SpinDog. "Let me teach this arrogant weakling about honor!"

"Nay, Stella," the broad-shouldered man said grimly. "Even my daughter must cleave to the law. This is a clan matter. And as to the stripling's question…

"I, hight Yannis al-Caoimhip ex-huscarlo, Patrisero of the Herdbane, First among the Sarmatchani," he went on, fixing his eyes first on Volo and then each of the Terrans. "I name Stabilo of the Sky People a liar, a cheat, and a coward. I call his people to account. Blood or treasure. At dawn tomorrow either will suffice."

309

Harry didn't say a word but heard a deep sigh from Rodriguez. These were the allies he'd been sent to find, all right. Just like every other joint operation with indigs, it was SNAFU.

Murphy's Law was in still in effect.

* * * * *

Get "Shakes" now at: https://www.amazon.com/dp/B0861F23KH

Find out more about Myrphy's Lawless and Beyond Terra Press at: https://chriskennedypublishing.com/imprints-authors/beyond-terra-press/

* * * * *

Made in United States
North Haven, CT
02 March 2025

66428724R00173